SPECIAL FORCES: THE RECRUIT

Cindy Dees

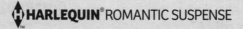

HARLEQUIN® ROMANTIC SUSPENSE

Recycling programs
for this product may
not exist in your area.

ISBN-13: 978-1-335-66199-9

Special Forces: The Recruit

Copyright © 2019 by Cynthia Dees

Printed in U.S.A.

New York Times and *USA TODAY* bestselling author **Cindy Dees** is the author of more than fifty novels. She draws upon her experience as a US Air Force pilot to write romantic suspense. She's a two-time winner of the prestigious RITA® Award for romance fiction, a two-time winner of the RT Reviewers' Choice Best Book Award for Romantic Suspense and an *RT Book Reviews* Career Achievement Best Author Award nominee. She loves to hear from readers at www.cindydees.com.

Visit Cindy's Author Profile page at Harlequin.com for more titles.

Chapter 1

Staggering a little as she ran, Tessa Wilkes spied the finish line maybe a half mile ahead through waves of heat and dust. Whatever bastard had decided to call a twenty-mile run carrying a forty-pound rucksack a "sprint" should be shot. Right now. She volunteered to pull the trigger.

Her body hurt in every way it was possible to hurt. Three months of grueling, around-the-clock physical training had taken its toll on her. She'd reached the end of her rope, and her fingers were slipping off the last bit of said rope with every agonizing step.

She'd known going in that just because it had become legal for women to begin Special Forces training, it didn't mean any were going to be allowed to finish the program and play with the big boys. The male instructors would keep doing BS like this run until they broke her. They were never going to back off.

Only she could make the pain stop. By quitting. By giving in. By accepting that she was never going to be one of them. She was sorely tempted to give up on her futile dream when she reached this one last finish line.

But no sooner had the impulse come to her than a wave of sheer, cussed stubbornness slammed through her. She was that horse who would die in the harness, still straining to pull its load.

Her face was on fire. Her lungs were self-combusting. The heavy pack hammered her feet into the ground with every step she took. But onward she staggered. Step after miserable step. At this point any reasonably fit person could walk beside her faster than she was running.

But she. Did. Not. Stop.

She'd asked for this insanity—begged for it, even—which made her misery even worse. It stripped away her right to complain. All she had left was anger.

She reached for her old friend, Fury. Born of rage at being powerless to control her life, it rose from her determination someday to become a strong, independent woman whom no man would ever push around.

Her steps stabilized. Her stride stretched back out into a full run. Less than a quarter mile to go now.

"Damn. Thought we had you there, Wilkes," a male voice said sardonically from behind her.

She didn't bother turning around to look. *Lambert.* A recently arrived instructor, he always wore mirrored shades and a baseball cap, which meant she had no idea what her latest tormenter actually looked like beyond that lean, chiseled jaw. And a physique modeled after the great masters of sculpture, of course. He never participated in harassing the trainees. He just watched. Mostly her.

He'd been hanging around pretty much continuously

the past few days. Either he was studying her for who knew what inscrutable reason, or he was stalking her. Whatever. They could throw their best head games at her and run her till she dropped. When she got back up, she would just keep on going.

"Ahh, well. We'll break you next time," he murmured from just behind her. "Or the time after that. If you won't quit coming after us, we won't quit coming after you."

His lightly delivered comment sent a chill through her. He was not lying. They would keep coming after her until they destroyed her.

The finish line of today's "sprint" loomed ahead, and she pushed herself to reach it by envisioning a big glass of ice water waiting for her. She crossed the finish line and stopped cold, not taking one more running step than necessary as she panted in the oven-like heat.

She'd done it. One more time they'd failed to break her. A stone-faced instructor looked at a stopwatch and recorded her time on a clipboard without comment. She caught Lambert looking over Clipboard Guy's shoulder. Both men pulled disgusted faces, then Lambert peeled off to head for the instructor's building.

Screw them. She'd given it everything she had. Just because her triumph was their failure didn't make it any less of a triumph for her. She bent over, planting her hands on her thighs, sucking in great, awful lungfuls of parched, scorching air.

"Wilkes!"

She looked up sharply at her barked last name.

"My office. Now."

Crap. That was Major Torsten summoning her. No one knew exactly what he did around here, but even the instructors treated him with deep respect. Frankly, he scared her to death.

In an act of bald-faced defiance, she forced her protesting legs to run to the door of the Quonset hut Torsten loomed in. One corner of his mouth quirked up for just an instant before settling back into its usual tight, disapproving line.

Torsten disappeared inside the building as she trotted up the steps after him.

"Sit." He pointed at a wooden chair in front of the desk he'd moved behind.

She slipped off her pack and sank into the chair not a moment too soon. Her legs felt entirely boneless. They would have collapsed on their own in a few more seconds. In fact, her entire body felt like a marionette's with the strings cut. She was going to hurt like a big dog in a few hours. Cool air-conditioning wafted down on her, as blissful as angel's breath.

"Enjoy the run?" Torsten asked drily.

As if she would give him the satisfaction of showing even a hint of weakness. Not a chance. She shrugged. "Nice scenery. And I've done worse." Which was a total lie.

He opened a cabinet behind his desk and tossed her a bottle of water. She snagged it neatly midair and downed it greedily. Meanwhile, he opened a brown manila folder on his desk and lifted out papers one by one, glancing through them at his leisure. She just enjoyed being still and letting her body temperature return to something resembling normal.

At length, he closed the file and stared at her long and hard enough that she had to consciously tell herself not to squirm. She'd gotten used to the mind games they played around here and had learned not to break awkward silences unless she had something specific to say.

"You're out," Torsten announced without warning.

Out? As in *out of training*? Her mind went completely blank. A single word took shape and popped out of her mouth. "Why?"

"You are underperforming. Your run and swim times aren't coming down fast enough and your physical fitness test scores are not coming up fast enough for you to stand a chance in the remainder of this course. You're out."

Shock slammed into her, wiping her mind clean.

Ten years. Ten grueling, miserable, painful years she'd been training in hopes of one day having a shot at the Special Forces—practically around the clock. God, the things she'd sacrificed for this. A normal social life. The relationships she'd let pass her by. The friendships lost. Jobs turned down. She'd geared her *entire life* around this.

It simply couldn't be over.

Besides. She already met all the minimum required scores to pass this training! And just like that, she was out?

"Are Jones and Peterson out, too?" she blurted. They were men in her class. Men whom she consistently outperformed and outscored.

"I'm not discussing any other trainees with you, Wilkes."

She looked up at him, then. Stared into ice-blue eyes that did not for a second flinch in the face of her silent outrage. Arguing with him would be useless. Both trainees and instructors called him the Iceberg behind his back because the bastard never thawed and never budged.

The Special Forces did not want her. They had tested her and found her wanting. And they were not going to debate the decision with her. Just, "You're out." Done. Pack your stuff and leave.

Anger exploded abruptly in her gut, knocking the air out of her lungs, and leaving her panting with fury. This sanctimonious bastard dared to hide his misogyny behind her performance numbers? Why not just call it what it was? These male chauvinist pigs just didn't want to let a girl into their little boys' club!

She pressed words past her clenched teeth. "I get why you are resisting allowing women into your hallowed band of brothers. But it's a mistake. Not many women have what it takes, but a few of us do."

He leaned back in his leather executive chair and merely continued to stare at her, his entire demeanor cold and emotionless.

She warmed to her subject and ignored his body language shouting at her to shut the heck up. "We have talents and skills that would be an asset to the teams. You guys are weaker because of our exclusion. Other countries are already figuring that out, and you'll end up scrambling to play catch-up. But by the time you catch on, the women you need will be so pissed off we'll have moved on to other jobs. Other lives. You'll be poison to the very women you need."

"Are you done?" he snapped.

She crossed her arms defensively over her chest and pressed her lips tightly together, the rest of the rant she so badly wanted to throw at him barely contained. Silently, she flung the worst names at him she could think of.

Out of good names, she reverted to her Venezuelan mother's native tongue for more.

He said more mildly, "You've got orders."

"To where?" she demanded. God, that was fast. He'd already gotten her assigned to some other base? The man didn't mess around when he tossed someone out of his unit.

"Phoenix."

What on earth did the Army have for her to do in Phoenix, Arizona? The only military base nearby was Luke Air Force Base in Glendale. She wasn't being cross-posted to the Air Force, was she?

"Lambo!" Torsten called.

Lambert of the gorgeous jaw poked his head in the door, hat and sunglasses gone for the first time, and she did a no-kidding, wrench-her-neck double take. She'd seen some beautiful men in her life, but behind the disguise, this one was in a class all his own. The guy was a walking recruitment poster. The motto on it would be, "Join the Army and become a living god."

His American flag–blue gaze took her in coolly. Thoroughly. And everywhere his scrutiny touched her, she abruptly felt naked. *On fire.*

He looked away from her like she was about as interesting as a cockroach. She sagged in her chair and let go of the breath she hadn't realized she was holding.

"Sir?" the god asked in a smooth, confident voice.

Oh, man. Her ovaries just melted.

Lambert stepped fully into the doorway and liquid heat pooled in her groin. The guy was hotness personified. Raw sex appeal rolled off him in waves that made her feel as if she was drowning in lust. Cripes. There should be nothing the least bit attractive about this guy. She wanted to *be* a Spec Ops warrior, not *do* a Spec Ops warrior.

"You have your orders, Beau. *Direct orders.*"

Lambert scowled fiercely at Torsten, and she looked back and forth between them. What was she missing? Why the emphasis on the words *direct orders*?

Torsten continued, "Escort Wilkes to the airfield. Put her on a plane and get her off my base. You know what her orders are. See to it she follows them."

Torsten didn't have to be nasty about it. He'd already won.

Lambert frowned thunderously, clearly not pleased—at all—at having to babysit her. He glared at Torsten, who glared back. If she didn't know better, she would say they were communicating silently through some secret warrior mind powers.

Lambert made a sound of disgust, and Torsten replied, "Your objections are duly noted. But we're doing this my way."

"It's a mistake—" Lambert started.

Torsten cut him off, snapping, "We've already had this discussion. Report back to me *after* you've gotten your head out of your ass."

Lambert spun on his heel, scowling. "Let's go, Wilkes. I've got places to go and things to do."

She hefted her pack wearily over one shoulder and headed for the door after "Lambo." She would lay odds he got that handle not entirely because of his last name but also in honor of a Lamborghini—the sleek, sexy Italian sports car.

"Hustle up, Wilkes," Torsten said sharply. "Your ride's already waiting. You're late."

She scowled. She couldn't very well be late for an appointment she didn't even know she had until ten seconds ago. "What about my gear back at the dorm?"

"It'll be shipped to you."

Wow. He really had it in for her, didn't he?

She paused in the doorway and looked back at him. She spoke with quiet certainty, not by way of a whine, but stating a fact. "You're making a mistake, Major."

"I'm absolutely certain I'm not. And someday you'll come to agree with me," he retorted.

Never.

Tears burned at her eyes and she blinked them back furiously. She would be *damned* if she cried in front of these jerks. They didn't deserve her tears. And she didn't deserve this rude treatment. She was a freaking Army officer with a distinguished career behind her *and* ahead of her.

The walk of shame from the Quonset hut to the parking lot with Captain America at her side like a jailer was perhaps the worst hundred yards of her life. She felt the eyes on her. Everyone…*everyone*…noted her departure. She could physically feel on her skin the satisfaction of the boys' club as it closed ranks against her. It was all she could do not to vomit up Torsten's bottle of water in her humiliation as she climbed into a Hummer, her head held high.

It was a fight, but she wrestled back another bout of threatening tears as Lambert started the Jeep's engine. She wasn't going to cry for this jerk, either. A girl had to have a little pride, after all.

Lambert backed out of the parking spot and headed for the airfield. She commented sourly, "I knew folks around here hated the idea of women special operators, but this dramatic show of expulsion is a little excessive."

"Take it up with Torsten. I'm just following orders."

Orders he sounded irritated as heck over. What did he have to be mad about? He wasn't the one being publicly humiliated. She had to get her mind off what was happening or she was going to break down and sob in front of all of them, and she would *never* give them that satisfaction. Searching desperately for a distraction, she mumbled, "What's in Phoenix?"

Her escort merely shrugged. Even that casual gesture of his shoulder, fraught with rippling muscle under smooth, bronzed skin and a tight black T-shirt, was sexy as hell. At least Torsten had given her one last piece of eye candy to enjoy before he dashed her dreams and ended her life.

Lambo drove her straight to the airfield without saying a word. But disapproval rolled off him in tangible waves. All these guys were flaming jerks. Too bad she was so wasted from the run she couldn't think up any better epithets to call him in her mind.

She spied an airplane, apparently waiting for her, and stared. It was a twin turboprop plane that would carry about eight passengers. Except there didn't appear to be any other passengers milling around waiting to go. Surely, Torsten hadn't ordered up an entire airplane just to get rid of her.

Lambert came around to open her door for her as she stared back and forth doubtfully between aircraft and man.

He smiled wryly at her. All the oxygen in her vicinity disappeared, and she caught herself swaying toward him slightly. Dang, that man was attractive. Like a giant, man-shaped electromagnet. The pull of him crackled through her individual cells, realigning them into his orbit whether she willed it or not.

Maybe she was reacting to him so strongly because she was frazzled from the run and her abrupt ejection from the Special Forces pipeline. Whatever the reason, being this close to Lambert was throwing her seriously off balance.

She took a step out of the vehicle—or tried to, at any rate—and pitched forward, straight into her escort.

Impressions assailed her from every direction. His

stomach was as hard and ridged with muscle as it looked. Heat poured off his body. He smelled like a forest on a lazy summer day. And he made her think of hot, sweaty sex.

He grabbed her by her upper arms and dragged her up his body deliciously. An unmistakably hard, impressively large bulge pressed against her belly. He acted as if he barely noticed her weight. His strength was breathtaking. Literally. She had trouble inhaling properly as her entire body melted in a puddle of unwilling lust. *Oh, who was she kidding? It was totally willing lust.*

Beau Lambert stared down at the smoking-hot woman plastered against him. Her skin was a totally edible shade of café au lait, her hair wavy and dark, coffee brown. But what really stood out were those eyes of hers, mint green and practically glowing against her darkly tanned skin. She wasn't model material unless modeling agencies went for exotic types, not quite beautiful but undeniably unforgettable. He would 100 percent buy her a drink if he saw her across a crowded bar.

At the moment her cheeks were flushed, her eyes wide with surprise. His nostrils flared at the sudden sexual awareness he sensed in her.

Dammit, this was exactly why he hated the idea of women special operators.

His stare dropped to the neck of her tank top and the curves of her upper breasts. How was a woman as buff as she was that bountifully endowed? Talk about winning the genetic lottery. This woman had hit the mega millions jackpot in that department.

Get your head out of your crotch, man. Tessa Wilkes was an Army officer, not a sex object. But he couldn't resist a last glance at that swelling cleavage. She checked pretty much every box on his hot female checklist. She even had the cocky attitude and sassy mouth he secretly loved.

He murmured, "If you can't stand on your own two feet, this little adventure is going to be over before it ever gets rolling."

"What adventure? What are your orders?" she demanded. "Let me guess. Put me on that plane and make sure I don't bolt before it goes airborne."

If only. He would love nothing better than to toss her on a plane and send her anywhere far, far from him. He'd argued stridently against the assignment Torsten had given him, but the bastard hadn't budged. Torsten was convinced that he, Beau Lambert, was the only man for the job.

Wilkes tried to stand on her own, grimacing in pain, but her legs weren't cooperating yet. He wasn't a complete ass, and he held her upright. Which, of course, meant more belly-to-belly, sex-fantasy-conjuring contact.

She hung in his arms like a rag doll devoid of bones. He remembered that level of exhaustion from his own initial training. A frisson of shared sympathy passed through him. But he shoved it aside. He had no time for sympathy for this woman. Not if he was going to prove Gunnar Torsten wrong.

She mumbled, "First a public humiliation, and now this. I'm so sorry."

She was right about the public part. His orders were to make sure everyone in the program saw him haul Wilkes out. There had to have been at least a hundred witnesses to her departure, all silently gleeful. But she was wrong about the humiliation part. Torsten had other plans for her altogether. If the other trainees and instructors knew what the boss was up to, they wouldn't be so smug to see Wilkes go.

He commented, "You're closer to the truth than you know."

She looked up at him quizzically, but he offered no explanation. All would become clear to her soon. And frankly, he was too ticked off at what came next to get all talkative with her about it.

He shifted his weight onto his bum leg, and a bolt of white-hot agony shot through him. He sucked in a sharp breath and froze, terrified he'd done something to wreck his knee even worse than it already was. He swore colorfully to himself.

When he'd leaped forward and caught her under the armpits, his right knee had given a mighty shout of protest, shooting daggers up and down his leg in retaliation for the stunt. He tuned in to that pain now, breathing through it until it gradually subsided.

Wilkes made no move to stand on her own. Probably couldn't. He knew all too well the agony of the human body transforming into one giant cramp.

His pain lessened until he was able to register once more the galvanizing sensation of a woman's body snuggled up close to his. She was curvy. And springy in the right places. Sex in a bottle.

"Aww, hell," he muttered. "You really are a girl, aren't you?"

She glanced down at her chest mashed against his. The display of cleavage above the neck of her olive drab tank top was impressive, to say the least. "Last time I checked, I'm still a girl," she declared.

An unwilling crack of laughter slipped out of him before he was able to bite it back.

She felt soft and feminine in his arms. Which went

against everything he knew about her. He'd seen her PFT scores and run times. She was a beast by female standards. Best they'd seen in a long time. All the more reason to ignore the blood surging into his loins. She was a job, not a date. But day-umm, she was hot.

The light green in her eyes was overtaken by black as her pupils dilated. She must have registered his wholly male reaction to her. Not much he could do about that. But then her gaze, peeking up through long, dark lashes, went a little languorous and a whole lot sensual.

Uh-oh. One of them had to be responsible here and do the right thing. At the moment it was going to have to be her because his pulse was pounding through an erection hard enough to hammer nails with.

Instead, she didn't do a blessed thing to stop every sexual part of her from pressing against every sexually corresponding part of him. Worse, she looked ready to have hot, sweaty sex with him this very second. All he had to do was say the word. And the word was hovering right on the tip of his tongue.

It took every ounce of discipline he had to force his feet to take a cautious step back. His knee held. Praise the Lord and pass the potatoes.

He continued to grasp her upper arms until her legs steadied. Or maybe it was his leg he was waiting on to settle down and accept his weight. Or maybe he was waiting for his hard-on to calm down enough that he wasn't on the verge of doubling over in pain around it. Either way, something primal and hungry roared through him as she stared up at him, her huge, green eyes more huge and more green than usual.

"You good?" he asked gruffly.

"I'm great," she breathed back. Lord, she sounded like Marilyn Monroe singing "Happy Birthday" to JFK.

He would bet she was great in bed. Out of bed. Against a wall. In a shower. In the back of a car. On the back of a car…

Stop.

Reluctantly, he set all of those smoking-hot curves and smooth muscles away from him. He had to get control of himself, and fast, or this assignment was going to go to hell in a handbasket of his own weaving.

His hands fell away from her, and something possessive inside him growled at the absence of her heated skin. As for her, she abruptly looked too tongue-tied and, truthfully, too obstinate to thank him. He couldn't help but be amused at her stubbornness. It was a quintessential Special Forces quality. *Pigheaded* was a term that got applied to him frequently, in fact.

He reached past her into the back of the vehicle for her pack. He slung it over his shoulder and led her over to the airplane as she stumbled along after him. He trotted up the unfolded steps and turned around, reaching a hand down to her.

"I can do this myself," she stated.

"You didn't leave everything you had out on the course earlier?" he asked in disappointment. Hell, her run time had been respectable even for a guy. Surely, she hadn't run that far, that fast, carrying that much weight, casually.

She stared at his outstretched hand for a long moment. Long enough that he wasn't sure she would accept help from him. Of course, that had been the big ding against her in her training file. She didn't trust men. Had trouble working in a group with others. Tended to be a loner.

But then her palm touched his, and just like that, lightning zinged through his hand and up his arm. It had nothing to do with resentment and everything to do with something else altogether. Man. All she needed was a crack of thunder to go with all that sexual lightning.

Her gaze lifted to his. They stared at each other for a second that stretched out to infinity. *Whoa.* The moment snapped back into real time sharply, like a rubber band, with the same painful slap against his skin.

He tugged and all but launched her airborne into the plane.

"Crud, you're strong," she breathed under her breath.

He didn't think she'd meant for him to hear it, but he replied, nonetheless. "All special operators have to be."

"I'm the first to admit that no woman will ever be as strong as a guy at the top of his fitness game. Not even someone like me who's ridiculously strong relative to most other women."

"Then why put yourself through the misery?"

"Just because I won't ever be as strong as a man doesn't mean I'm not strong enough to do the job. Strength comes in many forms."

She was right, of course, but he wasn't about to give her the satisfaction of saying so. "Take a seat," he ordered.

"No other passengers? This bird is just for me?" she asked.

He moved forward to a small cabinet behind the copilot's seat. He dug out several bottles of water and tossed them one by one to Wilkes. She caught each easily. Good reflexes. That was something, at least.

"Major Torsten is in a hurry to get you out of here," he replied as he moved back toward her.

She finished chugging a bottle of water, coming up for air and muttering, "Yeah, I got that memo."

She sounded a shade bitter. Like it was dawning on her that she really was not going to be a Special Forces operator. He knew the feeling. And he was definitely bitter about it, too. He wasn't about to accept the doctor's final word that his knee would never be strong enough for him to operate on the teams again.

He'd transformed from a scrawny, picked-on kid into a hard-core warrior, hadn't he? He could transform one lousy, busted knee into a joint strong enough to do the job. No way was he walking away from his brothers in arms. They were his family. His life. What would he do if he couldn't be a special operator?

He dropped into the seat across the aisle from her, and Wilkes stopped slugging the second bottle of water to squeak, "What are you doing?"

"You heard the major. He told me to see to it you get where you're going."

He realized he was massaging his right leg, just above the knee, and jerked his hand away. *No weakness. No pain. His knee was fine.*

She snapped, "I'm not going AWOL just because Torsten tossed me out. I'm going to be pissed off for the next several decades, but I'm not going to throw some giant, career-destroying tantrum over it."

He shrugged. "I've got my orders." As the engines cranked up outside, he leaned his seat back, closed his eyes and settled in for a nap. If she knew what was good for her, she would do the same.

Nope. She was feeling chatty apparently, for she said, "Just how crappy an assignment is Torsten sending me to? Is this punishment for my daring to try for the Special Forces?"

The plane started to taxi. Without opening he eyes, he said shortly, "Operations 101—eat and sleep whenever you get a chance to do either." Surely, she'd already learned that one. Didn't she know *anything*? God almighty, this mission was going to suck worse than he'd thought. And he already thought it was going to suck pretty damned hard.

The plane accelerated down the runway, and he caught her surreptitiously wiping tears away from her cheeks as she stared out the window, her face averted from him. Aww, hell. Now he felt bad for her. And that was the one emotion he couldn't afford where she was concerned.

Thankfully, she had no more inclination to talk. She reclined her seat and went unconscious in a matter of seconds. She had to be beat. He recalled his training as if it was yesterday, and saying it had been hell on earth would not be an exaggeration.

Of course, the real misery for her had just begun. Not that it was going to be any better for him. Someday, somehow, he would find a way to get even with Torsten for this.

Chapter 2

Tessa jolted awake as the plane bumped onto a runway. It was dark outside the small window at her elbow. She was disoriented. Groggy. *Airplane. Kicked out of the Special Forces pipeline. Orders from Torsten. A god sent along to deliver her to Phoenix.*

She peered out the windows and saw the tall, black silhouettes of trees crowding an unlit runway. Trees? In Phoenix?

She'd been to Arizona before. It had been a thousand degrees outside, and all that grew in the sandy desert were rocks and cacti. She peered out her window again. Not only were those trees, they also looked like a mix of moisture-loving deciduous species and conifers. Totally not trees that would survive the hellish heat of summer in Arizona. And the air in the plane was muggy. Humidity in Phoenix often ran in the single digits. It was warm wherever they had landed, though. And the air smelled strongly of…plant decay.

She glanced over at Lambert. "Do you know where we are?"

"Yup."

The man had the conversational skills of a caveman.

She waited for him to share, but *nada*. He just stared out his own window, jaw set and a grim expression on his face. "Well?" she demanded. "Where are we? This is obviously not Phoenix."

"Are you always this impatient?" he asked laconically.

"Guess I am. I have this funny thing about liking to know, oh, what *state* I'm in." One thing she knew for sure. This was *not* Arizona.

His lips twitched, but he didn't deign to enlighten her. Apparently, he was as stubborn as his boss. Jackasses, both of 'em. Yeah, well, she could play that game, too. She'd be darned if she asked *him* any more questions.

The jet came to a full stop. Deep silence fell as the engines shut down. The copilot came back to open the clamshell hatch and lower the steps. She smiled flirtatiously at the young Air Force officer and asked him, "Could you please tell me where we are?"

He glanced up at her in surprise. "Louisiana."

What on earth was *there* for her?

At least she'd caught what felt like a couple hours–long nap. If only she felt better after it. Not that anyone in the history of aviation had ever napped comfortably in an airplane seat. She hoisted herself out of the chair, every bit as stiff and agonized as she expected. Bent over in the low-ceilinged cabin, she hobbled to the exit.

She eyed the stairs warily. There were only four steps, yet that was enough to be problematic in her current state of pain. But no way was she going to ask Lambert, waiting impatiently at the bottom of the steps, for help. She made it down the first couple of steps, but her entire right leg cramped on the third step and collapsed out from under her. She pitched forward, straight into the arms of her SEAL babysitter. Again.

Dad gum it.

He growled in her ear, low and sexy, "Do you always throw yourself at men like this?"

His low voice sent a thrill rippling down her spine and vibrating deliciously through her lower abdomen before she remembered he was a jerk and she hated his guts.

His chest was hard, slabbed in resilient bulges of muscle, warm under the soft cotton of his black T-shirt. And he still smelled good. Which ticked her off to no end. She smelled like a landfill on a hot day, but there wasn't a thing she could do about it until she crossed paths with water and a bar of soap.

It never failed. She always ran into the sexy guys when she was a total mess or being a complete dork. She was not one of those girls who managed to be pulled together, poised and make positive first impressions on men. Ever.

"Are you done trying to face-plant?" he asked.

Crud. She was still plastered against him. She yanked free of his strong, supporting arms and forced her legs to bear her weight no matter how much they protested. The copilot passed her rucksack down to Lambert, and she didn't have the strength or give-a-crap factor to take it from him. She was already kicked out of training. She didn't have to try to impress anyone with how tough and self-sufficient she was anymore.

Which scared the bejeebers out of her. Her entire life had been devoted to convincing herself and everyone around her that she was the real deal. That she could hang with the big boys. That she was tough. Invulnerable. Safe from harm or abuse.

What was she supposed to do now? Trade in her combat boots for flowered dresses and aprons? Who was she supposed to be? She had no idea how to be a regular woman. Knowing Major Torsten, he'd seen to it she would be stuck in some secretarial job fit only for a June Cleaver wannabe, in his misogynistic estimation.

If she had to make coffee for anyone, she swore she was going to poison the stuff.

Waterworks threatened again, and she breathed deeply, repeating over and over to herself, *I will not cry. I will not cry.* But hopelessness washed over her, anyway. What had all the years of work and sacrifice been for in the end? God, the time she'd wasted on a hopeless dream.

Lambert took off, striding toward an open-topped Jeep parked at the edge of the tarmac. He limped the tiniest bit on his right leg. Had he not been moving directly away from her like that, she probably wouldn't have spotted the subtle anomaly in his motion. Not that the knee brace showing under his camo fatigue pants made him any less lethal.

She looked around the airfield, and the place was deserted. It was just a strip of asphalt in a clearing among the towering trees, not even a real airport. There were no buildings, no other vehicles, no people. If this guy was an ax murderer, he was totally going to get away with his crime.

"You comin'? Or are you just gonna stand there countin' mosquitoes?" he tossed over his shoulder. If she was not mistaken, his voice had taken on a distinctly more Southern drawl.

She hurried after him, sucking in a sharp breath as

a thousand hot knives stabbed her body from every direction. One thing the past few months of training with the big boys had taught her. There was sore, and then there was *sore*.

Lambert tossed her pack in the back of the Jeep and swung easily into the driver's seat, waiting impatiently for her to catch up and climb in. She couldn't help groaning a little as she levered her body into the vehicle, using the roll bar to help lift herself. She felt like death warmed over, for real.

"You always this creaky?" he asked.

"Not usually. Training was a little rougher than usual the past few days. No downtime to rest and recover. Nothing's wrong with me that a hot shower and a decent night's sleep won't fix."

A single chin lift was all the acknowledgment she got. At least he didn't feel obliged to comment that if she thought initial Spec Ops training was bad, she should try the real deal. Whether he was showing sensitivity to her having just been thrown out of the program or he figured it went without saying that real operations were worse, she was glad for his forbearance. Her patience was *way* too thin right now to deal with man-snark.

He turned on the headlights and she squinted into the illuminated swath, making out only a thicket of vines, brambles and more trees. "Where in Louisiana are we?"

"Southern Louisiana. Not close to anyplace you've ever heard of."

"What's here?"

"The next step in your career."

"What career?" she asked sourly.

He glanced over at her, his expression inscrutable. They bumped across a sandy field and turned onto an asphalt road crowded by towering trees. Cypress, mostly.

The night was noisy. Crickets and frogs and God knew what else were audible over the Jeep's engine.

"Why'd Torsten tell me I was going to Phoenix if your orders were to bring me to Louisiana?"

"Not the city of Phoenix. *Operation* Phoenix," was her escort's only, and cryptic, answer.

Huh? She leaned back to wait and see where he took her.

Lambert drove confidently, his hands moving on the steering wheel and gearshift with the ease and precision of a race-car driver. Bulging biceps flexed under the sleeve of his T-shirt, a sight she never got tired of. It had been one of the best perks of the training she'd just left. The man-candy factor had been through the roof.

Special operators weren't generally men who packed on weightlifter's muscle. They focused on stamina and high-repetition calisthenics that moved their own body weight. Their muscle was lean and hard as steel. And *hawt as heck*.

She'd put on some hard, lean muscle of her own over the past few months of training. But not enough, apparently. Lost in silently delivering the rant inside her head to the icy major who'd thrown her out for no good reason, she wasn't inclined to engage her taciturn babysitter in conversation.

After about a half hour, lights appeared ahead, and a sad-looking strip of ramshackle buildings that might once have been a reasonably prosperous little road stop came into sight. Lambert turned into the potholed parking lot of a one-story motel that had seen much better days.

He parked at the end farthest from the office and swung out of the Jeep, and she spied him using his hand to give his right leg a little boost. He snagged her pack before she could reach for it, and she was forced to follow him and her gear to a door whose paint was peeling back to expose rusting metal. The night air smelled of brine and rotting grass as Lambert fished a key attached to a plastic paddle out of his pocket. He opened the door and stepped back to allow her to enter first.

How in the hell did he already have a key to a room in this dive? Her hackles leaped to suspicious attention along the back of her neck. "What is this?" she asked, not moving forward.

"A motel room."

"You're hilarious." She rolled her eyes.

"You wanted a hot shower, right?"

Man, that was tempting. But in some guy's cheap motel room? Even if he was possibly the hottest guy she'd laid eyes on in, well, forever? She said wryly, "I don't have any idea who you are. Why on earth would I go into a motel room with you in a strange town whose name I don't even know? You can go ahead and cue up the ax-murderer theme music right now."

He shrugged. "It's no skin off my nose if you stink. We can head out to your assignment now, if you want."

Crud. A shower really was tempting. In the flickering red light of the busted neon sign spelling out *M-O-E*, he was one fine-looking man. His tanned skin was smooth and taut over razor-sharp cheekbones. His nose had been broken before and wasn't perfectly straight, but the slight imperfection made the perfection of the rest of his face even more pronounced. Even the hint of razor stubble on his jaw was hot.

She was usually immune to men like him. After all, she worked in the Army, which was chock-full of fit, well-groomed men of discipline and energy.

But this guy. He was a stud among studs. There was

an aura about the guys operating in the real world—a hardness, a confidence, self-awareness that called to her in some nameless, primitive way.

Not that she was looking to hook up with any man, thank you very much.

Lambert stepped inside, flipped on a light and paused to adjust the thermostat. Downward, hopefully. It was a sweltering night and sticky as sin. He glanced up without warning, catching her staring at his gorgeous profile. "You coming in?"

"Who are you really?" The question was out of her mouth before she could stop it. Dang, this guy messed her up. She never blurted stuff out like that.

"Just a guy doing a job. You can call me Beau."

"Lambo's your field handle, right? Let me guess. It's short for Lamborghini and not Lambert."

"Correct." His eyes briefly lit with approval.

Hah. She'd nailed it. "You got a rank, soldier?"

"Yes."

And, on cue, he went all caveman on her and didn't share said rank. It irritated her enough that she refused to ask him what his rank actually was. Major Jackass. *That* was his rank.

"With all due respect, Beau, why in the hell are we here? Wherever here is."

"Torsten didn't tell you?" he replied sharply.

"Obviously not, or I wouldn't be asking."

"Come in and close the door. You're letting in mosquitoes. And if I have to be in an enclosed space with you, please take a shower. You really do stink."

"Screw you," she said mildly.

His gaze snapped to hers, hot and willing. Her breath caught. Realizing belatedly what she'd just said, she rolled her eyes and stepped inside.

He held out her rucksack and she snagged it without comment as she passed by him, heading for the bathroom. She locked the door, stripped and turned the water on as hot as it would go. It was strange and disturbing knowing Lambert was right outside while she was in here, naked, like this.

Hyperawareness of her escort skittered across her skin, and it made her jumpy. It wasn't that she was a prude. Far from it. But she could still feel all those acres of yummy muscle against hers. Smell his deodorant.

No amount of vigorous scrubbing erased the feel of him off her body. And, truth be told, she wasn't sure she wanted to forget the sensations that had torn through her. They had been…amazing.

Irritated at whatever head game he was playing with her, she blasted the water, letting it pound her muscles until the water ran cold—which actually felt pretty good, too. Only then did she reluctantly pour the freebie bottle of shampoo over her head and scrub her hair blessedly clean. She soaped down her body, rinsed off and stepped out of the shower feeling like a new woman.

She toweled off and then stared down at the filthy mess that was her clothes. There were no clean ones in her rucksack, which held only combat and survival gear. She sighed and used the bar of soap in the bathtub to give her tank top, cargo pants and underwear a scrub and a rinse. God. How did women in the past wash all their clothes by hand like this?

She wrung out the garments as best she could, then pulled and plucked the soggy clothing onto her body. Oh, Lord. Beau was gonna love the wet T-shirt look. It didn't help that her nipples were puckering with cold underneath her damp sports bra and thin tank top. Bracing herself for his disdain, or at least a rude stare, she stepped out into the room…and was startled to find it empty. Where had he gone? Out for food, hopefully.

She guzzled down a bunch of sulfur-tasting water using the plastic cup by the sink and combed out her hair. She was startled to see in the mirror that it had grown out to nearly her shoulder blades in the past few months. More startling was the deep tan she also was sporting. It made her gray-green eyes look even lighter and brighter than usual.

She towel-dried her hair and pulled it up into a high ponytail. It was going to go full poodle puff on her, but there was no help for it. Without a round brush or straightening iron, no way was she corralling its natural curl.

Using the motel's blow-dryer, she worked at drying her clothes right on her body. They were still damp, but no longer clammy, when the door opened abruptly behind her and she spun, brandishing the blow-dryer like a six-shooter.

"Gonna take me down with that thing?" Beau asked drily.

Rats. No grocery bags or other sign of human sustenance. She would take calories right now in pretty much any form she could get them.

"I'm de-stinked," she announced. "Any chance there's somewhere nearby where I can grab a bite of real food?"

His cell phone rang just then and he fished it out of his jeans, answering tersely with, "Go." He listened for a moment. Then, "The package is almost delivered. Understood." He hung up.

She stowed the hair dryer in its wall mount and turned back to him. "Are you a drug dealer, or am I the package?"

"You would, in fact, be the package."

"Can we please feed the package?"

He jerked his head for her to follow him and headed outside. She noticed this time as she passed him that she was about six inches shorter than he was. She was not quite five foot eight, which made him a little over six feet tall. He probably had sixty pounds on her in weight, even though at a glance he looked lean. She'd developed a discerning eye for the muscle density of special operators in the course of her recent training.

He moved past her with deceptive speed for a guy with a bum leg and reached for her car door just as her hand moved toward the handle. He opened it with a flourish and she looked up at him, startled.

"Don't get used to it. I won't coddle you or get any doors for you after tonight. But let the record show my mama didn't raise a heathen."

"Duly noted," she replied, bemused as she slid into her seat and he closed the door. He went around to the driver's side and in seconds was backing out of the lot. He threw the Jeep in gear and took off down the road. A gas station next to the motel appeared operational, along with a titty bar that looked like a total dive. Oddly, a bait shop was open, too. Apparently, night fishing was a local thing.

Beau turned off the narrow asphalt road onto an even narrower dirt road, and she was pretty sure she would start hearing banjos any second.

They banged along the terrible road for maybe ten uncomfortable minutes before a building on high stilts came into sight ahead with a half dozen muddy trucks parked in front of it. Another half dozen shallow-bottom boats were tied up at a dock behind it.

"We're here," he announced.

"Where's here?"

"At the best steak joint in the Bayou Toucheaux."

She salivated at the mere mention of steak. He led her up a staircase to a rickety wraparound porch. The weathered building looked as if a stiff breeze would blow it over.

She followed Beau into the dim, smoky interior. Any fire marshal worth his salt would have a stroke at the plentiful cigars and flaming grill filling the wooden structure with smoke. Four rednecks in sleeveless shirts and baseball caps bellied up to the bar, and several couples sat at tables in the middle of the room.

"'Eyy, *chère*," one of the rednecks at the bar slurred as he spotted her. The guy strolled over to her, flashing a smile that had about one tooth for every three available slots. "You new come to dee parish, *oui*?"

Beau took a step forward, injecting himself between her and the drunk. "She new come to the parish with me."

"Bah. *Femme* like dat wan' de real man. Not girlie boy wit' de pretty face…" The drunk trailed off, peering at Beau closely. "Lambert? Beau Lambert? Dat y'all?"

"Farty Lambert?" one of the other drunks behind the first one hooted? "Y'all done growed up. Got yo'self some muscles 'n' all. Shee-it."

Clearly Beau had some sort of history with these yahoos. Based on the taunts, she gathered he'd lived here as a child. Rough place to have come from if the poverty she'd seen so far was typical.

The other three drunks closed ranks behind the first one. "Li'l Farty Lam-bear? I'll be damned. Never thought to see yo' face round he-uhh no mo'," one of them slurred.

Tessa's entire body tensed. She knew that tone of voice from her own childhood. It belonged to a bully.

One pumping himself up to inflict pain on someone weaker than he was. A bully enjoying his victim's fear. Oh, this was not going to go well.

Anger at a bunch of big, strong jerks picking on someone else rolled through her, hot and sharp. God, she hated bullies. She sized up the four men quickly. She and Beau could totally take them. Teach them a lesson—

Check that. Not only was it strictly forbidden for special operators to lose their cool in public and particularly against civilians, but failure to control anger was also a big, fat disqualifier for joining them. Anger clouded the mind. Impaired judgment. Still. It was hard to rein in the urge to remove the rest of these jerks' teeth.

As for Beau, he'd gone still and silent beside her. As in totally hunting-predator still and deeply, unnaturally silent. Menace poured off him like sublimated carbon off a block of dry ice. Surely, the four drunks weren't so far gone that they failed to sense the threat emanating from him.

The first drunk gave Beau a hard shove. Nope. Too far gone to realize Beau was not a man to bait and threaten anymore. Little Farty Lam-bear had grown up into a stone-cold killer.

Beau stepped back up beside her after the shove. He spoke quietly, calmly. "Walk away from me, Jimbo. And don't ever lay another hand on me. This is your only warning."

The four drunks hooted with laughter. She thought Beau had gone a little pale, the only indication that these assholes actually bothered him.

"Easy, Beau," she murmured low. "They're not worth it."

"Stay out of this, Tessa," he muttered back. "This has

been a long time coming. If they pick a fight with me, I'm within my rights to defend myself."

She winced. It wasn't a good idea for anyone to pick a fight with a trained Special Forces operative like him.

On cue, Jimbo took a clumsy swing at Beau. For his part, Beau dodged the meaty fist in negligent disdain, reaching up casually, gently even, to grasp Jimbo's fist. The big drunk dropped to his knees, yelping.

Beau leaned down and spoke in a low, almost caressing tone, "You think you can mess with me like back in the good old days, Jimbo? Take my girl? Humiliate me in public? Think again, my friend."

"Screw you," Jimbo growled.

Beau just laughed quietly and tightened his grip until the guy on the floor howled with pain.

"Need me to help kill him?" she asked under her breath.

Beau glanced up at her. His stare was flat. Emotionless. He looked like Death incarnate.

Which, of course, he was.

"Maybe you should cut him loose," she murmured. "I'm starving, and I don't want to get kicked out of here."

Beau released Jimbo's hand, or more precisely, he released the unfortunate thumb bent back nearly to the guy's wrist. The Cajun surged to his feet, right fist cocking back as he rose.

Mistake.

Beau moved so fast Tessa barely saw him slide past his foe. But all of a sudden Jimbo was facing her, and Beau was behind the guy, forearm around Jimbo's neck, and the drunk was rapidly turning an ugly shade of purple.

She spoke calmly and slowly. "Beau." She waited until he made eye contact with her to continue. "Toothless, here, has learned the error of his ways in trying to sucker punch you. Haven't you?" she asked Jimbo.

The drunk tried to nod within Beau's grasp but only managed to bug his eyes out a little more.

She glanced back at Beau. "How about you turn him loose so we can eat our dinner?"

He hesitated, but then nodded tersely and turned Jimbo loose.

The Cajun bent over at the waist, gasping and coughing. Tessa leaned down beside him and spoke coldly. "You're welcome. And for the record, he could've snapped your neck like a twig if he actually wanted to kill you. Walk away from Beau and don't ever mess with him again, or next time, I will let him break your neck."

Jimbo glared at her, spitting out something under his fetid breath about crazy bitches and their homicidal pretty boys. Whatever. She was more concerned about Beau.

She straightened and turned, coming face-to-face with him. "You okay?" she asked under her breath.

"Yeah. Fine. Why wouldn't I be?"

She stared at him, startled. He sounded utterly normal. Casual. The incident was a stark reminder of just how lethal these guys could be when crossed. They killed with cool, calculated precision. No anger, no emotion, just efficient violence in the blink of an eye.

"How long have you been waiting to do that to that guy?" she asked low.

"Awhile," Beau replied shortly.

She knew a thing or two about having old scores to settle.

Jimbo stumbled back toward his equally dentally challenged buddies, grumbling about jealous bastards who refused to share the hot chicks. At least somebody thought she was attractive. Of course, she still had all her teeth. By that measure alone, she was probably smoking hot to those losers.

Beau still stood rooted in place. Maybe he wasn't so unaffected, after all. She reached out to touch his elbow lightly. "Ready to eat?"

He shook himself a little. "Yes. You?"

She smiled. "Show me the meat, big guy."

His eyes glinted at her double entendre, but he didn't rise to the bait.

He glanced across the room toward a grill that was actually an oil drum split in half with metal mesh over the two halves. Beds of charcoal filled the drums. "'Ey, Marie," he called out.

A large woman wearing a New Orleans Saints jersey and standing by the grill turned around, wielding a long pair of tongs. She bellowed back, "Grab a table and yell out what y'all want. Damn waitress didn' show up t'night."

Tessa sank into a chair opposite Beau at a table for two, studying him closely. He had reacted the same way she would react if one of her mom's boyfriends tried to rough her up nowadays. She would go postal on his ass.

Beau scowled back at her as he caught her intent regard on him. Didn't like being psychoanalyzed, huh?

"Where do you know those guys from?" she asked.

"Everyone in these parts knows the Kimball brothers. I'm surprised all four of them are out of jail at the same time."

"Are they petty criminals or into bigger stuff?"

Beau shrugged. "They deal drugs. Run guns. Extort protection money from local businesses. Rumor has it they've killed a few folks who got in their way or refused to pay." He added sardonically, "They're just smart enough to stay one step ahead of the law. The sheriff puts them away for small stuff anytime he can catch them. But so far, they've avoided arrest for the more serious felonies everyone knows they've committed."

She eyed the big men across the room, memorizing their faces for future reference.

"How do you like your steak?" he asked, his voice a bit too tight. Predatory intensity rolled off him, and frankly, it turned her on like mad. Not that she would *ever* admit to him that she was secretly a bit of a Spec Ops groupie.

"Earth to Tessa, come in. Your steak?"

"Rare," she answered, mentally shaking herself. *Get a grip, girlfriend.*

"Pink rare or bleeding rare?"

"Marie can just walk my steak past the flame and call it good."

Beau called out, "Two steaks. Biggest ones you've got and rare as a virgin in a whorehouse."

Guffaws filled the room. The Kimball boys glowered, however. Their heads came together angrily as they muttered amongst themselves. She made a mental note to keep an eye on that bunch as the night progressed and the level of whiskey in the bottle in front of them went down.

Marie came over to their table carrying an armload of plates and bowls.

"It's been a while, Beau. Been, what? Fi'teen years since a Lambert come 'round these parts?"

"Something like that," he answered noncommittally.

Fifteen years? Wow. That was a long time to hold a grudge against Jimbo and company.

"Well, ain't y'all gone and got purty? Picture o' yo' daddy, you is. Good to have ya home, boy."

"Good to be he'uh." With every word he spoke, Tessa swore his Louisiana drawl got stronger. Why on earth would Torsten have sent the two of them to one of his men's hometown in the middle of Cajun country? The longer she was here, the more the questions were stacking up.

Marie plunked down a platter of toasted garlic bread, a mess of green beans and ham hocks, and a big bowl of red beans and rice with sausage so spicy it made Tessa's eyes water. When it came, a huge steak covered her entire plate and was tender enough to cut with a fork. She dug in with gusto.

It took a while for her to lay her napkin down and push her plate back. Another perk of her recent training: she could eat as much of anything she wanted and not gain an ounce. If anything, she'd lost a little weight even with putting on more muscle mass.

Someone fed the decrepit jukebox in the corner a handful of quarters, and twangy zydeco music abruptly filled the place. The talk got louder, the beer flowed more freely and women drifted into the bar and then out with men.

Under the din, Beau leaned forward. "Did Torsten tell you anything at all?"

"About what?"

Beau frowned.

She shrugged. "All he said to me was—and I quote—'You're out. You've got orders. Lambo, you have your orders. Get her off my base.' End quote."

He swore under his breath. "I'm gonna need a drink for this, then, and so are you." He called for some moonshine and two glasses.

"I don't like alcohol," she announced as Marie

thunked a mayonnaise jar of the local rotgut on the table along with two shot glasses.

"Tough. Drink up." He poured two shots of the stuff.

"Are you trying to get me drunk?" she demanded.

He shrugged. "Hey, if you can't roll like one of the boys, we don't have to have this conversation at all."

Scowling, she picked up the glass and tossed back the liquor, which burned like *fire* on the way down, shuddering at the powerful aftertaste. The alcohol went straight to her head, but at least it dulled the pain in her muscles while it was also dulling her brain function.

"Walk with me," Beau murmured.

He sounded tense as heck. What on earth was going on with him? He'd actually been reasonably pleasant during the meal. Admittedly, neither of them had talked much as they devoured their steaks.

Perplexed, she followed him out to the porch. He strolled around back to face a narrow canal that stretched away into the blackness. They were alone out here. Citronella tiki torches provided the only light, their flames flickering weakly against the dark. A cacophony of sound wrapped around the pungent odor of the swamp rising from below. Beau propped his elbows on the waist-high rail and stared into the bayou beyond.

Just being alone with him out here in the dark like this was a turn-on. She'd never, ever been alone with a guy so hot, nor so deadly…which made him even hotter.

"You're right about one thing," he said low enough that she had to lean down in a similar, elbow-propped pose to hear him. "The military is never going to publicly stand for women in the Special Forces."

She huffed in exasperation. "That horse is dead. You don't have to kick it for fun."

"But you're right about something else, too. There

is a place for women in special warfare. More to the point, Torsten agrees with you that we need women in the field."

"No freaking way. He hates women."

Beau snorted. "He hates everyone. But he loves the Special Forces. Wants us to be the best we can be. Male or female, he doesn't care."

"Why are you telling me this? He already booted me out."

Beau didn't answer her directly. Rather, he changed subject abruptly, asking, "Did you notice how publicly women are being tossed out of the various Special Forces courses?"

She snorted. "It's hard to miss. Every time a woman fails it practically makes national news."

"That publicity is intentional. We need the general public, hell, the world, to believe there are no American women operators and there will never be American women operators."

"Well, yeah. That's because there are none."

"That wasn't true once. There used to be an all-female Spec Ops team called the Medusas. Highly classified bunch. Operated for years and were wicked effective."

"What happened to them?"

"The original team worked together for about ten years and gradually retired from active duty. The second generation team was lost."

"As in they died?"

His voice no more than a sigh, he answered heavily, "Yeah."

"How?" she asked quietly.

"Not my story to tell, and too classified to discuss here."

Yikes. "And now? What's next?"

"Next, we'll try to build a new team." He glanced at her and then back out at the bayou. "Starting with you."

She stared at him. "Come again?"

"Torsten thinks you've got what it takes. He wants to train you to be a full-blown special operator. Not just a support type. A completely qualified combat specialist. That's the purpose of Operation Phoenix. To raise the Medusa Project from the dead."

She laughed in disbelief. "Right." She added sarcastically, "And that's why he threw me out of training and sent me across the country to a *swamp*."

"I'm serious. Do you want to be a Medusa or not?"

Chapter 3

Beau stared at the stunned woman beside him. *Please say no. Please say no.*

"Hell to the yes, I want to be one!" Tessa exclaimed.

Dammit. He *knew* she would say that. He was in no shape to be training anyone, let alone the next Medusa. What was Torsten thinking, throwing him into a scenario like this? The boss knew his knee was destroyed. That doctors said his career was over.

Of course, Torsten also knew Beau was determined to get back in the saddle and back onto the teams no matter how messed up his knee was.

Beau did have to give Tessa Wilkes credit for one thing. She was a good-looking woman. Sexy as wild hellfire. But that didn't necessarily mean she was cut out for the Medusas. Torsten had been clear. Assume she was not fit to be a Medusa. Test her. Push her. Make her prove she was Special Forces material.

And, as soon as he was done working with her, he could get back to the business of being an operator himself. Which could not happen soon enough for him.

Operation Phoenix. The reference to the mythical firebird rising from its own ashes didn't elude him. Torsten was resurrecting the Medusas after convincing the world the idea of an all-female Special Forces team was dead. He wondered, though, if Torsten had also chosen the name with him in mind. Was Gunnar trying to resurrect Beau's career from the ashes, as well?

If so, this was a hell of a strange way to go about it. Assigning him to work with a woman who would do nothing but slow him down.

He'd vehemently protested the idea of a woman operator when Torsten broached the assignment with him. Not that the boss had listened to a word of what he'd said. Just because Torsten thought this woman had the drive and mental toughness to play with the boys didn't mean she had the physical strength or stamina to hack it.

The compromise they'd reached was that Beau would try to train her. But he also retained the right to wash her out if she couldn't cut the training.

No way would he let her onto a Spec Ops team if she was going to be the weak link. Any team was only as strong as its weakest member. He wasn't about to let a woman get his brothers killed just so Torsten—and some wannabe chick—could prove a point.

He swore under his breath. If his boss thought that because his knee was busted up Beau would take it easy on Tessa, Gunnar Torsten was in for a surprise.

Everyone kept telling Beau he could contribute to the teams by training the next generation of special operators. But damned if he was going to accept that his field days were over and settle for playing nursemaid to anyone, male or female.

He was the first to admit it was a miracle he could walk. But the thing was, if he'd made it back this far, well beyond where the doctors had told him he could rehab his knee, why couldn't he rehab his knee all the way back to operational? One thing he was sure of: no way was he cut out to be an instructor. Torsten—in his infinite bloody wisdom—seemed to think this insane, waste-of-time mission would be good for him. *Bastard.*

"Why Louisiana?" the waste of time beside him asked, all eagerness now that she knew why they were really here.

"The idea is to keep your existence completely off the radar. We don't want *anyone* to know the Medusas are back."

"Is *that* why Major Torsten had you march me across camp this afternoon where everyone could see me leaving?"

"Affirmative."

"So Torsten's making a big fuss about tossing out the women and then...what? Bringing them here secretly to train?" she asked curiously.

"He's legitimately tossing out most of the women. But he saw something in you." He added reluctantly, the words acid on his tongue to even say aloud, "He thinks you've got what it takes to be one of us."

Silence fell between them as they stared at the sluggish black water below. It lapped around the stilts supporting the building, oily and thick. He could feel the mind of the woman beside him working overtime. One thing Torsten had gotten right: Tessa Wilkes was a sharp cookie. Observant as hell. She would need both to make it through the rest of this hypothetical training of hers.

Assuming he didn't end up just shooting himself, instead.

He caught himself rubbing his thigh, as had become his habit ever since surgery to remove the shrapnel that shredded his knee and quad muscle. He jerked his hand back to the railing. No way was he showing weakness to Tessa, particularly if he was supposed to train her.

"When do we start?" she asked.

"In the morning."

"Is there a hidden training base around here?"

He envisioned the ruin that would be their base of operations for the next few months. He had already humped in the bare basics they would need to survive, and his knee had thought the hard labor of repairing the old dock behind the house and crawling around repairing the roof were terrible ideas. He answered drily, "I suppose you could call it a base."

"Will you be training me?"

She sounded so damned enthusiastic. He restrained an urge to roll his eyes. She had no business being here. Women didn't belong in the Special Forces community. Period. The total loss of the second Medusa team had proven that, hadn't it?

He had no idea how he was actually going to train Tessa. He had no experience as an instructor, and with just the two of them out here by themselves, he couldn't rely on the same methods by which he'd been trained. "About training you. Here's the thing. I'm not an instructor. I'm a field operator. Or I was until I wrecked my knee a while back."

She looked down in quick sympathy at his leg. Sympathy he neither needed nor wanted. His plan was actually to use her training to get himself back into good enough shape to qualify for field ops again. He would

drag her along with him until he was field ready—
and until he had run her into the ground and made his
point—both to her and to Torsten.

"The first part of the Spec Ops training you went
through with the boys was mostly physical conditioning,
meant to weed out the faint of heart and the quitters. Torsten feels like he's seen enough from you to know you
would actually make it through the physical demands of
full Spec Ops training." He added wryly, "Torsten says
you don't know the meaning of the word *quit.*"

"He got that right," she muttered.

Spoken like a true operator. Beau smiled a little in
spite of himself.

Torsten had discussed with him at length where to
train her. This project needed a challenging, but se-
cluded, environment. Beau had been the one to suggest
reluctantly that his abandoned family homestead fit the
bill perfectly. The incredibly difficult bayou environment would force her to battle heat, humidity, muck,
critters and general squick factor.

"Will my training be like the men's course?" she
asked.

She sounded entirely too naive and eager. Poor kid
had no idea what she was in for. Torsten had been clear.
Push her right to the edge of breaking. Find out where
her limits lay and take her to them and beyond. And
while he was at it, figure out how to work with a woman.

Not. Happening.

"I'll be a real operator, right?"

"Don't count on it," he snapped.

"Then what the hell are we doing out here?" she shot
back.

Gun, I'm gonna kill you the next time I see you. He
straightened to his full height and a hot knife of pain

shot through his knee. He clenched his jaw until the pain subsided to bearable. "Assuming you survive, which is not a given, you would hypothetically be a no-kidding operator when it's said and done."

He added direly, "Don't get your hopes up. The odds of you being able to do everything you'll have to in order to work on an operational team are pretty much zero."

For a blink of an eye, trepidation shone in her eyes. But in the very next blink, steely resolve filled them. Unwillingly, he was impressed with her mental toughness. Even if it was useless. No way was he graduating her from this training. He wouldn't do that to his brothers.

"Why Louisiana?" she asked.

"Secret location. No prying eyes. Challenging environment." He added warningly, "The ocean may have sharks, but we've got gators out here. They're a whole lot sneakier than sharks, and you can't punch a gator on the nose and get him to back off. He'll eat your arm if you try it."

She turned her head to study him more fully, and her ponytail fell over her shoulder in soft curls that begged his fingers to run through them. Her gaze was intent. Focused on him like a laser. In that moment she looked just like a warrior...but with firm, round breasts filling out her T-shirt, a lush behind filling out her fatigue trousers and muscular legs a mile long.

Crap. Talk about messing with his head. A woman operator. And of course, she had to go and look like a freaking *Playboy* centerfold.

He had to give her credit: not many women looked this good without a stitch of makeup on, wearing combat boots, no less. Even her muscular shoulders and the pronounced veins in her bare arms were hot. Everything about her spoke of strength, confidence and badassery.

But it was all wrapped up in a package so sexy he could devour her like his steak earlier.

He shook his head to clear the thought. It didn't matter how sexy she was. He wasn't about to let her become a member of the club.

"Let's get out of here," he growled. "I owe you at least one decent night's sleep before we get this ball rolling." *Down a tall hill into a pile of manure.*

She was silent on the ride back to the motel, but her excitement was palpable. He just hoped his knee didn't give out before it was all said and done. He figured it was a 50/50 proposition. His doctors had argued vehemently against him attempting this comeback. They warned him that, if he overdid it on this op, he would blow his knee out, this time for good. But he refused to sit down and give up. He would go down fighting first.

They got back to the motel, and Tessa bounced out of the Jeep before he could get around to her side of the vehicle to open the door. He had to smile a little at her enthusiasm. He recalled all too well his own elation when he found out he'd been selected for special operations training all those years ago. Almost a decade.

Man, he'd been young and naive back then. He'd seen a whole lifetime's worth of action since. Would she be as jaded as he was ten years down the road, taciturn and tense, living life balanced on a razor's edge?

He closed the motel room's door and turned to face Tessa, who stood in the middle of the room, frowning. "Problem?" he asked.

"Well, yes. There's only one bed."

"You afraid to share it with me?" He arched an eyebrow in an open dare. "What are you going to do when you're bivouacking with a male team and all of you are crammed into a hide like sardines, spooning with each other?"

Her mint-green eyes narrowed. "*I've* got no problem sleeping with *you*. The question is—are you okay sleeping with me?"

He snorted. "Honey, I'm not sixteen. I've got my hormones firmly under control, thank you very much." Which might not be entirely true where she was concerned. All of the previous Medusas had lived and worked in very close quarters with their male counterparts. She had to learn to do the same. Starting with him. *Oh, joy.*

"Great," she said cheerfully. "Then you won't mind if I take my pants off. They're still a little wet."

Well, hell. Give the woman points for calling his bluff.

She kicked off her combat boots and stripped out of her fatigue pants right there in the middle of the room, revealing legs every bit as lean, muscular and wrap-around-his-hips-and-hang-on sexy as he'd thought they would be. His gaze slid down to her ankles and back up to her black bikini underwear, which stopped an inch short of the bottom of her olive green tank top.

Was that sweat popping out on his forehead? That strip of tanned stomach was almost more than he could stand. Her waist nipped in sharply, and then her chest flared in Coke-bottle curves that definitely were making him sweat. His palms itched to trace those curves. Memory of them mashed against his chest sent blood pounding to his groin.

Her chest was high and firm, and her nipples poked at the soft cotton of her shirt, taunting him. Daring him to take them in his mouth. To suck on them till she moaned. His hard-on all but doubled him over with its painful throbbing.

She stood there defiantly, staring back at him, daring him to say or do something about her display of general hotness.

Keep your eyes on her face.

Yeah, right. He could no more stop himself from letting his gaze wander down her body and back up than he could stop his body from leaping to attention at the sight of a woman like her standing half-naked in the middle of his hotel room practically daring him to do something about it.

His traitorous gaze traveled slowly and thoroughly down her body once more, taking in every juicy detail of her. Ho. Lee. Cow.

Okay, then. If that was how she wanted to play it… He reached for the back of the neck of his T-shirt and hauled it off over his head. He unbuckled his belt and shoved his pants down, as well. His Spandex sports briefs didn't do much to conceal his raging hard-on, but if she was going to play with the boys, she would have to get used to their reaction to her.

"Shall we?" he said casually. It took every last drop of his self-discipline to manage that light tone of voice.

Her bravado seemed knocked back a few notches by his matching strip-down. Good. She might as well learn early on just what a bad idea it was to dare an operator to do anything. Filters were not part of their mentality.

He reached for the light switch, and the room was abruptly swathed in darkness. The warmth and humidity of the night wrapped around him. The hum of the window air-conditioner and the thin stream of cold air coming from it teased his skin. The night was made for heavy breathing, sweaty skin on skin and the mindless plunge into hot, tight, female flesh—

Her silhouette slipped under the covers and the bed springs creaked under her weight, breaking him out of his fantasy. He felt brittle. On the verge of exploding. Cripes. And he hadn't even touched her yet.

Yet. Which implied intent to go there with her.

No can do, buddy, he told his raging erection. Not only was she off-limits, but he would also be damned if he would let her manipulate him into anything. Even if he wanted that thing worse than he wanted to keep breathing.

He moved over to the bed, lifted the covers and lay down beside her, an image of her body swimming in his mind's eye. Hell's bells. Her warmth radiated across the narrow strip of mattress separating them, along with simmering sexual tension that made him want to jump out of his skin.

It was a double bed, and they were not tiny people, which meant it was a tight fit. And he was neither a dead man nor a dummy. No way could he miss the fact that her nostrils flared whenever she looked at him and thought he wasn't looking. Nor could he miss how her pupils dilated anytime he had leaned close and smiled at her during dinner.

She was as hot for him as he was for her. Which was going to pose a massive problem on this op. Almost as massive as the woody tenting the sheets over his groin.

What would it be like to make love with a woman nearly as strong as he was, with stamina to match? A woman who could absorb everything he had to give and give as good as she got in return? If even half of his imagination was accurate, sex with Tessa would be epic. He was sure of it.

Of course, military fraternization rules prohibited instructors from sleeping with trainees. But he wasn't officially her instructor yet. Not until tomorrow. Besides, he was going to wash her out at the first opportunity, and they would each get on with their regularly scheduled lives. So there was nothing standing in the way of them scratching the itch between them. Right?

He couldn't find any flaw in the logic. His body jerked eagerly in response.

Nope. There was no reason at all they couldn't engage in a little extracurricular hanky-panky.

Other than the fact that she was going to hate his guts within the next twenty-four hours or so. And if he washed her out of the program like he planned to, she would hate his guts even worse. He tended to avoid sleeping with women who were going to become homicidal in the near future.

Disappointment coursed through his entire body.

I know, buddy. I know.

The scent of her shampoo drifted across the narrow space between them. It was sweet and floral and caressed him like a lover's hand, as seductive as hell. His body begged him to change his mind, and he clenched his teeth against its coaxing.

For her part, Tessa lay stiff and silent beside him. Tense, too, huh? Was she as turned on as he was? He would bet his next paycheck she was. He could practically smell her arousal.

The standoff stretched out between them, and with every passing minute, he became more determined not to be the one who broke first. But he couldn't remember being this uncomfortable since junior high when a hole in a wall had been enough to turn him on.

Their shoulders bumped every time one of them

shifted even the tiniest bit, sending him off into a new round of horny speculation, molar-grinding pain and reluctant refusal to give in.

This bed was entirely too small for the two of them.

Finally, in frustration, he muttered, "Turn on your side facing away from me."

"Why?" she blurted.

"That was an order. Just do it," he snapped.

She huffed and the mattress shifted beneath him. He rolled onto his side facing her and scooted forward until her warm, sexy body was tucked against his.

"What the hell are you doing?" she squawked.

"Getting comfortable so we can both sleep. Now you'll know where I am, and you won't lay there all night wondering if I'm going to jump your bones." He tucked his knees against the backs of hers, threw his arm over the inward curve of her waist and pulled her back against his front. Wow, she felt magnificent against him. They fit together like two spoons in the same set of silverware.

Of course they did. The torture wouldn't be complete if they didn't.

His male parts bulged against her in no uncertain terms, but there was no help for it. He was *not* going to have sex with her tonight, but neither was he going to treat her feminine sensibilities with kid gloves. If she planned to live and work with men like him, this was part of the deal.

She felt amazing in his arms. He couldn't remember the last time he'd done this platonic cuddling thing with a woman. Normally, he didn't stop to pay much attention to the finer details. The groupies just wanted to be bedded and then go on their merry way.

Maybe not so platonic, truth be told. His hands ached

to roam across her satin skin, to test her curves, to make her moan. He needed to lose himself in her body, to plunge into her mindlessly, to find bliss and then oblivion. His jaw clenched. He could do this. He could sleep with her without having sex with her. It was a *hell* of a fight not to act on his craving, but he corralled his lust.

"Go to sleep," he told her tightly.

By inches over the next few minutes, she gradually relaxed against him, which added a whole new set of temptations to his misery.

Get a grip, dude. He'd slept in war zones with mortars flying over his head and the deafening reports of shelling exploding around him. He'd slept with enemy forces closing in on him, and when completely surrounded by hostiles. He could bloody well sleep in a dark, quiet motel room in his hometown.

But he followed Tessa into sleep with great difficulty, ultimately having to resort to his sniper training to force his breathing to slow and deepen, to will himself to slide toward unconsciousness. She felt like a slice of heaven in his arms, soft and warm and relaxed. All the things his life was not.

He couldn't remember the last time he'd slept with a woman—actually *slept* with one. Most of his interactions involved horny, half-drunk sex and him leaving the woman's bed immediately after, before anything more could begin to develop. No attachments, no feelings. Just physical release. That was his mantra.

But Tessa Wilkes had already busted through that boundary in a big way. Even if they were mostly negative, he had definite feelings about being here with her.

Torsten owed him *huge*.

He eventually surprised himself by drifting off to

sleep. Maybe it was the companionship, or maybe it was how damned delicious Tessa felt in his arms.

He did wake up a couple of times during the night, tensing in anticipation of flashbacks from the night he should have died—the mission he'd been lucky to be medevaced away from with a destroyed leg and no future on the teams.

Nightmares were standard issue to men in his line of work. The shrinks said dreams were how guys like him worked out their emotional crap over killing people for a living. Whatever. He didn't run around spilling tears for his victims. They were bad people in need of killing.

But tonight the nightmares never came calling.

Nothing came to him except the sweet smell and quiet breathing of the woman snuggled up against him, filling the darkness with soft curves and comfort that lulled him back to sleep.

Too bad this was a onetime good deal. In the morning, he was going to unleash holy hell on her, and that would be the end of cuddles in the dark with Tessa Wilkes, wannabe Medusa and soon-to-be *former* trainee.

Chapter 4

Tessa arched her body in a cat stretch, moaning a little in the back of her throat as a confident male hand cupped her breast, thumb stroking lazily across her straining nipple. An arm was heavy across her waist, pinning her in place, and another heavily muscled arm acted as a pillow under her left ear. The smell and feel of man and muscle surrounded her, cocooning her completely in security.

Protection. A completely foreign concept to her, especially coming from a man. Slaps and fists were her childhood fare from most men. Her whole life, she'd been responsible for taking care of herself. Seeing to her own safety. If she didn't do it, no one else would. And yet, here was Beau, doing it unconsciously. As naturally as breathing.

Or maybe he was just copping a freebie feel.

Either way, she had never spent a full night with a

man before, and certainly not in a man's arms. It was shockingly…nice. The intimacy of it was staggering. It was something she could definitely get used to. Maybe not with this guy, and definitely not at this time in her life. But someday.

Her decision to pursue the Special Forces had pretty much precluded her having long-term relationships, given the time demands of her constant training. She was confident that, as long as she was on the teams, she would have to dedicate every waking minute to it.

The first new Medusa. Her. Who'd have thunk?

Deep satisfaction settled into her gut, along with a big dose of fist-pumping exultation. She'd climbed the impossible mountain and made it to the unattainable peak.

Although truth be told, she hadn't climbed the real mountain yet. She had no illusions about how hard her upcoming training was going to be. If the past few months had been a taste of things to come, the main meal was going to be a bona fide bitch. Particularly since her teacher didn't seem the least bit thrilled at the idea of her actually becoming a Medusa.

And as hard as it was going to be, she simply didn't have time for a personal life, no matter how nice it felt to snuggle with a hot guy. Correction: a smoking-hot guy who clearly was as turned on by her as she was by him. And yes, that made it worse. *Eyes on the prize, girlfriend. Eyes on the prize.*

Still. A pang of regret coursed through her. She really didn't need to have glimpsed this other existence she might have had.

Of course, she could have a life like this if she wanted it. A man to sleep with every night and wake up to every morning. All she had to do was quit. Walk away from Beau and the Medusas. She had no doubt his orders were to do everything in his power to make her give up; he wouldn't stop her if she decided she wanted this more than being a trained killer.

Thing was, she'd made it her life's work to become exactly what he was. To be stronger, badder and bolder than any jerkwad man she could ever possibly encounter. It was really no choice at all. She had to go for the chance to become a Medusa.

Her gut warned her, however, that she wasn't likely to feel this safe and protected again until she left the Medusas for good—either by choice or in a body bag.

Was a life of constant danger really what she wanted? It was all she had ever known growing up. But Beau had unwittingly—or maybe wittingly, knowing him—given her a glimpse of another world. Another way of life.

She lay there, caught between sleep and wakefulness, contemplating the choice. All the while, the big, strong warrior claimed his woman—

Whoa. Wait. What? She jolted the rest of the way to full consciousness with a mental lurch. She was nobody's woman! No matter that Beau was draped all over her and she was practically purring and rubbing herself against him like a cat in heat.

Apparently, their subconscious minds had no qualms about crawling all over each other. No matter that this man was about to be her trainer in a supersecret and superintense program that didn't officially exist. And no matter that she emphatically didn't want a long-term relationship with any guy. Ever. Not in this lifetime.

Obviously, there would be no rules during her training out here in the middle of nowhere. No oversight. No limits on what they could and would do. Did that mean there were no sexual boundaries, either?

She knew there would be mind games galore as part

of her training. They were part of any special operator's training. Was this semiseduction part of it?

Would Beau take this further?

More important, *would she let him?*

Belatedly, reason kicked in. This was Beau Lambert she was talking about. He clearly didn't like the idea of her becoming a Special Forces operative, but he'd been nothing but polite to her yesterday. He'd caught her when her strength had given out, holding her patiently until she could stand on her own two feet again. He'd fed her and seen to her needs, getting her water and a shower. Hell, he'd put Jimbo Kimball on the floor when the guy had made a rude advance to her.

Her gut told her in no uncertain terms that Beau Lambert was no creep. And she trusted her gut.

Sure, he was a healthy, red-blooded male, and his frequent, umm, male reactions, in her presence were a dead giveaway that he thought she was hot. But he'd spent an entire night in bed with her and not done a single thing about it.

She trusted him. More or less.

His palm cupped the weight of her breast and she gasped in spite of herself. Liquid lust shot straight from his hand to her crotch. She squeezed her thighs together tightly, but it didn't help. Her core throbbed hungrily, desperate for this man. It had been *way* too long since she'd had sex. It didn't help that she had utter faith he would know *exactly* how to appease that particular aching need.

She tried to move away from his hand subtly, without waking him. But the mattress was so narrow she had nowhere to go, and his arm tightened with easy strength, holding her snugly against him. Was he awake? Was this her first test?

Her eyes narrowed. She never had been the type to walk away from a challenge. She rolled over to face Beau and insinuated her thigh between his. The guy had an impressive erection going. Not lacking in that department at all, she noted. She rested her palms on his chest, tracing the gorgeous collection of muscles there and letting her hand drift around his narrow, muscular waist to his back. Her nose nestled against the junction of his neck and shoulder, the heat of the man furnace-like.

Abruptly, he came wide awake. He didn't move in any way to indicate to her that he'd woken up. One minute he was relaxed against her, and the next she was clinging to a deadly predator thrumming with tension, prepared to pounce at any second and eat her alive.

Beau was so appealing to the eye that it was easy to forget just how dangerous a man he was. His pretty-boy looks lulled a person into a false sense of security. She could see how Jimbo had made the mistake. Memory of that cold, flat, killer's calm in Beau's eyes last night in the restaurant flashed into her head. She wasn't just playing with fire here. She was playing with a lit blowtorch.

"What are you doing, Tessa?" he growled.

"Saying good morning," she replied brightly.

"You do like to live dangerously, don't you?"

"Don't you?" she challenged.

And just like that, she was on her back, her legs pinned beneath his thighs, his body weight smashing her down into the cheap mattress, her hands yanked up over her head, her wrists captured in an iron grip. He stared down at her from a range of about six inches. Their bodies fit together *perfectly*. "Don't tease me if you can't take the heat."

Gulp. She scraped together all the false bravado she could muster and replied lightly, "I can give back anything you dish out. I'm all the woman you can handle and more. You've never met a woman like me."

She stared up at him bravely, although doubt over the wisdom of engaging in this little game of cat and mouse with a pissed off lion shivered down her spine.

One corner of his mouth turned up. Whether it was in amusement or disbelief, she couldn't tell. He spoke with quiet certainty. "I guarantee you've never met a man like me. I'm going to warn you once, and once only. Don't play games with me. You *will* lose."

Yeah, but losing to him didn't sound too bad at the moment, not with his arousal pressing at the juncture of her thighs, and his weight and strength making her feel sweetly overpowered.

He pressed up and away from her abruptly, leaving the bed shaking in his absence. A little voice in the back of her head swore angrily at her for letting him go, and she shamelessly watched him retreat into the bathroom. The man had a rear end fully as sculpted and magnificent as the rest of him. Nope, her personal instructor was not hard on the eye. Not at all.

She bounded out of bed, feeling better than she expected. Maybe it was the adrenaline in anticipation of what was to come, or maybe it was last night's protein bomb of steak and muscle relaxant of whiskey that had helped her recover overnight.

Or maybe, a little voice in the back of her head whispered, *it was sleeping in Beau's arms that had her feeling so fantastic this morning*. She told the voice to shut up and reached for her pants and combat boots.

"Hungry?" Beau bit out from the doorway of the bathroom as she finished dressing.

"I know I'm never supposed to turn down an opportunity to eat, but I'm actually not hungry after that huge meal last night."

"Load up on water, then," he instructed her tersely.

Oh, God. What did he have planned for her? He wasn't going to hold it against her that she'd rubbed herself all over him before they'd entirely woken up, was he? It had been his idea in the first place to spoon all blasted night. Irritation at him for doing it and at herself for liking it coursed through her.

She downed a bunch of water, and ominously, he did the same. They got into the Jeep and drove south for about thirty minutes. The morning sun felt good on her skin, and the moist breeze in her face made her feel free and alive.

Beau was silent on the drive, and she followed suit. Major Torsten had reprimanded her training class leader once with a brusque comment that had stuck with her. *Try not to ruin a good silence.*

"What are you smiling about?" Beau asked.

She repeated Torsten's pearl of wisdom and Beau replied, "Big talker, your class leader?"

"Obsessively. Couldn't shut up long enough to let anyone else share a decent idea."

"Important leadership skill, listening to your guys."

He turned off the main road and parked just short of a tall sand dune. They slogged over the dune, and the Gulf of Mexico stretched away at their feet. The surf was quiet, swishing onto the shore serenely. A few distant figures dotted the beach, but no people were close.

Beau set down a pair of two-liter water bottles and partially buried them in the sand at the base of a wooden sign pointing at the parking lot behind them. He stripped off his T-shirt and tossed it over the bottles.

She gulped at the sight of all that glorious muscle,

and her hand remembered the feel of them sliding under her palms. She actually felt her pupils dilating. Dang it. They were a dead giveaway that she was affected by the sight of him shirtless. Sure enough, he smirked at her.

"Let's go," Beau said. "Down the beach and back."

She was tempted to ask how far down the beach, but she knew better. Run distances tended to increase exponentially in the face of whining or complaining about them. The sand was soggy and hard-packed, but hand-sized flakes of it gave way unpredictably under her combat boots, making each step she took unstable. Sand running used an entirely different set of muscles than road running. Stabilizer muscles in the ankles and knees got viciously overused, and fatigue and pain set in fast.

Today was worse than most. Beau really seemed to have it in for her. Maybe he was pissed off, too, that he'd liked spooning last night.

Screw him. It had been his stupid idea.

She didn't think Beau was ever going to turn around and head back toward the Jeep. Nope, he was all glistening skin, flexing muscle, deep breathing and long stride. His gold-touched brown hair was tousled by the breeze, and his bronzed torso was lightly dusted with sand that her fingers itched to brush off him.

"You think you can seriously become a Medusa?" he grunted.

"Yeah," she grunted back. She kept her response short so he wouldn't hear her panting for breath between phrases. This pace was a killer. As if he was trying to run her into the ground. "What's your problem with women?"

"No problem. I like women. Just don't like the idea of them on the teams."

Oh, yeah? Then she would just have to prove him

wrong and show him women did belong in the Special Forces.

He picked up the pace, and she stuck to his side like a sandbur, determined to show him she could hack anything he threw at her. A stitch developed in her side, and she focused on breathing more deeply and getting more oxygen to her starved muscles.

He scowled and picked up the pace again.

Jerk.

As her thighs and calves protested more stridently, she searched for something, anything, to distract her from the pain. Unfortunately, her mind latched onto the question of how in the *world* it was possible for any human being to look so hot while slogging through shifting sand that made every step a person took treacherous as all get out. She would purely hate the guy if she didn't reluctantly admire anyone who could look so good while sweating profusely.

She estimated they were a solid three miles down the beach before he finally turned around. Crud. She was wiped out *now*, and they still had the entire run back to do.

Beau glanced over at her. "You good?"

"Yup," she lied. "Let's do it."

She caught a flash of pain on his face as they turned around. A moment's triumph quickly gave way in her brain to wondering just how screwed up his knee was. Her undergraduate degree had been in kinesiology, and that training kicked in now. This sand running should be good for it—low impact, with lots of strength training for the muscles that would support the joint—*if* he didn't take a bad step and blow the whole thing out.

She was starting to labor, her legs and her lungs tiring. But no way was she going to give Beau the satisfaction of stopping. She glanced over at him, and he was scowling. Ticked off that she could hack the pace he'd set, maybe?

As for her own pain, she knew how to deal with it. She settled into the zen state of detachment from body that had gotten her through half a dozen triathlons, a dozen marathons and countless beatings from her mother's more violent boyfriends. She was a machine. Pain had no meaning, and fatigue was the attempt of a lazy body to get out of doing its job.

The dune with its big wooden sign pointing to the parking lot came into sight in the distance. Almost there. Thank goodness.

She still had a smidgen of energy left, and she used it to deliver a silent screw-you to the chauvinist beside her. Her stride lengthened. She loved running, and the morning was crisp, the breeze in her face just strong enough to cool her without impeding her speed. She left Beau behind and tore along the beach, arms pumping, sand flying.

The dune loomed close, the lettering on the sign becoming legible. Almost there. A hundred yards. Fifty. She put on one last burst of speed and reached deep for everything she had. She blasted past the sign and eased off the accelerator with a huge mental sigh of relief, gratefully letting her speed coast down to a walk. She turned around to grin at Beau.

He looked genuinely ticked off as he caught up with her. Maybe it hadn't been the smartest thing she ever did to show up her instructor like that. Especially with his messed up leg and all. He caught up with her and—

What the heck? He kept on running. He passed her and drew away steadily.

Son of a—

Swearing mentally, she mustered her physical and mental resources. Gathered herself. And took off running after him. It took her a couple of minutes to catch up with Beau, who did not once look back over his shoulder to check on her. Not that she expected him to.

The second she did pull up by his shoulder, though, he smirked…and sped up. Not to a killer charge, but into a plenty brisk run. Jeez. How much farther was he going to drag her?

Her eyes narrowed. Trying to wear her down, was he? Hoping she would cry *uncle* and give up? Take her girlie toys and go home? Not freaking likely. She dug deep and plowed on, hell-bent not to give him the satisfaction of winning.

He glanced over at her, determination glinting in his eyes, as well. He was obviously just as hell-bent on breaking her. The silent battle of wills continued as they raced down the beach.

She had stumbled a couple of times and painfully wrenched her ankle on a misstep before it dawned on her that she'd lost mental focus. She was locked into being annoyed that he'd lied about the length of the run and into proving she was as good as he was. She wasn't paying enough attention to what she was doing right now.

Was there was an actual point to this competition from hell other than proving she wasn't fast enough to run with the big dogs?

Ahh. The lesson dawned on her. Just because she'd thought the run was over didn't mean the situation couldn't change at a moment's notice. Same deal out in the field. Just because a team thought a mission was over didn't mean the mission couldn't change or encounter a last-minute complication that extended it indefinitely. A run—or a mission—wasn't over until it was over.

She settled down, brought her mind back into focus on the mechanics of her running. She let go of the frustration, calmed her emotions and dropped back into the calm state that would allow her to keep on running as long as necessary or until her body collapsed out from under her.

No sooner had she done that, than Beau turned around and headed back toward the Jeep. This time, when they reached the sign, she didn't break stride until he did. She was prepared to run all the way back down that damned beach if she had to.

He slowed to a walk, and she did the same beside him. Gratefully. He dug the water bottles out of the sand at the base of the sign and handed one to her. They downed their respective drinks and caught their breath in silence.

"How's your knee?" she asked.

"Fine," he snapped.

"I'm not the enemy, Beau. I was an athletic trainer in college. I'm on your side and want to see your knee come back for you."

He glared at her for a long moment, and then jerked his head in a single, tight nod.

She knew that nod for the concession that it was. It had been a silent acknowledgment of alliance in pursuit of a common goal. And it was as good a starting place as any with him.

They climbed in the Jeep, and Beau pointed it back toward Motel MOE. "You passed the training exercise," he tossed at her.

So. That unexpected bonus run *had* been the whole point of today's outing. She'd analyzed it correctly. Leaning back in satisfaction, a horrifying thought occurred to her. It wasn't even close to noon yet. What if the lessons weren't over? What if he had some additional massive torture in store for her this afternoon?

As soon as the notion occurred to her, certainty that she was right set in. Better grab whatever rest she could right now. She closed her eyes and consciously relaxed every muscle in her body. It wasn't sleep, but it was the next best form of rest for recovery purposes.

Chapter 5

Tessa napped in the room while Beau showered. Then, while she washed up, he went out and came back with sandwiches, fruit and drinks. She matched his rapid consumption of the meal, and when he reached for his combat boots she did the same. Suspiciously.

"Blouse your pants," Beau ordered. "There'll be snakes and biting insects galore where we're going."

Great. Without voicing her distaste for creepy-crawlies, she hooked stretchy elastic bands around the tops of her boots and tucked the bottoms of her pant legs under the elastics, creating a snug seal from boot leather to trouser that would let nothing crawl up inside her pants.

Beau could crawl inside her pants—

Hush up, little voice.

They took off in the Jeep and quickly left the main highway for roads that would be more properly classed as shock-absorber-destroying trails. She had to duck branches, and on more than one occasion, brace herself against the overhead roll bar to avoid being thrown out of the Jeep.

"Grab me a protein bar from the glove compartment," Beau said after one such near ejection. "Get a couple for yourself, too."

She wasn't particularly hungry after their recent lunch, but she did as he directed. The protein bars turned out to be military issue—2000 calories in a compressed bar she knew from experience tasted like sawdust and lard. She stowed several in her rucksack.

The road ended without warning at the bank of a body of water, overhung by black-trunked cypresses draped in gray Spanish moss. It was every bit as atmospherically creepy as she could hope for in a bayou. All it lacked was an alligator or two sliding off the bank into the inky black water. Beau turned off the ignition.

"We're on foot the rest of the way," he announced. He shouldered a hefty backpack while she strapped on her rucksack. The thick vegetation here was as unlike the California desert of her youth as it was possible for terrain to be. Comparing it to a sauna didn't begin to do justice to the cloying mugginess.

"Don't run ahead of me out here. You'll get lost, or you'll get into trouble."

Annoyed that she'd showed him up this morning, huh? She highly doubted if his knee was healthy she'd have been able to keep up with him, let alone outrun him.

The intent in bringing her out here was obvious. Maximum misery. Test her character. Challenge her will to stay the course and prevail.

Beau headed out along the edge of the water, following the faintest of trails. There was no path to speak of, just a broken branch or a flattened clump of grass to indicate someone had come this way before. He pointed out the trail signs to her as they moved deeper into the gloom of the bayou. A subtle art, tracking.

She gathered this was how he planned to teach her—by sharing tidbits as they came up until he'd passed on enough information for her to operate in the field. Her job would be to register every little piece of advice he gave her, learn it and apply it. Fair enough.

They fell into a rhythm holding branches back for each other, murmuring warnings about footing and pointing out hazards. It felt as if an invisible rope connected them; every movement he made vibrated down its length into her. It was a hyperawareness bordering on psychic.

Did all operators have this when they worked together, or was this just the simmering attraction between them manifesting itself?

She hoped it was the former but feared it was the latter. What was she going to do about it if she couldn't get past her raging attraction to him? More to the point, what would he do about it?

The earth beneath her feet had a spongy quality that she found vaguely unsettling. After a rainstorm, she suspected this path would be impassable.

Somebody, Beau probably, had already hacked through the stands of vining kudzu and brambles that occasionally blocked their path. He moved quickly enough that she had to walk fast and breathe hard to keep up with him. Not that he ever looked back at her.

They race-hiked for a solid hour before he stopped at the end of a spit of land jutting out into a bog. "Waterproof your gear," he ordered.

Groaning mentally, she pulled out a large, waterproof

bag and zipped her entire rucksack into it while he did the same with his backpack.

"Not like that. Capture air in the bag so it'll float. Saves you having to drag it along as dead weight under the water. If we were moving covertly, you'd want to take the air out and add rocks if necessary to sink it. But for today's purposes, float it."

She unzipped her waterproof sack a little, blew air into it like a balloon and resealed the thing. And so it went. Every few minutes he passed along some technique or taught her some new trick. It was a humbling demonstration in how much she had to learn.

They spotted alligators now and then. Mostly, they looked like bumpy gray logs as they slid silently into the water and disappeared when she and Beau got close. Tessa sincerely hoped they were all swimming in the opposite direction.

He picked up a makeshift walking stick, and she did the same, unsure why she was going to need it...until he walked out into the bog. Beau used his stick to test each spongy mass of dead grass and debris before he stepped on it.

She sank nearly to her knees in black, brackish water with each step, and her pants became coated in black muck. Not only did she have no trouble envisioning snakes, alligators and other nasty critters rising up out of the goop, but the water had to be chock-full of nasty parasites and microbes, too. Ick.

She kept up with Beau until she had one tiny lapse of concentration and failed to test a step. Her right leg sank to midthigh and promptly got stuck.

"Beau!" she called as he moved ahead of her.

He turned around and took stock of her predicament. "How are you going to get yourself out?" he asked.

She swore to herself. Ideally, he would reach a hand out and give her a tug. Barring that, this was going to suck. She tested the hold the muck had on her foot. Her whole boot was pretty securely sucked down into the sludgy sediment. She wedged her walking stick into a bush to one side of her and rested the other end atop a cypress stump jutting up on her other side. She gave an experimental tug on the makeshift pull-up bar. No movement. At all.

No amount of wiggling, jiggling or pulling loosened up the mud around her boot. She was well and truly stuck. She sighed and looked up at Beau. "I'm going to have to dig myself out by hand, aren't I?"

He merely shrugged.

No help there. It was tempting to call him names for refusing to help her, but she understood what he was doing. He was making her be self-reliant. Solve problems.

She took a deep breath, screwed her eyes shut and ducked her head under the disgusting water, running her hand down her leg until it encountered the sticky glop trapping her foot. Working fast, she grabbed handfuls of it, digging around the edges of her boot until it came loose all at once and tipped her over on her side, submerging her completely.

She righted herself, sputtering, and dashed the water and debris away from her eyes before she risked opening them.

Her entire body looked like she'd gotten wet and rolled around in a bag of black topsoil. Where there wasn't black muck, there was green pond slime. The foul odor of it nearly gagged her. It was completely disgusting.

She wiped a string of algae off her face and grinned

gamely through her coating of filth at Beau. "Good times," she declared.

He nodded back, a look of reluctant approval on his face. Hah. This had been a test, too. Self-reliance, and the ability to find humor in a sucky situation, maybe?

"You look like a rougarou," he commented.

"Rouga who?" she asked.

"Rougarou. Swamp monster said to inhabit the bayou. Human by day, people-attacking monster by night."

"Like a werewolf?"

"Close enough. Tender, sweet morsel like you will be right up the rougarou's alley."

She rolled her eyes at him. "If you're trying to scare me, you'll have to do better than that."

She joined him on a patch of relatively dry ground, and he took a hasty step back from her. "Whew. You stink. That a habit with you?"

Tessa shrugged, unconcerned. "There's a time to smell good and a time to smell bad. Perfume out here would only draw mosquitoes."

"Sensible attitude for a woman."

Her gaze narrowed. "That's the problem with you men. You make the mistake of expecting me to act and think differently than you because I'm a girl. Quit thinking of me as a woman and just think of me as a soldier."

His gaze raked down her body and back up to her face. "Kinda hard to forget you're a woman with curves like that."

She made a sound of irritation. "What do you want me to do? Wear a burlap sack in the field? It's not my problem if men look at me and think of sex."

"It is your problem if it affects the functioning of the team you're on."

"If I'm on the Medusas, it'll be all women and not a problem," she shot back.

"Assuming we can find enough women to field an all-female team. Until then, you'll have to run with guys."

Oh.

None of her instructors to date had been willing to talk about this 600-pound gorilla lurking in the corner, and she leaped on the opportunity to get inside the head of a male special operator.

"I always thought the big hang-up was that women aren't physically strong enough to be on a team. But if I'm hearing you correctly, you think the problem is sex, not strength."

He turned and took off walking, but thankfully continued the conversation. "Lack of upper body strength is a real problem. A team is only as strong as its weakest member."

"But you think my gender is the bigger problem?"

"Not your gender. The way you look."

She considered herself okay-looking—a six, maybe. She was too unconventional to be considered beautiful. But hey. Give the man points for honesty. "So you think my—" she searched for words "—general hotness…is the problem?"

"Team dynamics are important in the field. All the power struggles and personality issues have to get worked out in training so that, by the time a team hits an op, no personal crap distracts them."

"Isn't that hard to achieve? You guys are known to have big egos and a lot of testosterone."

"Egos are okay in bars when the guys are picking up women. But they have no place on a mission." He shrugged. "Besides, there's always somebody more bad-ass than you to keep you humble."

She considered his comments as they hiked in silence for a while. If she was not mistaken, he was gradually picking up the pace of their hike. She was having to work even harder to keep up with him now.

Abruptly, Beau declared, "You think too damned loud."

"Excuse me?"

"I can hear you thinking back there. What's running through your head?"

She was startled. Her instructors to date hadn't had the slightest interest in knowing what she was thinking. They had just wanted to run her into the ground and force her into a physical collapse.

"Why do you want to know what I'm thinking?"

"Most civilians think of this kind of training only as physically grueling. But the mental aspects are actually more important. It's about finding your breaking points and learning how to overcome not only fatigue and physical pain but also fear, stress, anger or any other thought or emotion that could get you killed on an op. I know how guys think. But I've got no clue how you think."

She frowned at his back and answered slowly, "I'm not afraid of physical pain. I learned a long time ago how to use my mind to overcome it. That part of the game is never going to be a problem for me."

He offered up in a reluctant voice, "That was Torsten's assessment of you."

"Really?" she exclaimed. "He noticed?"

"The guy's like a spider sitting in the middle of his web. Nothing escapes his notice. He's freakishly accurate in forecasting who will and won't make it through Spec Ops training."

"What else did he have to say about me?"

"Do I look stupid?" Beau threw over his shoulder. "I'm not giving up all my secrets to you."

She laughed quietly behind him. "I thought that was my line."

Beau's only answer was to pick up the pace. Significantly.

Cautious after her misstep earlier, she struggled to splash along behind him and keep herself from taking another plunge in the swamp. The afternoon heated up even more, and the air was so thick with humidity and so utterly still it felt as if she was swimming through it. The stench clinging to her hair and clothes reeked powerfully enough to make her feel sick.

She drank all her bottled water and began to consider where she was going to get more clean drinking water. It was frustrating being surrounded by so much of the stuff and none of it drinkable. The swamp water would need to be filtered, distilled and treated with purification tablets before she would even think about giving it a try. Setting up a distilling rig would take some time and a fire. A fire would take dry kindling to start, and there was precious little of that out here.

Suspicious of Beau after he'd let her flail in the muck alone, she started collecting dry, dead twigs as she came across them and stuffing them into a pocket of her rucksack. At some point in the miserable race through the bayou, they passed a cedar stump poking above the water line. It was heavily decayed and crumbling. Gleefully, she stashed handfuls of resin-soaked cedar shards in her pack. Even wet, the highly flammable fatwood would light off with a simple match to start it burning.

She was just zipping the last pocket on her rucksack when Beau startled her, speaking directly in her ear. "What are you doing?"

She jumped about a foot straight up in the air and whipped around to glare at him. He loomed so close she could see his individual eyelashes, thick and dark and long.

"Nice startle reflex you've got there, Wilkes."

"Screw you, Lambo," she muttered.

"Seriously. What were you doing?"

"Gathering fatwood."

"Why?"

"Fire starter. I figure you're going to make me get my own water, and I plan to distill it before I drink any of that filth."

He nodded. "Thinking ahead and contingency planning can save your hide." He added casually, "Hate me yet?"

She blinked up at him, surprised at the question. Deliberately, he stripped off his gloves and tucked them in his belt. Then he shocked her by reaching out to tuck a wayward strand of her hair behind her ear. His fingertips traced the rim of her ear lightly, and her gaze snapped up to his. Whoa. His eyes flared as hot as a blast furnace as he stared down at her. An ember of something equally molten ignited low in her belly, incinerating her from the inside out.

The invisible rope between them tightened, and she swayed toward him. He, too, seemed to feel the pull and he leaned closer, bringing them chest to chest. His lips parted slightly, and darned if hers didn't do the same. His breath touched her cheek as lightly as his fingers had touched her ear.

How her right hand came to rest on his chest, she had no idea. But she felt his heart thudding slow and steady beneath her palm. Vital. Masculine. Strong.

"Man, you're tempting," he breathed.

"Hello, pot. Meet kettle," she murmured back. He shifted restlessly beneath her palm, and his hands came up to encompass both sides of her head, tilting her face up slightly. At just the right angle for kissing. His heart-beat leaped erratically beneath her hand, and her breath hitched in response.

She wanted to kiss him so much she could hardly stand it. Did she dare? All she had to do was stand on her tiptoes, lean in a little more, plaster her body against the smoking-hot length of his and touch that sexy mouth with hers. Breathe him in, taste him, take off his shirt, shove her hands down his pants and grasp his throbbing—

He stepped back sharply.

Shoot! Was the guy a mind reader or something? Lust raged through her, clawing at her angrily.

One corner of his mouth quirked up knowingly as if he sensed her sexual frustration. "There's more than one way to get you to hate me."

"Why do you want me to hate you?"

"You'll figure it out." He shrugged. "Guess I'll have to pick up the pace."

Of what? Seducing her? Please God, yes, pick up the pace!

She thought she heard him swear under his breath. "Let's go," he ordered briskly, whirling and striding off into the swamp.

Mentally, she groaned. Her legs were not in top shape after yesterday's run and this morning's, and the boggy terrain was forcing her to lift her feet unnaturally high, often having to pull her boot free of the clutching muck under the water in the process. It was exhausting going. It made the most sadistic stair-climbing machine look like kid stuff. Not that she would ever voice a complaint aloud to him, of course.

Good thing his rear end was so nice to look at.

After announcing his intent to provoke her hatred by speeding up, he kept his word. She had to splash along clumsily, half running, to match his long strides.

The man was a freaking machine. Marching and running were areas she pretty much always kept up with the boys, but Beau made mincemeat of her out here. Twice he had to stop and wait for her to catch up lest they lose sight of each other entirely in the dense vegetation. He was not happy either time she caught up with him, his lips pressed tightly together and his sapphire eyes glinting in disapproval, but he didn't say anything. He just turned and pressed on.

Not that it entered her mind to quit. He would have to kill her to get her to stop trying to keep up.

Okay, she was starting to hate him a little. It wasn't fair for any one person to be that strong or have that much stamina. Her mind boggled at the prospect of sex with a man like him. He would wear her *out*. Imagining it was enough to keep her slogging along after him for at least another hour.

In spite of the awesome distraction of fantasizing about sleeping with Beau, the afternoon stretched on interminably, a slow roasting oven that cooked her alive. It didn't help that she had no more water. A dehydration headache pounded at her skull, her thighs screamed in protest, her stomach tried to gnaw a hole through her spine, she was covered in dried, black, swamp gook, she itched, she stunk and she hurt from head to foot. To top it all off, she was horny as heck. In a nutshell, it was awful.

But hey. She could be sitting in an office pushing paper and pouring coffee. She supposed it was a matter of picking her poison.

Desire to cry *uncle* warred with knowing that Beau

was trying to get her to do precisely that. No way would she give him the satisfaction. She didn't like it when anyone got inside her head, particularly her personal, smoking-hot commando.

She'd had more than enough of that as a child. Her mother's string of crappy boyfriends had excelled in messing with her, and she'd learned early to throw up emotional walls against their teasing and outright cruelty. Who'd have thought the day would come when she would actually be grateful to the slimy jerks her mother'd had a gift for finding and bringing home?

"You're thinking loudly again," Beau announced.

She looked up at him, startled. He shot her a single, cocked eyebrow that demanded to know what was going on in her noggin. "I was thinking about my mother's boyfriends."

"Kinky."

She scowled. "Hardly. I never thought I'd be grateful to them for being jackasses."

Beau cracked a smile. "That's more like it."

"What do you mean?" she challenged.

"I was wondering how long I would have to run you around in circles out here before you'd finally get fed up."

"We've been going in circles?" she exclaimed. Now, that actually did hack her off.

His grin widened. "Round and round."

"Okay, I hate you now."

He laughed outright. "Excellent. Let's head for camp, then."

Camp? Out here? Oh, joy. She generally loved being outdoors. In fact, she despised being cooped up behind walls as a rule. But this place had an ee-yew factor that was hard to overlook. Beyond the alligators she'd already seen, she knew there were rattlesnakes, cottonmouths, copperheads, scorpions and a host of other venomous critters lurking out here. Ah, well. It wasn't like special operators got to choose their environments. And at least no one was shooting at her.

Yet.

Chapter 6

The sun had gone down and twilight wreathed the mist starting to rise off the swamp when suddenly, her feet touched solid ground. Thank God.

This never-ending day had all but done her in. Her boots squished with each step and her feet felt totally waterlogged, but she couldn't care less. She could actually walk without having to lift her feet knee-high.

She stopped and stared as they moved farther ashore. Two arrow-straight, parallel rows of huge, arching live oak trees stretched away into the gathering darkness in shades of gray and black. It was an incongruous sign of human civilization tucked away in the middle of nowhere. The ancient trees were thickly festooned with Spanish moss like twin lines of stooping old women with long, straggly, witch's hair.

Hints of gravel beneath her feet spoke of a driveway of some kind having once run between the looming trees. Those massive oaks had to be at least a hundred years old. Who on earth could have planted them? And why would anyone settle in this godforsaken spot?

Beau strode confidently between the trees as if he had a destination in mind. She followed along, intrigued in spite of herself. She made out a shape ahead, tucked into the deep shadows of a cluster of giant live oaks.

Square. Man-made.

She squinted into the gloom. Was that a house?

It looked as old as the trees. If the siding had ever seen paint, it was long gone, leaving behind gray, weathered wood that looked older than time. The house, a sprawling, one-story plantation-style home stood unnaturally high off the ground on telephone-pole-sized stilts. Shutters hung at crazy angles, and a wide, covered porch wrapped around the entire thing, supported by gray pillars in desperate need of paint. A set of broad, graceful steps led up to it.

"What is this place?" she asked cautiously as Beau came to a stop in front of the ruin.

"It was a hideout for pirates. Or rather their women. Story has it this place was originally built as a brothel for pirate doxies."

"Cool! Which pirate?"

"One too smart to let his name get bandied about and get so famous the authorities came after him."

Awareness of being entirely alone with a man who could easily overpower her and do whatever he wanted to her washed over her. Cold fingers of fear crept up her spine at the notion. She'd been groped by men and been powerless to stop it too many times as a kid to be comfortable now.

At least the motel had offered the illusion of other humans nearby who would hear her screams and call for help. But in this place she would be completely at Beau's mercy. She'd decided just this morning that she trusted him. Did that still hold true out here?

"Is it safe to go inside?" she asked, testing the first step cautiously with her foot.

"I repaired the steps before you got here. They're safe. Just don't explore beneath them. An aggressively unpleasant nest of cottonmouths is living there."

While her mind wanted to dwell on the mention of snakes, she was more interested in the notion of him preparing for her arrival. "How long have you known I was coming?" she asked sharply.

"You would have to take that up with Torsten."

"I'm taking it up with you."

He exhaled hard. "He gave me a heads-up two weeks ago that he wanted me to bring a female candidate here for training."

"Why did he let me suffer through the past two weeks with the men if he was just going to pull me out and send me here?"

"Probably wanted to see how you dealt with the last set of training exercises. They come pretty close to approximating the physical challenges of actual operations."

She snorted. "The instructors hounded me day and night. Nothing I did was good enough for them. I have never been screamed at so much in my entire life."

"Torsten liked what he saw when his guys pushed you, or you wouldn't be here."

"Bastard," she grumbled.

"You have no idea," Beau bit out. He turned and strode up the long, sweeping staircase.

She followed him, asking curiously, "What did he do to you?"

"He sent me to a freaking swamp to train a girl wannabe."

"Aww, c'mon. It's not that bad running around with me, is it?" she joked to disguise the pang of hurt his snapped reply caused her.

He didn't deign to answer. Instead, he threw open the front door and stood back to let her enter.

A sense of impending doom swept over her. Her old fears kicked up, in spite of her conscious effort to suppress them. Going inside, allowing herself to be trapped behind walls with a man, was madness. She knew better!

But this was Beau. He didn't count in the grand scheme of men who were not to be trusted. She entered the house. It was a stupid little thing, but she mentally counted it as a private triumph over her rotten past.

No surprise, the architecture of the plantation home was traditional. A wide hallway ran from front to back with rooms opening off each side of it, and the house stretched back much deeper than she'd guessed at first glance. The inside wasn't anywhere near as decrepit as the outside. What little furniture there was appeared to be in decent condition, if hopelessly dated. It struck her as 1940s-era decor.

She turned right, slid between a mostly closed set of pocket doors and looked around at a parlor, she supposed it would have been called.

Beau filled the doorway behind her as she examined a fireplace mantel carved from green marble and in pristine condition. The stone was cool and smooth and soothing beneath her fingertips. Everything the man behind her was not.

She turned to face him. In the gloom, she could barely make out his features, and what she could see gave nothing away.

"Look, Wilkes. My being here has nothing to do with you." A pause. "Well, it does to the extent that I'm supposed to train you until you wash out."

What if she didn't wash out? Then what? Was he prepared to admit he was wrong and that women—she—could cut it in Spec Ops?

Beau added, "Torsten sent me here for reasons that have nothing to do with you."

"Care to share?" she asked when he didn't continue.

"Nope."

And the monosyllabic caveman was back. Great.

"Show me around the place?" she asked.

"Parlor," he commented, gesturing to the room at large. She followed him back out into the main hall. He pointed at a set of closed pocket doors across the hall. "Billiard room." He strode down the hallway, not checking to see if she followed. Which, of course, she did. He pointed to his right. "Dining room." He pointed across the hall. "Sitting room. Converted to an office a while back.

"Two bedrooms, one on each side of the hall." He pointed at twin pairs of doors as he passed them. "Next, bathroom on the left. Toilet flushes if you dump a bucket of water in the tank. None of the other plumbing works. Staircase to the attic on the right. Four more bedrooms and a bathroom upstairs under the rafters. For maids or the new girls."

Right. Pirate brothel. Many bedrooms. Got it.

"Last two bedrooms in the back of the ground floor were converted to a modern kitchen in the nineteen-twenties. It runs the full width of the house."

The layout was simple. Efficient. And as she recalled, this shotgun style allowed for maximum breezes to cool a home. "I gather this house is on stilts because of flooding?"

"Hurricane storm surges mostly."

She wandered into the kitchen, which was a wreck. But she spied something that made her smile. "A still?" she asked. "The pirates did a little moonshining on the side?"

"Squatters brought that in."

"Where are these squatters now?"

A shrug. "I chased them out. We're here now."

"Are we the new squatters in town?"

"I own the place."

"Not much for upkeep of your stuff, huh?" she commented.

"Haven't been home in a while. I inherited it a few years back, and it was already decrepit then. Maybe when I get out of the military I'll restore the place."

"Assuming anything is left by then to restore."

"Let's hope that's the problem," he muttered under his breath.

Worried about staying on the teams, was he? Interesting. No wonder he was tense about his knee injury. He thought it was bad enough that it might end his career, apparently. She would be chippy, too, if she thought her whole future was at stake.

Oh, wait. It was.

She moved over to the still to look it over. "Copper tubing looks to be in good shape. With a few small modifications, I should be able to distill water with this."

"Be my guest."

That sounded suspiciously like a challenge. Fine. She'd always been mechanical. One of her mother's less awful boyfriends had taught her how to repair cars, and she was comfortable around tools and tubes and wires.

She spent the next half hour modifying the still and moving it to the backyard, leery of burning the house down if she set a fire on the kitchen floor. Using her bits of fatwood, she started a fire to heat the steel water drum. In the amount of time it took her to gather a good-sized pile of firewood and stack it beside the barrel, distilled water was starting to drip out of a glass tube into a bucket she'd wiped out and placed under the nozzle. It would take a good chunk of the night to distill enough water to sustain them both, but once the setup was running smoothly, they ought to get plenty of drinking water.

She rinsed off as best she could with a bucket of water she scooped out of the surrounding bayou and a bar of soap out of her pack. It wasn't a great bath, but it was better than nothing. Cleanliness mattered in the field. Jungle rot was a constant threat to armpits, groins and toes, not to mention the risk of bacterial infections to any cuts or scrapes she might have picked up and failed to disinfect.

Beau helped her roll a big log over next to the distiller, and they sat down to dry their feet next to the fire. Trench foot, where the bottom of the foot died and sloughed off, was a real danger when feet spent hours on end soaked in filthy water. They stripped off their boots and socks and stuck their feet as close to the flames as they could stand to warm and thoroughly dry their skin.

Munching energy bars, they watched the flames and listened to the night sounds. Beau kicked back, looking relaxed, but she felt stretched as tight as a wire. He identified what kinds of owls were hooting for her, named the night birds and toads behind various calls and trills and told her which species of insects clicked and whirred beyond the circle of firelight.

But then a deep, roaring sound split the night. Beau grinned broadly.

"What's that?" she asked sharply.

"Gator. Big bull by the sound of him. Looking for a girlfriend."

She looked around quickly at the margins of the clearing. "How close is he?"

"A deep sound like that carries a long ways. He might be as much as a half mile away."

"He sounds closer," she declared. She pointed her high-intensity flashlight around the edges of the clearing. No eyes glowed back at her out of the night. Thank God.

"Afraid, Wilkes? Ready to quit yet?"

"Not on your life."

"Why do you want to do this?" he surprised her by asking.

"Why not?"

"I'm serious. Why this?"

She balled up her protein bar's wrapper and tossed it into the fire. Then she answered honestly, "I hate the idea of being a victim. And I hate being trapped in offices." She hesitated and then added, "As a kid, I never felt good enough. I wasn't strong enough, smart enough or tough enough. Over the years I've made it my goal to be…enough."

Beau was silent.

"What about you?" she ventured to ask.

He shrugged. "I like to shoot things and blow stuff up."

"That's a cop-out answer," she muttered.

Beau scowled and silence fell between them.

He surprised her by saying several minutes later, "I

wanted to do something for my country. Something that would matter."

She got that. It was comforting to know their motives for pursuing this extreme career were similar. Maybe just maybe, she and Beau weren't that different, after all.

When her feet and socks were bone-dry, she picked up the socks and stood up, looking down at Beau. "Now what?"

"Bed."

And there went her blood pressure the rest of the way to sky-high. Instantly, images of him pinning her down, his eyes glinting with heat above her, flashed through her mind's eye unbidden.

Thunder rolled ominously in the distance, muted by the heavy vegetation.

"Roof's sound," he said into the quiet that followed. "I fixed it while I was waiting for you."

Waiting for her. God, if only she could interpret that romantically. Instead, the comment made her skin crawl. Which was totally unfair to him. He hadn't done anything to indicate he was a creepy stalker.

Jerkily, she banked the fire under the distiller. The drum was wide enough that even if it rained hard, the hot coals should stay dry enough to keep the distiller working.

The first cold drops of water hit her face and she raced after Beau into the house. Thunder rolled again, low and deep, vibrating through her being.

"You have a bedroom staked out for yourself?" she asked.

"Ground floor. East side of the hall."

"Guess I'll take the one across from that, then." She stepped into the abandoned room. A wooden chair sat in one corner, and a steel-springed bed frame with no mattress occupied one wall.

She shone her flashlight into the corners, checking carefully for rats and spiders. She batted down a few cobwebs but had the place more or less to herself. Beau must have given the house a thorough cleaning for it to be so free of visitors.

A knock on her door spun her around. She threw it open nervously. Beau stood there with an old-fashioned hurricane lamp glowing softly in his hand. "Thought you might like a little light. I know how you girls are afraid of the dark."

Her eyes narrowed. "I like it. Easier to sneak around killing people at night."

He snorted. "You wish."

Since the only words passing through her mind were too filthy to utter aloud to her instructor, she took the oil lamp in silence and set it on the chair seat. He leaned a shoulder against the doorjamb and crossed his arms.

Irritated, she muttered, "You're thinking loudly, Lambo. What do you want?"

He shoved off the doorjamb, and her entire body tensed, poised for battle. Long years of ingrained defensiveness were hard to overcome. Gradually, she forced her body to relax. He wouldn't hurt her. At least not in *that* way.

"We need to talk," he announced.

Professional alarm shot through her. "Okay. Talk."

"Sit."

Crap. That was how Torsten started his "You're out" speech. She perched awkwardly on the edge of the bed frame. Beau made a restless lap around the narrow room, stopping to prop his right leg up on the far end of the bed frame. He rubbed his knee absently.

He did that a lot, which led her to believe his knee was hurting him more than he was letting on. She knew exercises to stretch and strengthen the joint, but it wasn't her place to intrude. Not to mention, she had faith he would not take kindly to her giving him rehab advice.

If she wasn't mistaken, the joint looked swollen under his pant leg. It was nice to know that today had taken at least a little toll on him, too.

He spoke abruptly. "Torsten's right. You do have the operator mind-set. You don't need me to beat physicality into you or push you to prove to you how much you can take. You'll go until you drop dead if I ask you to."

"Umm, thanks, I think?"

He continued grimly, "I don't think running you around a swamp for weeks on end is going to teach you anything you don't already know about yourself."

"Thank God," she breathed.

"Don't thank me yet. I'm still going to bust your ass. Just in other ways."

She nodded, pleased.

"After initial training, the guys who pass go through another six months of Qual training. Then they spend as much as a year training with their future team before they go out into the field. I don't have the facilities or other trainees to do team-building stuff with you, so Torsten instructed me essentially to move on to Qual training with you. It's still physical and you'll need to bring up your fitness level even more, but it focuses on the technical skills you'll need to be a Medusa."

Wow. Just…wow. This was really happening. Elation leaped in her belly.

Beau took a deep breath, and she tuned in past her exultation. Whatever he was about to say next was important to him, and she listened with every ounce of her attention. "Look, Tessa. I'm coming off an injury. Trying to get myself back into fighting shape."

His injury wasn't news to her. "I actually have some expertise with rehabbing injuries. If you'd let me help you, I think we can get your knee up to speed."

"What can you do that the docs haven't already done?" he asked bitterly.

"I have specialized training in soft tissue rehab. Breaking up scar tissue. And I have a ton of training in functional strength and flexibility. Stuff beyond what most physical therapists study."

He stared at her a long time and then nodded once.

She knew it for the giant concession that it was and nodded back.

He said, "I'm going to push through my conditioning regimen, and if you can keep up with me, then you're good enough physically to be a Medusa. Fair?"

"Fair," she replied, surprised. And more than she'd expected from him, given his obvious distaste for the idea of women operators.

"We'll have to figure out the rest of it as we go along."

Her initial gut reaction was to be suspicious. Figure out what?

"Make no mistake, Wilkes. I'm not here to hold your hand. When you can't hack it, you're done."

Was he hinting that he planned to wash her out no matter how she performed? She frowned, alarmed. Surely, he was going to give her a fighting chance to succeed. Wasn't he?

Something gradually shifted between them as she stared at him and he stared back. It stopped being about her future and started being about the crackling attraction between them. The invisible rope drawing them closer was back, electric and alive, coiling between them. It was fascinating and dangerous.

A huge crash of thunder made her jump, and it effectively broke the intense sexual tension of the moment.

"Right, then. G'night, Tessa."

"'Night, Beau."

He retreated, leaving the warm, golden glow of the lamp behind. She stripped off her damp pants and shirt and laid them out carefully to dry overnight. Until she got some more clothes, these were all she had, and it was important to take care of them. She was tempted to jam the chair underneath her doorknob but forcibly restrained herself from doing it. It wasn't like he was a specialist at breaching locked doors or anything.

She stretched out on the thin foam bedroll that had been strapped to the bottom of her rucksack. Laying it over the bed springs made for a reasonably comfortable bed. She was exhausted but found herself lying awake listening to the rainstorm roll in.

One day down. Who knew how many more to go. Not that it mattered. She would take each one as it came.

Beau retreated to his bedroom and leaned against the closed door to catch his breath. This was a nightmare. Every minute he was alone with her and not tromping around in a swamp, he was thinking about bedding her.

Too restless to sleep yet, he stepped out into the hallway and stared at Tessa's door in supreme frustration. It didn't help matters that he *knew* she wanted him every bit as much as he wanted her.

But that would ruin everything. His career. His future. The trust Gunnar Torsten had in him.

He grabbed a towel and all but ran down the hall to the back door, bursting outside just as the skies opened up and a torrent of rain poured down. He stripped off his clothes, stepped into the rain, and let it sluice down over his raging body.

He threw his head back and let the rain strike his face. It ran down his body, washing the day's sweat and grime off of him, and blessedly cooling off his ardor. A little.

He ran up onto the porch, shivering, and grabbed the towel. He rubbed himself dry briskly, and damned if his body wasn't stirring again already at the mere thought of Tessa, warm and soft inside the house. He seriously didn't need to spend all night standing out here in the rain, but he might just have no choice if he couldn't calm his body the hell down.

He sighed and pulled on his pants. There was one surefire cure for this driving need of his. And he'd been avoiding it all day.

He sat down on the porch swing and pulled out his cell phone, a snazzy signal-boosted model that got coverage via satellite anywhere on earth. He dialed Gunnar Torsten's number and waited grimly for his boss to pick up.

"Hey, Beau. Little late for you to be calling in, isn't it?" Torsten said.

"I didn't wake you up, did I?" Beau asked in surprise. It was barely 9:00 p.m. on the West Coast.

"Not even close. How's your girl?"

Tessa was not his girl! It was on the tip of his tongue to say so—forcefully—but he expected that protesting too hard on the subject would only raise questions he didn't want to answer.

"How did your first day of training go with Lieutenant Wilkes?" Torsten asked.

"It went." He added reluctantly, "You weren't wrong that she's got no quit in her. I dragged her up and down the beach for nearly two hours, and she barely missed a step. Hell, I was sucking wind. But she didn't utter a single word of complaint."

"I told you she was good," Torsten said archly.

"That doesn't mean she'll make it," Beau snapped back. "Just because she can run doesn't mean a damned thing."

"How's she doing mentally?" Torsten asked.

"She's thrilled at the idea of becoming a Medusa," he reported sourly.

"How's she relating to you?"

"Uhh, we're getting along okay," he answered. God, he hoped that didn't sound evasive.

"Still convinced women can't be special operators?" Torsten asked.

"More than ever, sir."

"I thought you said she did fine."

Beau scowled at the black night beyond the porch. "I did," he ground out.

"But?" Torsten demanded.

He huffed. "But it's weird working with a woman."

"Define weird."

"I dunno," he mumbled. "Weird. The whole boy-girl dynamic being inserted into our ops is going to be a problem."

A long silence greeted his observation.

Then Torsten asked, "You gonna have a problem keeping it professional between you?"

"Of course not!" Beau lied. "I'm just saying that I can see where attraction and sex are potentially going to get in the way of—" he searched for a word "—morale," he finally came up with.

Torsten sighed. "I was afraid of that." A pause, then, "You've got to find a way to work around it, Lambo. I'm counting on you. You're going to have to teach all the other instructors who work with the new Medusa team how to work around it, too."

"Are you kidding me?" Beau demanded. The words were out of his mouth before he could stop them from tumbling out.

Torsten replied, "Men worked successfully with the Medusas for years. We can do it again. You just have to see them as colleagues and not sex objects."

He sighed. "I'm trying. I'm just new to this coed Special Forces idea."

"You'll get the hang of it, Beau," Torsten said in a placating tone.

"Look, boss. You're the one who stuck me out here with her in the middle of nowhere. And you know how she looks. You had to know this was going to come up at some point."

Torsten sighed. "Yes, I did."

Hah. So he wasn't a complete schmuck for noticing that Tessa Wilkes was hot!

Torsten asked, "Has Lieutenant Wilkes shown any discomfort at being alone with you?"

Discomfort? That surprised him. "What do you mean?" Beau asked.

"Discomfort. Fear. Trepidation. Nervousness."

"Why?" Beau followed up, not seeing what he was getting at.

Torsten said reluctantly, "Lieutenant Wilkes is known to have a rather negative history with men. Does she seem uncomfortable or afraid of being alone with you?"

He flashed back to her brazenly stripping in front of him in the motel room, and then that sexy as hell wake-up the morning after where she practically crawled all over him. "Nope. No discomfort," he answered.

"Huh. Interesting."

Now, why in the hell was that? He half listened as Torsten gave him instructions for the next few days' worth of training. Beau disconnected the call, still mulling over why Tessa Wilkes, badass extraordinaire, would be afraid of men.

Chapter 7

Tessa woke to a muffled moan that made her blood run cold. She lay perfectly still, assessing and listening. A few raindrops slapped her window. Surely, that wasn't what had jerked her from a dead sleep so abruptly.

There it was again. A low groan.

Crap. Beau.

She exploded to her feet and was across the hall in a single breath. Crouching low, she eased open his door and spun into his room, ready to *hurt* whoever was messing with her teammate.

His room was dark, but her night-adjusted vision aggressively probed every shadow for the problem. No visible intruder. A movement, and she lasered in on it. Mattress. In the corner. Thrashing. Another moan.

She exhaled in relief. Beau was having a bad dream. Jeez, he'd scared her there for a minute. She moved over to the mattress on the floor and knelt beside it.

"Beau," she whispered. "Wake up."

She expected him to jolt awake as sharply as she had, but he didn't. He flung an arm toward her and then rolled onto his back, his hands twitching. "Oh, my God," he groaned. "No."

He sounded like he'd just watched his best friend die horribly. Her heart ached for his pain. She reached out to touch his shoulder.

Beau's hands whipped out, grabbing her around the neck and throwing her down with shocking violence. He was on top of her, strangling her, so fast she hardly knew what had happened. Terror exploded in a red mist behind her eyeballs.

"Beau," she rasped, barely able to make a sound past the vise around her neck. Instinct warned her against fighting back. He would meet aggression with even more aggression. But she couldn't help herself. She panicked. No matter how hard she thrashed or kicked or swung her fists at him, his hands tightened more and more around her neck.

His heavy body pinned hers down. She was ten years old again, and he was a full-grown man. Spots danced before her eyes and her vision narrowed down to an even darker tunnel within the shadows of his room. Must. Break. Free.

Desperate and near passing out, she went entirely limp in his grasp. Maybe if his dreaming mind thought he'd killed her he would let go of her neck so she could breathe.

His fingers loosened and she sucked in a gasping breath.

Black eyes glared down at her grimly. Beau was awake. *Now* he woke up…after he'd half killed her!

She glared back at him, throat aching, still gasping

for oxygen. Eventually, it dawned on her that he was straddling her hips. And sheesh, it was suggestive. His thighs were powerful against hers, his bare chest impossibly broad and muscular.

Her panting began to take on a faint sexual undertone.

The expression in his eyes changed, shifting from angry, to wry, to more thoughtful than could possibly be good for her. Darned if that man didn't seem to have a gift for peering straight into her soul.

He had no business poking in her private thoughts and fears. Her personal stuff was, well, personal. It had nothing to do with her becoming a Medusa—

Fine. It did to the extent that it had motivated her to become the powerful, self-reliant woman she was today. But that was it.

He knew. Somehow, Beau knew about her childhood fear of being molested. Anger abruptly supplanted her residual terror at nearly being strangled.

Surely, he hadn't attacked her intentionally. He'd been asleep for crying out loud. Belligerence flared in her gut. His attack had *better* not have been intentional. She was going to have a serious problem with him if that nightmare had been a ruse so he could assault her.

"What the hell are you doing in my room?" Beau growled.

She thrashed, trying to throw him off and free herself, but he grabbed her shoulders and forcibly held her down. The ease with which he did it threatened to overwhelm her aggravation and turn it back into abject fear.

She ground out, "I was trying to wake you up from a nightmare, you butthead. But then you attacked me."

"You know better than to grab a sleeping Spec Ops guy."

"I only touched your shoulder."

"You should've put your hand over my mouth. I'd have known it was a teammate. Or you could've touched me on the foot and stood back."

She nodded. Next time she wouldn't forget.

Her gaze dropped to his glorious, shirtless chest. The sprinkling of hair was just right, not too much and not too little. It was tempting to offer to help him forget his nightmare, but she wasn't that cheesy, and he was her instructor. Not to mention, the military took a dim view of superiors sleeping with their subordinates under any circumstances.

Anyway, it wasn't her job to fix his nightmares.

"You're thinking hella loud, Wilkes."

Drat. She was back to being Wilkes. "Sometimes I think too much," she mumbled. "It would be nice if there was an off switch for my brain."

"Ain't that the truth," he agreed wryly.

Her gaze kept sliding down his torso, taking in his rock-solid body and sharply cut muscles. It was a fight not to put her hands on him.

"You're gonna have to quit looking at me like that," he said grimly.

"Sorry. It has been a while since I've been around a shirtless guy."

"What the hell are you talking about? Didn't Torsten put you in the same dorm with your male classmates? You were there for months."

"Yes, he did. But those were my classmates, and we were so miserable and focused on surviving from one minute to the next that I had no time to register them as male, let alone as sexy males."

"A) Thank you for thinking I'm sexy. B) We're going to have to figure out this male-female thing if you expect to go operational. One of my taskings was to figure out how to work with women so I can teach other guys how to do it. Clearly, this is going to be an issue."

It was easy to forget how smart special operators were. After a day like today, the tendency was to focus on what a physical beast Beau was and to discount the keen observational skills and insightful analytical processes he also possessed.

His gaze had wandered downward, taking in her braless state and her skimpy tank top. The man had to be getting a heck of a view. But with her arms pinned at her sides, it wasn't like she could cover herself. Not that she would, anyway. If he wanted to look, who was she to stop him? She wasn't going to cut off her breasts like Viking warrior women had supposedly done. She was beginning to understand why they'd done it, though.

Abruptly, Beau pushed up and away from her, rising to his feet. He flexed his right knee and winced. If rising from a crouch to his feet hurt, that meant he had a hamstring issue on top of his knee problems. Probably wasn't stretching his hammies enough.

She stood up, as well. And suddenly, they were chest to chest in the dark. Rain pattered against the window, and thunder rumbled low in the distance. It was a night made for sex. Slow and sensual, to the sound of the rain. And they were here. Alone. In the dark. In the middle of the night. Scantily clad. Standing so close she could feel his body heat against her skin. Just the two of them and the rain.

"Jeez, Wilkes," he muttered, taking a quick step back. "Sit over there." He pointed at the chair in the far corner.

She watched him light a hurricane lamp on the tiny table in the corner. His back muscles flexed in an anatomy chart display that was mesmerizing. Only when he started to turn around to face her did she move over to the chair he'd indicated.

He wanted her out of arm's—and temptation's—reach, did he? It was gratifying to know he wasn't the only one struggling with this thing between them.

He slid down the wall to his mattress on the floor, his good leg bent at the knee, an elbow propped casually on it. Now that the room was lit, she noticed the titanium brace encasing his bad knee, stretched out straight in front of him. Thank God today hadn't been a walk in the park for him, either.

She sank gingerly onto the rickety chair.

"So what are you going to do in the future when you're attracted to a guy your team is working with?" he asked her baldly.

She shrugged. "I'll do what everyone in the workplace does about it. I'll follow regulations and keep things professional."

"Military men and women date off duty all the time," he replied. "What if you want to be with a teammate off the clock?"

Her pulse just jumped by about fifty beats per minute. Was he suggesting that they should date off the clock? Hoo baby. Sign her up! Aloud, she asked cautiously, "Are you suggesting the Medusas create a flat no-military-dating policy?" she responded.

Talk about thinking loudly. She could hear his mental wheels spinning at near supersonic speed in response to her question.

At length, he replied heavily, "I don't see how to handle it any other way."

"Why?" she asked, genuinely curious.

"Take you and me, for example."

She was tempted to say, "Let's not." She had no desire to dissect her attraction to him like a bug under a microscope.

He continued, "Let's say we decided to date each other."

Her pulse jumped even more wildly, shocking her into stillness. Was that what she wanted from this man? A relationship? She hadn't even considered the idea of a relationship since she'd found out the military was going to open up *every* career field to women. From that day forward, she'd dedicated her entire life to becoming a special operator.

Beau was speaking again. "At work, we would have to set our feelings for each other aside completely. It would have to be only work. Nothing personal."

She frowned, not seeing where he was going.

"But if you're my teammate, I want you to have feelings for me." He frowned, obviously searching for words. "I want you to be fiercely protective of me. Be prepared to die for me if necessary. My teammates are my brothers. You'd need to be my sister. And there's no way in hell I would sleep with my sister, let alone have romantic feelings for her."

Tessa frowned. Where was all of this coming from? Beau didn't strike her as the type to drill down into interpersonal relationship issues for funsies. Still, she considered his words. She'd never had a brother, but out of general principles, she imagined it would be gross to have romantic feelings for one.

She said slowly, "So if you and I were da—" her voice cracked, but she forged onward "—dating, you and I could have, umm, romantic feelings for each other on the side, but have only platonic—brotherly/sisterly— feelings at work."

"Basically," he agreed.

"So what's the problem?" she asked.

He shot back, "Can you compartmentalize your feelings like that?"

She stared at him in dismay, seeing the problem.

"Could you love me one minute like a man, but then only love me the next minute as a brother in arms?"

She answered honestly, "I don't know. I've never tried."

His stare bored into her as if he was trying to see her innermost feelings and thoughts. He declared, "I can tell you right now, I couldn't do it."

This was a conversation she would really rather not have, but she also saw the necessity of laying all these particular cards on the table between them. If nothing else, she owed this talk to all the Medusas who would come after her.

To that end, she said thoughtfully, "What if men and women didn't have to separate out their private feelings from their work feelings? Why wouldn't it be okay for me to be in love with you—hypothetically—and still work with you?"

"Would you be willing to let me die if it became necessary? If you were my team leader and had to send me into a fight I might not come home from, could you do it?" he retorted.

She sighed. "I see the dilemma."

"Only way it would work would be for the job to come first."

"Isn't that how it is for most Special Forces types?" she asked curiously.

"Hence the high divorce rate," he retorted. "The guys whose marriages survive have wives who understand they play second fiddle for as long as their husband is on the teams. But once he leaves the military, he'll spend the rest of his life being there for her."

She snorted. "No one ever said being a military wife was easy."

"But for a both-military couple, the oath to country, the commitment to the job, would have to come first for both of them."

"Which would basically doom the romance," she finished for him.

He shrugged. "Maybe not for all people, but it would for me. When I love a woman, I'll do it with everything I have. I'll most certainly be willing to die to protect her, and I'll do everything in my power to keep her safe."

His words rattled through her with the force of prophecy. What would it be like to have a man love her like that? Unconditionally. To death and beyond. It sounded like pure heaven.

It also sounded like pure crap. No man she'd ever met was capable of that kind of selflessness and self-sacrifice.

"Part of Qual training is for the guys on a team to get to know the person they're training. To form the rapport necessary to work together. That's what you and I are supposed to be doing out here over the next few months."

Which she gathered was his way of saying that they could never have anything more than a platonic work relationship.

Talk about feeling like a fool. What an idiot she'd been! She'd practically thrown herself at him in the motel. And on cue, tears burned at the backs of her eyes and her throat felt unnaturally tight. *No way* was she going to cry in front of him, particularly not moments after he'd told her they couldn't have a relationship with each other.

She stood up quickly and moved over to the door. She paused, forcing words past the clog in her throat. "Message received loud and clear. And thanks for the talk. I know that was a whole lot of words for you to string together all at once."

A crack of laughter escaped him. "Screw you, Wilkes."

"Right back atchya, Lambo."

And the line in the sand was drawn. Look but don't touch. Think but don't act. Imagine but don't ever, *ever* make it real between them.

She lay back down on her bed and stared up at the ceiling, listening to the rain pound against her window. She'd already sacrificed so much to get here. She wasn't about to blow it all now over a guy with great abs and a killer caboose. He wasn't worth it.

Right?

Right?

Gunnar Torsten was a dead man. Beau tossed and turned, his gut burning with embarrassment and discomfort. The last thing he'd ever expected to have to do was have a birds-and-the-bees talk with a Medusa candidate.

Particularly one who had him sporting a hard-on pretty much every moment she was around him.

Talk about awkward.

Worse, he didn't believe a single word he'd said to her. Well, he was pretty sure he was right about the separating work and personal life stuff. But his ability to follow through on his big statement? That was another matter, altogether.

Man, he dreaded tomorrow. And the day after that, and the day after that.

He stared up at the ceiling for hours, listening to the rain come and go. He didn't know what he was more terrified of: the woman across the hall or the nightmares waiting for him if he closed his eyes.

He resorted to his sniper breathing exercises eventually and finally managed to drift off to sleep.

She was waiting for him in his dream.

Of course, she was.

Her thick, wavy hair loose around her shoulders, her shoulders bare, her eyes sultry.

"Let me help you forget your nightmare," dream-Tessa murmured low.

He shook his head. "You don't understand what you're offering."

"Show me."

Tessa tossed and turned, sleeping restlessly. *Even asleep, she was more nervous than she wanted to admit when Beau showed up in her dream, shirtless. Smoking hot. Looking at her like he wanted to eat her alive.*

Fear coursed through her. Along with confusion. Wait. She wasn't afraid of Beau. Special operators were honorable men. Good soldiers. She couldn't live in fear of them.

Reaching up, she tugged on dream-Beau's neck, pulling his head down toward her.

His hands landed on the mattress on either side of her head. Her hands drifted across his powerful shoulders and down his arms to wrap around those biceps.

He lowered himself in a slow-motion press that stole her breath away as his stare never left hers, weighing her response, testing her reaction to him.

"We should stop," he said with considerably less conviction.

"Kiss me, Beau," she whispered.

"You're sure?"

She gulped. It was all or nothing. She either beat the monster in her head or she was done as a Medusa. Right here. Right now. "I'm sure," she whispered.

His mouth captured hers and dream-reality evaporated, leaving behind only a vast, empty darkness cocooning the two of them in a private world of their own.

Okay. This wasn't so bad. She kissed him back tentatively.

Beau inhaled sharply in his sleep, tensed enough to momentarily wake up and then exhaled as he settled back into his dream.

His tongue plunged into her mouth. She met the invasion with her own tongue, testing and tasting him as he claimed her in no uncertain terms. Her body moved against his, and he gasped at the amazing sensation of her strength and femininity mingling together.

He couldn't have remained still if his life depended on it as she kissed him hungrily, her hands roaming across his back, measuring the width of his shoulders, sliding down his ribs to his hips. Everywhere she touched him, he burned for her. Lord, she was addictive.

She matched his lust with abandon, kissing him like she'd been looking for him her whole life. His hand skimmed up her side, past the indentation of her waist and forward to cup her breast.

"Been a while?" he muttered.

"You have no idea."

A short grunt. "I might."

Tessa groaned as her dream intensified, flinging her arms wide, restless.

She slipped her hand between them to grasp his erec-

tion. Sensations slammed into her. Hard. Satin-smooth. Pulsing. "Oh, my goodness," her dreaming self breathed.

A silent gust of laughter escaped dreaming-him. "And nothing but goodness," he growled as he pushed on her shoulder, rolling her to her back and looming over her. He asked darkly, "Are you okay with this?"

"Try me," she challenged.

"You really shouldn't throw down dares in front of men like me," he muttered warningly. And then he was all heat and motion and muscle and hot skin against her.

"Beau, please," she begged.

"Please what?"

"Now. Take me now." Her limbs moved restlessly and her entire body strained toward him.

"You gonna freak out on me?" he challenged.

"No. I'm fine." And shockingly, she was. Surrendering to this man didn't scare her. "Go ahead. I dare you."

"Positive?" he ground out.

"Never been more positive," she declared.

Beau plunged into Tessa, sheathing himself to the hilt. Her groan wrapped around him like her body did.

Terrible tension stretched his entire body into a taut bow, pleasure bordering on pain, it was so intense. He reveled in torturing himself and her by holding himself still as long as he could.

Or until she begged.

She obliged without hesitation. "Please. I can't stand it anymore. I swear I won't break. Let go."

Still, he held back.

"Oh, for the love of Mike, Beau. That was me saying, will you just go for it already?"

He half laughed, half groaned and gave in all at once in his dream, plunging into her with all the power and *abandon he could muster. She rode the storm with him, matching his passion with unbridled lust of her own, matching thrust for thrust, groan for groan and shout for shout.*

He woke abruptly, breathing hard, drenched in sweat. He was in serious, *serious* trouble.

Chapter 8

Tessa flopped onto her back, so wiped out she couldn't move a muscle if she had to. At least Beau was equally wiped out, stretched beside her on the front porch. He had just put both of them through a calisthenics workout a professional athlete would envy. Cripes. If she never did a burpee again as long as she lived, that wouldn't be soon enough.

Let the record show, the man did not do anything halfway.

They'd spent the past two weeks running, climbing, crawling, hiking and swimming over every inch of the bayou in these parts. They'd been there for over two months, and day by day, the regimen got harder.

He'd finally agreed to let her do deep tissue massage on his knee, and she'd broken up most of the leftover scar tissue. He'd even consented to do daily stretching and strengthening exercises for his hamstrings, quads and knee. It was a slow road back, but his knee was coming along nicely. She couldn't be prouder if it had been her own knee.

But no matter how exhausted she was when she fell into bed each night, the dreams kept coming. Always a variation on a single theme—sex and more sex with Beau. And her imagination was getting hotter over time. Lately, she'd been dreaming some downright wild stuff with him.

The sound of Beau's hoarse breath reminded her sharply of her erotic dream last night, this one involving oil and full body massage. Languid warmth flowed through her joints that had nothing to do with push-ups and sit-ups.

"I think you've killed me," he muttered.

"I *know* you've killed me," she retorted, still panting.

"That was…" he searched for a word.

What would he mutter after sex with her? "Epic?" she supplied.

"Energizing."

Liar. "Yes," she agreed. "That." Of course, she was lying, too.

He lifted his head to stare down at her. "Ready to go another round with me?"

Like in her dream? "Oh, hell to the yes."

He made a sound that might be taken for unwilling laughter. He looked at her sideways as if he'd caught a hint of what she was envisioning. Abruptly, he rolled away from her. He was obviously attempting to distance himself from her. Again. She had to give him credit for trying to do the right thing like they'd talked about that first night at the cabin. She was trying, too. But damn, it was hard. Especially when her dreaming mind kept betraying her so completely.

She felt his withdrawal like a physical blow. Crap. She *had* to get control of this raging attraction to him.

But seriously. What woman wouldn't be attracted to a man like him, shirtless and sweaty, sprawled out like a god beside her, radiating raw sex appeal? She didn't care what big speeches he made about how they couldn't be together. The man spent a good portion of the time he was near her aroused. Either that was his normal state of existence, or he thought she was hot, too.

She sighed. Regardless of her lust for Beau, she had to play along with his stupid no-romance rule. To that end, she propped herself up on an elbow to gaze down at him. She asked lightly, "How did you sleep last night?"

For just an instant, his eyes darkened to a deep, deep shade of blue, like the ocean on a clear, sunny day, stretching away into forever. Memory of a dream came into his eyes, turbulent and sensual. Sexual tension poured off him like the sweat from their workout, and her breath hitched at the heavy-lidded look he threw her.

The instant passed, and his expression became impassive once more. But it had been enough for her to know. He hadn't slept any better than she had and had possibly experienced dreams along the same line as hers.

Hah! She did get under his rhinoceros-tough hide!

She asked blandly, "Until there are more Medusas, will you be on the same team as me?"

"Don't count on it."

Really? Did that mean they could date each other… hypothetically? If they didn't work together, did that mean the whole brotherly love argument was moot?

Aloud, she asked, "Why wouldn't we work together?"

He sighed heavily. "Who the hell knows what Torsten has planned for you? He hasn't shared his intentions with me." He added heavily, "And besides, I'm on my way out. My body's beat up. I've been on more missions than I can count. I'm—" he took a deep breath and plunged on "—getting old. You don't need a dead weight like me hanging around your neck."

"Ohh, puh-lease." She rolled her eyes. "You ran me into the ground today, and you're at least twice as strong as me. Not to mention, you've probably forgotten more about how to operate in the field than I'll learn for years to come."

"Like I said. Old."

She snorted. "If you're that decrepit, what we just did would have given you a coronary."

He smiled a little, involuntarily.

"Your knee's coming along great. In a few months I see no reason you can't go fully operational—"

"Don't worry about it. Not your problem."

"Aww, c'mon. For now we're on the same team. I'm just helping you out like I would help any of my team-mates."

He scowled, which she took to mean that he wanted to disagree with her but realized how stupid doing so would sound.

She warmed to her pep talk. "I have a vested interest in getting you back out in the field. After all, you're the first and only guy besides Torsten to even entertain the possibility that I might have something useful to offer the Spec Ops community."

He snorted. "I'm also the only guy to train with you."

"You haven't washed me out yet." Which frankly surprised her. She'd gotten the definite impression when they first came out here that he would yank the plug on her the second she messed up. And Lord knew she did that on a daily basis. But he shrugged off her mistakes, saying they were normal and that all newbies made them. The key was not to make them twice.

Beau was speaking. "...giving me way too much credit. I was not happy when Gunnar Torsten told me he wanted to train more women. To be dead honest, I still hate the idea."

"Are you at least willing to entertain the possibility now that women might be able to hack this job?" she asked.

"Shockingly, yes." He added, "But it's not like there are many women like you out there."

"I'm not *that* unusual. I mean, I get that not every woman wants to put herself through the training I've had to. But if I can do it, so can other women, if they really want to."

"Honestly, you've surprised me with your fitness."

Hark. Was that a compliment from Mr. Grumpy Pants? "Thank you. For the record, I appreciate everything you're doing for me."

He replied sharply, "Don't. I'm not your friend."

"Huh. Had me fooled."

"Your judgment is clouded, Wilkes." A pause. "You're going to have to get over your crush on me before I can release you to go operational."

She pressed up and away from him in a quick push-up that popped her to her feet. She planted her hands on her hips and glared down at him.

"That's the first sexist, misogynistic, patronizing thing you've said to me, Beau. And I sincerely hope it's the last. Otherwise, you and I are going to have a serious problem."

Beau swore under his breath as Tessa stormed inside and then shut the door behind her so gently she might as well have slammed it right off the hinges. She was not wrong. That had been a rotten thing to say.

Problem was, Torsten had been clear in his latest instructions. She had to become immune emotionally to the men she was going to work with.

Beau didn't know any other way to do that except to piss her off, provoke her and exploit her weak spots to toughen her up.

But he felt like a jerk for doing it. Which surprised him. He didn't want any woman in the Spec Ops community. Didn't need her on his team. And he seriously didn't plan to stand by and watch her endanger his brothers.

He *had* been sexist, misogynistic and patronizing, though, when he accused her of having a crush on him, particularly since he was suffering from a crush on her, as well. Talk about hypocritical.

If one of them was in trouble, it was him. His dreams were only getting more vivid. They were beginning to scare him, in fact. Imagining epic sex with Tessa had replaced his nightmares of the ambush that wrecked his knee.

He *had* to keep his hands off her. Had to corral his feelings for her. Harden his emotions. Remember to despise her and everything she stood for. But every day he spent with her was making that harder. She was funny and straightforward, smart and kind. She was deeply likable, dammit.

He shoved a hand through his hair and climbed to his feet awkwardly. His knee was killing him today, in spite of her words of encouragement. A woman had been able to keep up with him and walk away unaffected by a workout that had left him limping. Granted, she was a ridiculously fit woman. But still. He'd been shown up by a woman.

How was he ever going to get back onto the teams at this rate? Was he deluding himself to even try?

Of course, self-delusion was what got his leg torn up in the first place. He'd fallen into the trap of believing that he could do anything. That his body had no limits, his abilities had no boundaries and that an IED with his name on it would never come along. *Dumbass.*

He'd paid the price, though. And a half dozen good men had nearly died because of it. He and his teammates had been stupidly lucky that US Marine Force Recon patrol had come over that ridge instead of reinforcements to the rebels mowing them down.

He and his guys had been out of ammo, out of batteries for their radios, and were busted up, shot up and done in. Worst of all, he admitted privately to himself as he stared out into the bayou, he'd been out of ideas that day. Out of hope. Almost ready to give up.

It was the cardinal sin of Special Ops. You died believing you were going to win. You never, *ever* gave up. It was the single fastest way to get bounced off the teams. And he'd almost gone there.

He'd told the truth to Tessa. He was washed up. She had no business holding him up as a role model.

Which raised the question of why he was training her. When he'd posed that exact question to his boss a few days ago, Torsten's only response was that he thought the two of them would be good for each other.

What the hell was that supposed to mean?

The only truly good thing he could do for Tessa was keep her off the teams so she could live to the bitter, feminist old age awaiting her if she didn't get that Special-Forces-or-bust chip off her shoulder.

He couldn't keep having smoking-hot dreams. He would lose his mind if he had to keep enduring those nightly and pretend all day long that he felt nothing for her. She'd gotten too damned far inside his head already.

Too restless to return to the house, he grabbed his toolbox and went to work on the electric pump connected to the well that supplied fresh water to this place.

It took him most of the afternoon, but the house had running water again. In a few hours the water heater would even put out hot water. That should make Tessa happy. He frowned. Not that he should be worrying about her happiness.

He flopped in the old swing under the porch overhang to watch the sunset.

Maybe it was time for him to retire. To settle down and grow old swigging a beer in a swing like this, reminiscing about the good old days. He wouldn't mind it so much if he had a woman like Tessa to share it with.

But the adventure was just starting for her. Maybe he had no right to get in her way. She should get a chance to save the world…or try until she got cynical. Until she got sick of death and war. *Or until she died.*

If only he could show her a taste of what she was headed into. It would scare any sane person off the romance of being a special operator.

Now that was an interesting idea. Maybe he could stage an op here. Something that would show her what being operational was really like…

A few days later Tessa was shocked to hear a stranger's voice shout a hello from the direction of the dock. Beau, who was teaching her how to make slap charges—small explosive charges used to defeat locking mechanisms on doors—looked up and grinned.

"Who is it?" she asked.

"Come meet him."

She followed Beau to the boat dock and squealed in delight as she spotted her duffel bag slung over the shoulder of a clean cut, dark-haired stranger just climbing out of a sleek speedboat. She raced forward and took the bag, thrilled to have her clothes and toiletries back.

"Tessa, this is Neville Thorpe. Nev, Tessa."

"Pleased to meet you." The man's British accent was smooth and sexy. But it didn't make her insides melt the way Beau's easy drawl did.

"Help me unload your toys, Lambo." Neville passed several heavy metal boxes to Beau. "Next time you can hump in your own ammo, my friend."

Beau laughed, and the two men traded insults. Then Beau asked, "How about I fire up the grill and fry some fish?"

"Brilliant. I'm starving."

In short order, they lounged in lawn chairs, eating succulent catfish and drinking the beers on ice Neville had brought with them.

"So, Tessa," Neville asked. "How's your training getting along?"

She shrugged. "You'd have to ask Beau."

Neville's gaze shifted to Beau and one British eyebrow arched questioningly.

"It's going," Beau answered reluctantly.

Neville's next words surprised her. "Major Torsten sent me out here to observe for a day or two."

"Why?" Beau demanded.

"We're working on profiling a mission that might benefit from Lieutenant Wilkes's participation. We need to know what her capabilities are before we build it."

Tessa leaned forward in interest. "What kind of mission?"

Neville smiled a little. "The kind that won't happen

for a while. We're helping an OGA set up and take down a bad guy."

"OGA?" Tessa asked.

"Other Government Agency," Beau murmured. "The alphabet guys. CIA, FBI, NSA, DIA, HSA, etcetera."

She nodded. "I'll try to be ready by the time you need me."

They cleaned up after the meal and then headed out for the afternoon's training evolution—learning to use the slap charges they'd spent the morning making. They moved on to breaching charges, and blew a dozen man-size holes in the side of an abandoned barn.

The next day they walked through a series of fire control exercises—the men teaching Tessa where to move and shoot in confined spaces to prevent hitting her teammates or getting shot herself. They practiced advancing and retreating as a team, providing cover for each other. The dynamic was different enough with three of them versus two that she was grateful for the opportunity.

On the third day they practiced evacuating a two-hundred-pound dummy Beau had fashioned from burlap sacks, tag teaming hauling it on a stretcher for miles at a run.

Tessa was trashed physically by the end of that training evolution. Not that she would ever admit it to the guys. But as she lay in bed that night, aching from head to foot, she did secretly worry about finding herself in a situation where she had to carry a teammate whose life depended on her being strong enough to hump him to safety.

She dreaded rolling out of the bed the next morning, and it hurt every bit as bad as she feared it would. How she was going to get through today was an open question. Beau and Neville might just have found her physical breaking point.

The smell of bacon frying wafted down the hall and she followed it, strolling into the kitchen to see Neville pulling an omelet out of the oven that had to be three inches tall.

"Good grief, man. That almost looks like a soufflé!" she exclaimed.

Neville smiled over the cast iron skillet. "I can make soufflés, but you didn't have the ingredients. Sadly, you'll have to settle for a humble omelet."

"A tragedy, but I'll deal," she replied, grinning. She dug into her breakfast enthusiastically. "Tell me more about your team, Nev."

He shrugged. "If you survive fun with Lambo in the bayou, you'll meet them yourself. They're good men. The kind you want to have your back."

She risked following up with, "Will they be okay with me?"

Neville pinned her with a serious stare. "We all worked with the last Medusas. If you can do the job, you'll be welcome."

Tears actually welled up in her eyes, and she looked away quickly. She nodded, too choked up to speak. When her throat muscles finally loosened up, she murmured, "I'll do my best to be worthy of you guys."

He snorted. "If you can make it past Beau, you'll be worthy."

He stood up, and as he moved past her toward the sink, his hand landed on her shoulder for a quick squeeze.

That tiny gesture of support meant more to her than any words of encouragement he could possibly have said aloud.

She was sad to see him go when he packed up after

breakfast and headed back to civilization. As the sound of Neville's boat motor faded in the distance, she asked, "What's next, boss?"

Beau snorted. "Don't call me *boss*. That's Torsten's job." He rubbed his leg, and she frowned. Their gazes met, and the worry he usually kept hidden from her was there, naked and exposed in his eyes.

"You'll make it back, Beau. I've seen worse knees. We can do this together." She hadn't seen much worse knees that had recovered, but she'd seen a few.

"From your mouth to God's ear," he muttered.

He nodded, and she nodded back. He was awful at talking about his feelings, but she was gradually learning his silent signals. That single, simple nod was an acknowledgment of equality. Of teamwork. Maybe even of friendship.

Well, dang. This had turned into a red-letter day. First Neville expressed acceptance of her, then Beau had, too, after a fashion. Goodness knew Beau was a much tougher nut to crack than the charming Brit.

The next day Beau took off into the swamp so fast she had to actually track him to catch up with him. When she finally did, panting, she asked, "What did I do to piss you off?"

"Nothing." He took off again, but this time at a pace she could match.

From behind him she said, "Whatever it was, I didn't mean to offend you."

"I'm not offended."

"You sound offended."

"I said I wasn't, and I'm not," he snapped.

Liar, liar, pants on fire. She got that men like him didn't typically want to talk about their feelings or even admit that they had feelings. But she had nobody else. He was her only ongoing peek into the minds of the male operators she would be asked to work with down the road.

Had he freaked out after their rapprochement yesterday? Was this he retrenching in his fortress of male solitude?

He stopped abruptly enough that she actually plowed into his back.

"Pay attention, Wilkes," he snapped.

"Sorry."

"When you're running with a team and your weapons are hot, a collision like that could cause someone to fire accidentally. Not only do you risk shooting a teammate, but you'd give away your position and potentially get the whole team killed."

"Yes, sir," she said contritely.

"Don't *sir* me," he bit out. "We don't stand on rank in the teams."

Sheesh. Apparently, she couldn't do anything right today.

He unslung the Dragunov sniper rifle he'd been carrying across his back and unfolded the stock. "This is the squad support weapon in most Eastern European countries and in a bunch of crappy spots around the world that import Russian surplus weaponry. It's also widely available on the black market. Hence, it's a weapon you need to be familiar with. On top of that, it's a nice little sniper rig. Tell me what you know about it."

She replied, "It's semiautomatic. Uses a short-stroke-gas-piston system with a manual, two-position gas regulator to set recoil velocity. The barrel breach is locked with a rotating bolt. It has a chrome-lined barrel with four right-hand grooves along a portion of the barrel. Newer models have an increased twist, which reduces overall accuracy significantly, particularly at long range. The standard box magazine holds ten rounds. It fires 7N14 rounds at a little over eight hundred meters per second and can fire seven point six-two millimeter rounds, as well." She paused for air and then added drily, "Shall I continue?"

Beau merely scowled at her recitation.

C'mon. That was impressive as hell. Actually, the coach of her rifle team in college happened to own one and had let the students handle and fire it. But still. How many women anywhere could rattle off that stuff, and furthermore, know what it all meant?

"How well can you shoot it?" Beau asked.

"Passably," she answered humbly. She'd been a champion markswoman in college, but she suspected that real military snipers could shoot circles around her.

Beau passed her the rifle, pulled out a spotter's scope and knelt down. "I'll call the shots. Let's see what you've got, Wilkes."

She stretched out on her belly beside the weapon. This was familiar territory to her. She'd always loved the mental silence required for shooting, and welcomed it now. She breathed slow and deep, sinking into a state of full body relaxation.

"Five hundred yards downrange, twelve degrees left. A black human silhouette." He called a minor windage adjustment. She did the math and adjusted her sight one click left and a half click up.

"Fire when ready," Beau muttered.

She exhaled then pulled smoothly through the trigger.

"Four inches high two inches right," he announced. "Again."

She made the adjustments, sighting in the scope until he was calling out bull's-eyes. He started pointing out targets at greater range. Eight hundred yards, and then a thousand yards. As they reached the outer limits of the weapon's ability her accuracy dropped, but that was a function of the wobble induced by the rifle and not her lack of skill.

By the time Beau called a break, her right shoulder ached, and her back cramped from lying still for so long.

Beau passed her a protein bar and unwrapped one for himself. "You've got a future as a sniper, kid."

She shrugged. "Thanks. I like shooting a lot."

"Ever shot live targets?"

"Nah. I'm not into killing bunnies and Bambis."

He snorted. "You will be when you have nothing to eat."

"That's different. That's survival. I just don't enjoy hunting for sport."

"That's the correct answer for a sniper," he commented.

"Why?"

He shot her an are-you-kidding look. "Do you seriously want someone who kills people for a living to enjoy hunting for sport?"

She winced. "Good point."

"If you decide to pursue sniper training, you'll have to pass an exhaustive battery of psych tests to make sure you don't have any psychopathic tendencies. Uncle Sam can't afford to teach a crazy how to kill people and get away with it."

She snorted. "I had to take those tests to even apply to the Special Forces. Women are getting screened pretty hard before we're allowed to make a run at all of this. The military is calling it *research*, of course."

He shrugged. "It wouldn't do anyone any good to have women going mental when they fail."

She laughed a little. "I came close when Torsten told me I was out and then you dragged me off base in front of everyone."

"Sorry about that. But Gun ordered me to make your departure public."

"I get it." A pause. "Now."

"You looked like you were plotting my death when I put you on that plane."

"It did cross my mind."

"You wouldn't be Medusa material if it didn't."

So. He was starting to think of her as Medusa material, was he? *Cool.* Rock by rock, she was going to tear down his wall of objections to her, even if she had to do it with her bare hands.

He stuffed the wrapper in his pocket. "Okay. Your turn to spot for me."

And so it went. She listened and learned, and he stuck purely to business. No personal conversation, no joking around, no more flirting.

Even if they did end up lying side by side, their thighs pressed together from hip to knee in a shooter's nest he taught her how to build.

Nope, nothing going on here…except near orgasms at the contact with him.

Her shooting accuracy plummeted, and he snapped, "Get your head in the game. Focus."

That was the problem. She *was* intensely focused. On him.

Clearly, being plastered to her side like this wasn't bothering him at all. He'd put up a giant emotional barricade to prevent anything more between them. Lucky bastard.

It wasn't like she'd never crashed and burned with a guy before. On the contrary. Once men found out she was training in hopes of becoming a commando, they usually ran screaming.

She'd just never taken it personally before now. But it was really hard not to from a man whose approval meant so much to her and to her future. Worse, she genuinely liked Beau on top of finding him unbelievably attractive. He was smart, funny, generally considerate and decent. It was a lethal combination as it turned out.

She should just take the training and move on with her life. But unfortunately, she couldn't seem to get past her unwavering attraction to him.

Like it or not, she couldn't afford to fall into any traditional female stereotype—including craving approval from people around her. But it was impossible not to crave both the man and his elusive approval.

Chapter 9

A few deeply sexually frustrating days later, she woke up to Beau standing over her bed, staring down at her impatiently. The fact that he was even in her room was shocking.

"What's up?" she mumbled up at him, her voice sleep-roughened.

"Trip to town today. We need to get going."

Recalling the all-day trek from hell it had been to get here a lifetime ago, she groaned and pushed wearily to her feet. "You gonna stand there and watch me dress?" she snapped.

He spun and left the room abruptly. Almost as if he hadn't realized he was staring at her until she had pointed it out. If she wasn't mistaken, his ears were red as he swept out of her room. Excellent. He could use a little embarrassment. Maybe *that* would knock him out of his stupid ivory tower.

She desperately needed more clothes. And food. She was really tired of fish. Granted, the catfish, crawfish and bass Beau had been catching and cooking had been delicious. But she was ready for some variation in her diet. The thought of a salad of store-bought lettuce was enough to make her slightly orgasmic.

She grabbed her rucksack and threw in some basic survival gear. Weird how accustomed she'd grown to having a KA-BAR knife at hand. And rope, and a multi-tool. She went outside to wait and looked up as Beau jogged down the back steps toward her. His legs were powerful, his body rippling with muscle, the whole of him oozing aggressive masculine confidence.

Lord, that man was beautiful. She tried not to think about it, to ignore the visceral reaction in her gut to his masculinity. But when he caught her by surprise like this, she couldn't stop a tornado of attraction in her gut.

He moved with the fluid grace of an athlete. Where he got off calling himself old, she had no idea. His knee seemed to have been doing great the past couple of days. But they also hadn't been running around the swamp as much.

She followed him across the backyard to a raised wooden walkway about two feet wide. It took a sharp right turn, proceeded a half dozen more yards and turned into a dock with a shallow-draft airboat tied to it.

"Hop in," he directed as he untied the front mooring line and tossed it aboard.

She stepped into the boat and caught the rear mooring line from him as he stepped into the vessel. She stowed the line as he started the engine. It caught with a roar.

Beau steered away from the dock and into the bayou. They turned into a big, straight canal, and he opened up the throttle. They skimmed across the water and she laughed aloud, loving the speed and freedom. Her eyes watered, and she didn't want to think about how long it was going to take her to brush the tangles out of her hair, but she'd really needed this break.

The canal emptied into a lakelike body of water. He guided the airboat north along the coast for perhaps five minutes to a dock. A shopping center stretched along the waterfront.

She jumped ashore and caught the line Beau tossed her. She lashed it to a mooring cleat on the dock while Beau did the same with the back line.

"Wow," she commented. "Real people. I haven't seen a child in six months."

He glanced sidelong at her and murmured, "It's a shock to the system, isn't it?"

She hit a women's clothing store first and carried her purchases back to the boat. Beau had loaded up on ammunition and supplies for fixing up the house. He locked their haul in a storage box on the airboat and then led her to the grocery store.

In front of it, he said sardonically, "I know you haven't seen one of these for a long time. It's where Mommy and Daddy go to buy food. And this is a buggy. You put your food in it."

"Very funny. And where I come from, they're called grocery carts."

"Damn Yankee," he declared cheerfully.

He was joking with her? Had the iceman actually thawed? *Shock.*

She was delighted to find—luxury of luxuries— deodorant. Her blissful trip down the cosmetics aisle also yielded shampoo and conditioner, sunblock, lip balm and facial moisturizer. She even sneaked a tube of mascara into the cart.

And then she turned her attention to food.

Beau led her to the canned goods section, where they stocked up heavily. They were about halfway down an aisle when Tessa noticed a large man coming around the corner ahead of them. He looked familiar.

The face clicked. The drunk who had hit on her at the restaurant that first night. One of the Kimball brothers. What had Beau called him? Jimbo. That was it.

"Let's turn around," she murmured to Beau, whose irritated expression indicated that he'd spotted their old acquaintance.

"Can't," he replied low. "Two of his brothers are behind us."

Another man turned into the aisle in front of them, nearly as big and brawny as Jimbo. The last Kimball brother. Four on two. In close quarters. She had faith that she and Beau would win. But who wanted to fight in a grocery store and terrify the housewives and kids?

"Well, isn't this special?" she said casually. "A complete, matched set of Kimballs."

Beau commented from beside her, "Let's take this outside, fellas. No sense making a huge mess in aisle five for someone to have to clean up."

She followed him to the checkout counter and couldn't believe that he calmly paid for the groceries and even helped the bag boy put them in the cart. He did ask the manager to watch the cart for a few minutes inside the front door while he took care of a bit of business.

The manager looked nervous. Must've seen the Kimball boys head outside to lie in wait for them. The guy said, "Y'all be careful, now, heah'? 'Dem boys is trouble."

Beau thanked the man quietly for the warning, then

said, "Wait two minutes and call the sheriff, if you wouldn't mind."

The manager nodded jerkily, his face pale and sweaty.

"Can we just walk away?" she muttered at Beau as they approached the automatic doors.

"Not a chance they'll let us. You stay out of this. I'm going to have my hands full without having to look after you, too."

As if. He was her teammate, and they were in this together.

"Get behind me," Beau ordered low. "They'll be in the alley just beyond the buggies waiting to jump us. Put your back to the building and don't let them get behind us. I'll cover you from the front."

"I can help—"

"Stay right on my back. They won't be able to hit you there."

"I know how to fight—"

"Not like these guys," he bit out. "Grab one of those buggies and cover my left if you can." He pointed at the long row of carts stacked together outside.

She tried again. "Beau—"

"Later."

She had eight years of Krav Maga training, for God's sake. She could handle herself with these amateur thugs and even the odds considerably.

Nonetheless, Beau was expecting her to follow orders and he would make decisions in the fight based on knowing where she was and what she would be doing.

Frustrated, she slid behind him and grabbed on to the handle of a cart to use it as a makeshift shield. They stepped past the cart line, and sure enough, all four Kimballs came out of the alley.

"Hello, gentlemen," she said pleasantly to Jimbo and his gigantic brothers. "How are you today?"

"About to be a far sight better," Kimball growled.

"How's that?" she asked calmly.

"Swing left," Beau muttered.

She half turned to her left, and on cue, two of the Kimballs stepped left to confront her, while the other two slid right.

Beau's shoulder blade touched her back. He would use the light contact to keep tabs on where she was during the fight. She mimicked his loose relaxation, preparing her body to move with maximum speed when the time came.

"Gonna get me a can of whup-ass and dump it on yo' pretty boy's face. Won' be so pretty when I'm done wit' 'im."

She replied sympathetically, "I suppose it's hard to pronounce English properly with so many teeth missing, isn't it? Shame. Makes you sound like an ignorant hick."

Beau would know what she was doing, of course. It was Combat 101 to provoke the enemy into an ill-advised attack based on emotion rather than sound combat strategy and timing.

Jimbo growled. "Mouthy-whoring-bitch-slut."

"Wow. That's a lot of words. I had no idea you knew so many," she quipped lightly. The guy would rush her any second.

"I'll kick yo' skinny ass, too, bitch," he growled.

Beau tensed against her back. "You and what army?" she retorted. She was careful not to overtly threaten Jimbo. She was an active duty military officer, and the Army had no sense of humor about its officers picking fights, particularly with civilians. Even if they were total jerkwads.

Beau chimed in, his voice flat and cold. "Guys, we don't want any trouble. Consider this fair warning that for legal purposes my hands are classed as lethal weapons. Please turn around and walk away from this."

She was impressed at how he managed to pitch his voice to be both threatening and conciliatory like that. She added, "And while we're on the subject of lethal hands, mine are also legally classified as weapons."

Martial artists and boxers at a certain level were required to warn people before attacking them, lest they face criminal charges for the damage they inflicted in a fight. Beau's shoulder blades tensed briefly in surprise. Of course, he probably thought she was bluffing.

Legal necessities out of the way, she and Beau were both in the clear now to kick butt and take names.

"Big talk, li'l girl."

She shrugged. "You've been warned."

Jimbo swore luridly and charged. She took in torsos and fists and feet simultaneously as her targets approached, assessing them coolly. These guys would be strong, and potentially fairly fast. Probably would rely on their fists over their feet. They would also be overly aggressive, uncontrolled and overconfident because she was a woman. Two on one wasn't ideal, but she'd practiced against multiple attackers. She could handle this.

Mental assessment complete in the blink of an eye, she waited the last few milliseconds for the men to come into range. She jammed the heavy grocery cart at Jimbo's brother, nailing him in the gut and breaking the momentum of his charge.

Momentarily down to one attacker, she made a feint with her fist in hopes of drawing all of Jimbo's attention to her hands. Sure enough, his enraged glare zeroed in on her fist. She lashed out with her steel-toed boot, nailing him squarely in the kneecap. Hard. He howled, but followed through with the big right hook he'd thrown just as she kicked.

She threw up her left forearm and took the blow on her arm. He was strong, all right, and drove her arm back into her forehead painfully, albeit harmlessly. As he yanked his arm back to reload, she grabbed his fist with her left hand and maintained contact with it as she chopped up from below with her right fist. She punched up as hard as she could into his solar plexus. He exhaled hard and doubled over, driving his face down onto her knee just as she jerked it up.

The result was spectacular. Blood exploded out of his nose and he reeled back, screaming bloody murder. It was enough to give his brother pause for an instant to stare at him.

Which was a mistake. She took a quick step forward and clocked the brother with all her strength on the chin. The guy went down like a rock. Jimbo started to come up for another go and she nailed him in the temple with her elbow, driving it out hard from her side. It was a vicious blow, and he dropped on top of his brother in a heap. She spun to help Beau.

Not that he needed any help from her. He'd just spun around to defend her, as it turned out. "Look out!" he bit out sharply.

She registered the direction of his gaze and ducked, catching only a glancing blow on top of her scalp, which probably saved her from a serious concussion or worse. Beau leaped past her and chopped Jimbo's brother in the throat with the side of his hand, bladelike. The guy staggered back, gurgling. Beau scooped up an empty beer bottle and smashed it over the guy's head. Jimbo's brother collapsed, unconscious.

"Thanks," Tessa muttered, chagrined. She should have finished off her own attackers and not left it to Beau to save her from her overconfidence.

"No problem. You good?" he bit out.

"Peachy keen. You?" she replied.

Adrenaline was screaming through her blood and she became aware of the most amazing side effect. She was so turned on she could hardly stop from throwing herself at Beau and ripping his clothes off. Right here. Right now. Fire burned through her, pounding through her core, demanding the slap of sweaty skin on sweaty skin, panting, pounding sex, rough and randy.

Beau's gaze met hers, and his entire body tensed. His nostrils flared, his eyes went black and a promise of exactly the sex she craved poured off him. He was primal and male. He'd violently defended his woman, and now he was going to drag her back to his cave and have his way with her.

Yes. Please.

She'd barely cracked a sweat in the fight, but looking at Beau now, her pulse exploded and lust stole her breath completely away.

His voice was unnaturally rough. "Let's go before the boys wake up." He put his hand on the small of her back and she about came out of her skin. It was all she could do not to slam him back against the brick wall behind him, crawl all over his glorious body and ride him until they both howled like wild creatures.

He muttered, "Jeez, Tessa. Rein it in until we're in private."

He'd noticed she was about to have her way with him, huh? At least he had the good grace to sound a little out of breath, too.

He spoke more loudly. "Nothing to see here, folks."

She looked up, startled to see that a dozen people had gathered to watch the comeuppance of the Kimballs. Broad grins wreathed the bystanders' faces.

While she tried to form coherent thoughts beyond needing immediate, passionate, wildly unrestrained sex, Beau fetched their cart of groceries and pushed it outside.

Sirens became audible in the distance. She and Beau grabbed the grocery bags and carried them to the airboat with dispatch.

They were just casting off the lines when a police car pulled into the parking lot. One of the Kimballs charged out of the alley like a rampaging bull and ran smackdab into a deputy, who looked prepared to have a long and detailed discussion with him about physical contact with officers of the law.

Aww. Too bad, so sad.

Not.

As the airboat's engine vibrated through her nether regions until she hummed on the edge of an orgasm, one thought galvanized her mind. When they got back to the house, she and Beau would be *all* alone.

Chapter 10

Beau raced the airboat across the lake at full throttle, so turned on he could hardly see to steer. It had taken everything he had not to grab Tessa and take her right there, on the spot, after the fight. The desire rolling off her had been so potent he could hardly resist it. Thank goodness he'd looked up and seen that crowd of bystanders, or he might have embarrassed them both. Bad.

He was no stranger to post-mission adrenaline and the urgent lust it provoked. What he wasn't accustomed to was hitting the adrenaline wall with a woman around who'd also just slammed headfirst into it.

And not just any woman. Tessa, whom he'd wanted ever since he first laid eyes on her. Tessa, who was all the things he'd ever wanted in a woman. Tessa, who wanted him every bit as badly as he wanted her.

He practically missed the entrance to the side channel that would circle around behind the house and approach from the other direction. Out of long habit, he never went home the exact same way he went to a place. It was basic security ops not to.

Of course, it was no secret where the old Lambert place was. And it wasn't like the Kimball boys didn't know every square inch of the Bayou Toucheaux. They weren't successful drug dealers and smugglers for nothing.

Truth be told, he was taking the long way home to give his raging lust some time to cool down. Not that it was working. He swore under his breath.

Man, it felt good to drop those jerks. Funny how life had brought him full circle, back to his roots like this. When he'd left home to join the Army, he'd never planned to come back here. It had been worth it, though, just for the opportunity to kick some Kimball butt.

And getting to do it with Tessa? Well, that was a bonus. He should have guessed she would be some sort of martial arts expert. Cripes, it had been hot to turn around and see her making mincemeat of the bullies who'd tormented him as a kid.

As much as he hated to admit it, she was absolutely cut out for the Medusas. The very fact that she'd come out of the Kimball fight jacked up and ready for more proved the point. Hell, she'd even reacted like an operator by getting wildly turned on after the fight.

Dammit, he almost missed another turn. He swung into a narrow channel, banking up so hard he was looking almost straight down at water from his seat.

Focus, you idiot.

His post-mission adrenaline rush gradually calmed to semihuman proportions, until Tessa was no longer in danger of him blindly taking her up on her unspoken offer of mindless, blow-off-steam sex. Well, not *grave* danger.

He slowed the boat and eased into the perpetual gloom of the true bayou beneath towering stands of cypress. Spanish moss hung everywhere, and the tannin from the plentiful oaks turned the water as black as crude oil. This was the swamp primordial that people thought about when they heard the word *bayou*. Even though he'd grown up here, it was still creepy. He just knew his way around in it.

Now that the engine noise was not too loud to be heard over, he asked Tessa, "Where did you learn to fight like that? If I'd known you were a killing machine, I'd have left all of them for you to take down."

"I got into martial arts as an after-school thing to stay off the street. I kept it up through high school and college. Helped me work out my anger issues. And I did try to tell you."

Beau cut the engine completely and the boat drifted to the dock that appeared out of the gloom. He jumped ashore and Tessa tossed him the lines. After tying off the boat, Beau automatically offered her a hand to help her disembark.

She laid her hand in his, and lightning might as well have struck him. Rocked to his core, he concentrated on the strength of her grip. What would that feel like around his—

Dammit! He had to find a way to resist her!

He helped her to the dock and she surprised him by not releasing his hand. "Thanks for letting me help you with the Kimballs."

"Thanks for having my back," he replied roughly.

They stared into each other's eyes, and it was all there. The overpowering attraction. The knee-buckling lust. The intense connection. And on top of it, a healthy dose of adrenaline still thrummed through his blood.

Need to make this woman his, to make smoking-hot love with her, roared through him.

Tessa looked up at him sidelong. Her eyes burned like molten lava and were fully as turbulent. His gaze raked down her body possessively, visually stripping off her clothes. She took a wobbly breath and swayed forward.

How was he supposed to keep his hands off her when she crackled with all this pent-up desire? He was supposed to have supreme self-control. Hell, they both were. But this...this was bigger than he was, crushing his will in its path.

So much for weeks of setting all of this turbulent heat between them aside and pretending like they weren't totally into each other.

He ground out, "I can't get you out of my head. I've tried everything. But it's not working."

"Then don't try." She laid her palms on his chest, and something primitive inside him twisted hungrily. It felt like a sleeping dragon coming to life in his gut, roaring for his mate.

He put his hands on her waist with the intent to set her away from him. But instead, his hands urged her hips forward. Not that he had to urge very hard.

She groaned under her breath. Cripes. She might as well have thrown back her head and let out a mating call to the dragon inside him.

He stared at her, the crazy sexual charge between them snapping and crackling like a static buildup on the verge of exploding. A promise of epic sex hung *right there*, stealing all the oxygen from the air and making him light-headed.

"So...what do you want to do about this? About us?"

he asked roughly. He sure as hell knew how he would answer that question, but he was *not* going to fall on her like the beast he apparently was.

Teeth clenched, he hung on to his sanity. Barely.

Tessa stared up at Beau. His eyes were black, his nostrils flared, the muscles in his jaw rippling. Desire rolled off him, almost violent in its intensity.

She'd never had a man like him want her like this. It was…intoxicating.

What *did* she want to do about their lust-inspired race toward mutual self-assured destruction?

As if she had any answer at all but "bring it on." Crud. He might have pushed the brake handle to this runaway train at her, but it wasn't like she had any wish whatsoever to pull it. She didn't even know if they *could* stop what was happening between them at this point, let alone if she wanted to stop it.

Which she didn't. At all.

Which was insane.

But there she had it. She'd officially lost her mind.

And it was kind of amazing.

It was as if two versions of her were at war inside her head. The rational, logical version of her shouted that this was madness. A terrible, disastrous idea that would ruin their careers and lives.

But the other version of her purred with satisfaction. They were finally going to have raucous, raw, mind-blowing sex, and it was going to be everything she'd ever fantasized about and more.

"We shouldn't," she managed to choke out.

"No doubt." He inched closer, and the last of the smile faded from his eyes, replaced by intensity that was literally breath-stealing.

"But I can't stop wanting it. Wanting you…" she confessed.

"Me, neither," he agreed, leaning in.

"It's career suicide," she tried desperately, her resolve crumbling with every millimeter closer he came. "We can't have a relationship…feelings…"

"No relationship then," he ground out. "No feelings."

"Right," she breathed. "Just sex."

His mouth closed on hers and she all but sobbed with relief. He dragged her up against him, and she wrapped her arms around his neck, dragging him to her, as well. They clashed in a kiss of carnal hunger that erased all remaining rational thought from her mind. His tongue swirled around hers; he bit her lip and she bit back. She tugged at his hair, pulling him even deeper into the kiss. She wanted him down her throat.

His hands plunged inside her clothes and were hot against her skin.

Oh, yes.

All the adrenaline screaming through her system released, morphing into desire so intense she actually saw a red haze behind her eyelids.

He pulled on her ponytail not quite painfully, exposing her neck to him. "Welcome to post-mission sex," he mumbled against her skin.

The peaks of her breasts rubbed against his chest through the thin cotton layers of their T-shirts and her bra, and she moaned aloud. She arched her chest into him intentionally, rubbing her pebble-hard nipples back and forth against him.

"I've wanted this since the moment I first saw you," he muttered, kissing his way across her jaw. "Something fierce." He claimed her mouth again, devouring her ravenously.

Experiencing the same raging hunger, she wrapped her arms around his neck, plastering her entire body against his. Between hot, wet, tongue-tangling kisses, she panted, "I've wanted you so bad. I keep dreaming about you. About having hot, gnarly sex with you."

"You, too?" He released her momentarily and she nearly growled aloud in frustration. He stepped onto the boat but returned immediately. He tossed a thick blanket down on the dock and then tugged her down with him to kneel on it.

He tightened his arms roughly around her and twisted, carrying her down to the dock. He pinned her thighs with his larger, more muscular ones, and he leaned his considerable weight into his hands, which gripped her shoulders.

Never, ever, had a lover been able to overpower her like this. And from another man, it would have scared her to death. But from Beau—it was exhilarating.

He lowered his big body by slow degrees until he was deliciously crushing her, and she sighed in bliss at the weight of him. "You okay?" he checked in.

"Getting better by the minute," she answered.

She loved that he was bigger and heavier than she was. It made her feel small and feminine, both of which were novel sensations. He shifted his elbows to either side of her head, and her hands skimmed down his back, reveling in the taut flex of muscles and the barely leashed desire emanating from him.

He was voracious, and she met him halfway, inhaling him as hungrily as he was inhaling her. He lifted his body to fumble at their pants and to shove the clothing down around their ankles. She kicked one leg free and laughed as he did the same impatiently.

"This is a mistake," he ground out as he positioned

himself between her thighs. His arms tensed as he held himself over her, veins bulging and muscles tight. Good grief, he was a sight to see. A warrior in his prime, all male and about to be all hers.

"No doubt it's a mistake," she echoed.

"We ought to stop. But I'm not sure I can."

"Me, neither," she replied breathlessly.

Understanding passed through his hooded gaze. They couldn't go on like they had been, circling each other and snarling like a pair of hungry bears. Something had to give. And this was it.

"Nobody can ever know," he mumbled. "This has to stay between us."

She tugged his head down to his and captured his mouth with hers. "My lips are sealed. Well, maybe not *sealed*..."

A gust of laughter escaped him. His hand swept down the bare flesh of her stomach and then lower. His fingers stroked between her feminine folds and she jolted hard against him. Even his slightest touch made wild pleasure rip through her. He did it again, and she gasped, bucking hard against his hand. Impatience tore through her. She wanted him inside her so bad she could hardly stand it.

"Do you need me to show you what comes next?" she gritted out.

He grinned against her mouth. "Nah, I got it. Anyone ever tell you you're a pushy female, Wilkes?"

"Maybe. But you love it," she retorted. "Admit it."

"Yeah. I do."

"Still no action yet, Lambert. You sure you don't need some pointers?"

More laughter. "God almighty, woman. It's a good thing I have fantastic self-esteem, or you'd be stealing my mojo."

"If you don't *mo* my *jo*—like, right now—I'm gonna have to take over this show."

His eyes glinting with laughter, and something darker and sexier that stole her breath away, he positioned himself.

"Any day now—" She broke off as he pressed into her, filling her so full she thought she might burst. "Ahh, yes."

He withdrew a little and pressed home again, a little more forcefully this time. She shuddered with delight and already an orgasm clawed at her, trying to break free.

"Where's the big talk now, Wilkes?"

"More," she demanded.

"As the lady wishes." He crashed into her this time, setting up a rhythm that practically made her eyes roll back into her head with pleasure. He didn't hold back any of his formidable strength. But then, neither did she. Her hips surged up against his, and she met him stroke for stroke. Her heels dug into his cheeks, urging him onward.

She'd never experienced anything remotely like this. Beau didn't treat her like she was fragile or breakable. He was demanding but not obnoxious, generous with his body while taking freely of the pleasures of hers. And he knew. Just. Where. To. Go.

He kissed her deeply, his tongue plunging in and out of her mouth in time with their lovemaking. The combination was incendiary. She groaned, and then moaned, and then she screamed into his mouth as pleasure tore her to shreds.

"That's more like it," he murmured. "That's how I like my women. Shouting incoherently."

"You'll shout for me, too," she gasped back, her internal muscles clenching him, daring him not to be as loud as she was.

Her boneless languor transformed once again into taut, torturous pleasure pulsing through her until all she could do was ride the waves of ecstasy. A second orgasm, and a third, ripped through her.

And still he drove into her. Her body gathered itself for yet another explosive release. And then, inexplicably, he stopped. She groaned and reached down to urge him on.

"So impatient," he chided.

"So slow on the uptake," she retorted. "I want *more*."

"We're agreed then, that I do know what I'm doing?"

"Sure. Fine. You know. Just don't stop."

Laughter shook his chest, and he resumed moving inside her. But this time he picked up the pace, stroking faster and faster until she was a continuous, gelatinous mass of orgasmic bliss. She arched up into him, crying out again and again as he stoked the fire in her to unbearable heat.

She clung to his hips with her legs, and her hands roamed up and down his back. Everywhere she touched him, he was muscle and sweat and restless movement. She reveled in his power and flung her entire being at him with no fear of hurting him. It was liberating and utterly amazing.

Not that she could have held back if she wanted to. And she didn't want to. She cried out against the hollow of his neck, shuddering in ecstasy. He was making her whole from the soul out, and she never wanted it to end.

"You make me crazy," he gritted out from between clenched teeth. "I totally lose control around you."

"Perfect," she panted back. "I hate self-control."

"I noticed."

"Don't hold out on me. Take me over the edge with you."

He moved again, and the glide of slick, hot steel within her made her positively delirious.

"You're perfect," he gasped. His entire body arched into her, pressing her down into the hard dock, and she didn't care at all. It was glorious. She adored the wildness, loved the fact that she could pull this passion from him.

He stared down at her, his eyes glazed with pleasure. But he clearly saw *her*. He stared straight into her eyes, stripping her bare and laying her soul wide open. Mesmerized, she couldn't look away as a terrible tension built between them, higher, and yet higher.

Finally, with an entirely gratifying shout, he capitulated. His body spasmed violently against hers and she met him thrust for frantic thrust as epic orgasms tore free of their straining bodies and soared, taking them along for the ride.

They crashed back to reality in a tangle of sweaty limbs, panting breath, heaving chests and incredulous smiles that had no need of words.

She stared up at him in amazement, while he stared down at her in something akin to awe. After what felt like a long time, she finally was able to string words together. "That was even better than my dreams."

He just shook his head.

"What? You don't agree? Please tell me that's not average in your world."

He laughed shortly. "Honey, that would be mindblowing in any man's world. That was the gold medal standard of sex."

A smile unfolded across her face as relief unfolded inside her chest. "Really?"

"I would not joke about something like that," he said with a touch of reverence in his voice.

She smiled at him, and her heart sang when he smiled back at her. "Please promise me something, Beau."

He rolled onto his back and took her with him, drawing her across his chest with an arm casually around her shoulders. He was infinitely more comfortable to lie on than the hard dock. "What's that?" he murmured.

"Don't retreat into your emotional fortress of solitude again. If you need me to back off, just say so. I'll give you whatever space you need."

"Aww, Tessa. It's not you. It's my head that's messed up."

"How's that?" She would dearly love to press up onto her elbows and look at him, but she was leery of such direct contact with him. Better to stay where she was and keep the conversational tone light. Nonthreatening.

"I'm not ready to quit Spec Ops. But I don't know if I can get my knee back into good enough shape. It—" He exhaled hard before continuing. "It scares the hell out of me."

Holy cow. He was actually talking about his feelings with her.

She said carefully, "You handled yourself well in the grocery store. Your knee seems to have come out of that just fine." *And it had held up through some highly athletic sex.*

He shrugged beneath her ear. "The Kimballs are amateurs. I was able to use my hands to drop them. No strain on my knee. As a test, they don't count."

Just like this sex didn't count. By mutual agreement, this meant nothing. It was a physical release. Nothing more. Keep the conversation neutral. Nonthreatening. She cast about for something innocuous to say.

"What about you shifting to being a sniper special-ist?" she suggested. "Those guys don't usually engage the enemy up close. And you're a heck of a shot." *And a heck of a lover.* How was she supposed to walk away from what they'd just shared and never do that again?

"Maybe," he said doubtfully. "My knee would still have to hold up for ingresses and egresses. And I might not be any good at it."

As if he wouldn't be spectacular at anything he put his mind to. Hah. "I've seen you shoot, Beau. I don't think you'd have any trouble extending your effective range to sniper distances. We could work on it together. I need the long-range practice, too." *Anything to maintain this temporary truce between us, where he is treating me like a human being and, furthermore, like a woman.*

He went very still beneath her. Crap, crap, crap. Had she overstepped her bounds with him? Was she doomed always to stick her foot in her mouth with him? She hated this uncertainty. A little voice in the back of her head warned her she couldn't hope to sustain a long-term re-lationship with him if she always had to guard her words and measure what she was going to say before she said it.

Whoa there. Rewind. They'd already agreed there would be no feelings out of this. *No* relationship.

"Been thinking about my future, have you?" he asked.

What I wouldn't give to think about our future. To-gether. "Maybe," she replied cautiously. "Could you use a spotter?" *Or a friend with benefits? A lover? An actual girlfriend, maybe?*

He pressed up on an elbow, dumping her on her side and bringing them eye to eye. "You volunteering for the job?"

If only. "Somebody's got to spot for you."

"It wouldn't be a bad idea for you to get sniper training yourself," he said slowly.

Is there a chance for us, after all? Elation leaped in her gut.

"How are you at mental math?" he asked.

"Fantastic. I won every multiplication bee in the fourth grade."

He grinned and leaned forward to kiss her fast and hard before pressing to his feet and holding a hand down to her. She took it and he lifted her up into his arms and a long, lingering kiss.

Ohmigod, ohmigod, ohmigod. He wanted more of what they'd just shared. She was sure of it!

"Just promise me one thing, Tessa."

"What's that?"

"Don't fall for me."

"Why not?" she exclaimed.

"A future together for you and me is not in the cards. We'll have no control over where we're sent or how long we'll be apart. And if we do end up together on a team, we both know this can't ever happen between us again. I don't want to see you get hurt. Keep your heart out of this."

Crushing disappointment slammed into her, so heavy she was having trouble breathing. He was right, of course. But his warning had come too late.

Her heart was already totally involved.

Chapter 11

Beau followed Tessa into the house, admiring the way her tush twitched as she jogged up the steps. One thing he could say about recreating the Medusas—the scenery would be a whole lot better with them around.

But the other complications…not so much. He *knew* better than to have sex with her. *Mistake. Mistake. Mistake!*

But what an incredible mistake. Sex with her had been every bit as great as he'd imagined, and he had a terrific imagination.

He should have expected the adrenaline high to hit them both after the fight with the Kimballs. But it had totally broadsided him. It hadn't dawned on him that Tessa would experience the same rush of driving lust and need for release after the fight. Sure, after a dicey patrol, all the guys wanted to find the first willing female and get laid. But who knew a woman would react the exact same way?

He wouldn't be reporting *that* little detail to Torsten.

The sex was all his fault. He should have seen it coming and headed it off. But he'd been completely unable and unwilling to corral his lust and resist her. Not that he was having any success working up even a smidgeon of real regret for having had that outrageous sex with her.

But therein lay the problem. It hadn't been just sex for him. No matter how vehemently he swore that it was just physical, that there would be no emotional involvement, and that it meant nothing, his gut warned him it wasn't that simple. Not for him, and not for Tessa.

He was neither stupid nor unobservant. They had more simmering between them than just smoking-hot sex. They connected. Hell, they fit each other. Not just physically. She got him. Knew how he thought. Understood his world better than any woman he'd even been around. And that was only going to intensify as she continued her training.

Grimly, he helped her unpack the groceries and stack cans in the cupboards. He caught Tessa studying him thoughtfully, and an urge to kiss her until she couldn't think straight enough to psychoanalyze him came over him.

Irritated with himself, he went outside, picked up a paint scraper, climbed a ladder and vented his frustration on the wood siding of the house. He might as well keep doing repairs on the place while he was here. *Get a head start on your retirement*, a voice in his head commented bitterly.

Tessa came outside wearing that sexy little muscle shirt she'd had on the day he brought her here. Without speaking to him, she picked up the other paint scraper, and silently got to work below him. The view down the front of her tank top was spectacular. Her breasts were round and full, and he knew now exactly how those berry-ripe nipples pressing against the thin cotton tasted.

Aww, hell. The whole point of coming out here to work was to distract himself from having more sex with her. Now he wasn't going to get any relief from his fixation on that.

What was she doing out here? Was this a demonstration that she could separate work and play as well as the next guy? Or was it a blatant reminder to him of how irresistible she was? Surely, she wasn't trying to get inside his head and mess with him…or was she? If so, it was damned well working.

He thought about her every waking second. If he wasn't thinking about the many ways he'd like to have sex with her, he was thinking about her training. The multiple trains of thought in his head—what she would need to know to survive and not mess up a Special Forces team, how to find a way to wash her out of training, and how to talk her out of being a Medusa were mentally exhausting to juggle. The end result was that his whole world revolved around her.

He understood that her whole world had to revolve around him. He was the final arbiter of whether or not she got to pursue her most cherished dream. He knew now just how bad she wanted to be a Medusa—as much or more than any man he'd ever seen come through the pipeline, in fact. His resolve to rip her dream away from her actually wavered now and then in the face of her desperate desire to succeed.

Worse, he was reluctantly forced to agree with Gunnar Torsten. She'd been born to be a Medusa. If any woman on earth existed who was more suited to it than she was, he had a hard time believing it.

Of *course* they'd eventually given in and had sex with each other. The intensity of what they were doing out here combined with being in close quarters with each other 24/7 had made it pretty much inevitable. It was no use beating himself up over it. The sex had happened. It had been freaking awesome. And now it was over. Itch scratched. Box checked. Case closed.

He glanced down at Tessa, scraping the siding vigorously below him, and the sight of her breasts jiggling with her effort all but knocked him off the ladder.

Who was he kidding? He wanted to have sex with her again. And next time they would do it right. In a bed. Naked. Take their time—

Negative. Not happening. Nope, nope, nope.

What did she think about all of this, anyway? He would be interested to know.

Which was weird as all get-out for him. He'd never paid attention to what any woman thought before. Sure, he picked them up in bars on the rare Saturday night he had off, and he liked sex as much as the next guy, but he'd never had any reason to care seriously what was going on inside one's head or heart.

Tessa worked hard on the siding with him. Whether she was working off stress of her own or engaging in her usual feminist competition to keep up with him, he couldn't say. But they finished scraping the entire house before the light began to fail.

Plenty of time for him to come to the reluctant conclusion that his original plan of action was still the right one. Today's encounter with Tessa on the dock had cemented his certainty that he was terrified of her becoming a Medusa, in spite of the fact that she actually could do the job.

He had to convince Tessa to quit. Now, before she went and got herself killed. Because like it or not, the idea of her going out in the field and dying was completely unacceptable to him.

Grimly, he formulated a plan. He would put it into motion at supper.

Forcing his mind away from kissing her—which was no easy feat—he sat down across from her at the kitchen table. "Talk to me about today's incident," he said.

She glanced at him sidelong, and his groin stirred hopefully. *Down, boy.*

"Well," she said lightly, "the sex was a bit slow to get going, but once you figured out which widget went where, you were a reasonably quick learner—"

He cut her off. "Very funny. Talk to me about the Kimball fight."

"What do you want to know?"

He studied her closely. "How did you drop those guys? I was tied up with the two who jumped me and didn't see what you did."

She shrugged, a quick flex of leaned, sharply defined shoulder muscles, and even that casual movement was sexy.

She explained, "I shoved the cart into one's gut so I only had to fight one on one. Then I kicked Jimbo in the knee and followed up with a punch to the solar plexus. When he doubled over, I broke his nose."

"You dropped Jimbo Kimball just like that? The dude's twice your size and tough as nails."

"I tried to tell you I had martial arts training, but

you wouldn't listen. You were busy going all caveman, protect-the-little-woman on me."

Chagrin coursed through him. She was, of course, correct. "We may have a bit of a problem with the Kimball boys going forward. People who cross them have a history of going missing or turning up dead."

"I have heard that tends to happen around meth dealers," she commented drily.

"What makes you think they're dealing meth?" he asked curiously. The Kimballs had been hard drinkers and pot smokers in high school, but they hadn't messed with the hard stuff.

"Did you see their mouths?" Tessa retorted. "Meth rots teeth. Not to mention I smelled lye on their clothes. Sodium hydroxide is one of the main ingredients in production of methamphetamine. Trust me. They're cooking meth."

"And you know the smell of a meth lab how?"

Her gaze slid away from his. "Let's just say my mom didn't have the greatest taste in guys."

Ahh. The crappy boyfriends who'd made her so hinky about men. Anger seethed in his gut on behalf of the scared, victimized little girl she must have been. A need to track down those old boyfriends of her mom's and beat the snot out of them made his fists clench.

Although, had it not been for those jerks, Tessa probably wouldn't be sitting here beside him today. He supposed that, in point of fact, he owed them a thank-you... and *then* he would beat the snot out of them.

"How do you know the Kimball boys?" Tessa asked, startling him out of his violent thoughts.

"Went to school with a couple of them."

"Hah. So this is your hometown!" she exclaimed.

"I grew up in this house. My grandparents raised me here. How else do you think I knew of its existence, way out here in the middle of the swamp?"

It was the one place on earth he'd been loved and happy and safe. Not that he was going to share something personal like that with her. She was already way too far inside his head. He was *not* letting her in any further.

"Problem is, the Kimball boys also know where this place is," he explained.

Tessa leaped to the obvious conclusion. "Which means we should be expecting them to show up and try to finish the fight from the grocery store."

He shrugged. "They don't take kindly to losing nor to being made to look foolish. We handed them both today. It's not going to sit well with them that we kicked their asses so publicly."

"Still. That was fun. Admit it." Tessa grinned over at him, and he couldn't help grinning back. Hell, yeah, it had been fun.

"What's the plan?" she asked. "We gonna set up a watch rotation?"

"Yup. Do you want the first watch?" he asked Tessa as the deep dark of night settled around them.

"I don't care."

"Always take first watch if you have a choice," he instructed. "It allows you to get a longer block of uninterrupted sleep later during the hours of the night when your Circadian rhythms think you should be sleeping."

"Okay, then. First watch it is for me."

A hand over his mouth yanked him to full consciousness and battle alert sometime later. He heard immediately what had caused Tessa to wake him. A boat motor was approaching. Even as he listened, it cut off. But too late. The Kimball boys had made their first tactical mistake.

Second mistake: they appeared to be headed for the dock. He'd told Tessa the Kimballs would be that obvious in their approach, and she had argued that they wouldn't be that arrogant or ignorant. He glanced over at her in triumph now, and she just shook her head in disgust.

Mistake number two meant the Kimball boys were about to make mistake number three: walking right into the thick of the traps he and Tessa had laid for them. This should be fun.

Tessa crawled over to the smaller of the two sniper rigs with a rubber round already chambered in the weapon. Rubber bullets would stop a target and cause a fair amount of blunt impact trauma, but they weren't made to kill a person.

He picked up the shotgun lying at the ready and chambered a beanbag round quietly. Then he picked up a spotter's scope and dialed in the distance to the south end of the peninsula where the Kimballs were about to get several nasty shocks.

The first tripwire beyond the dock was simple. Each end of it was attached to a big cluster of stinging nettles that would be dragged in on the members of party behind the first guy whose boot caught the wire.

Sure enough, in a few seconds, sounds of thrashing drifted on the still night air to the hide. Tessa grinned beside him.

Next up was a pile of rolling logs in the path. Another simple trap, but effective, particularly for half-drunk bubbas stumbling around in the dark without night vision equipment. The trap sprung, several logs rolled into the path and muffled swearing erupted this time. It sounded like all of the Kimball boys were here. No one had stayed behind with the boat. Mistake number four.

A voice complained clearly in the darkness, "Jeebus, Jimbo. Git off me."

"If you see the bastard, shoot 'im. Hurt 'im but don't kill 'im. We's gonna have ourselves some fun first."

Beau's humor evaporated. So. That was how they wanted to play it, huh? The older Kimball, Travis, came into view in his scope. Range: sixty yards. Zero windage. Elevation: effectively nil. He flashed the numbers to Tessa by way of hand signals, and she flashed them back in confirmation. He nodded and she dialed in her sight. She could take this shot blindfolded, but treating easy shots the exact same way as hard shots helped build good shooting habits.

The Kimballs staggered clear of the logs a little farther to the right than he and Tessa had planned for. She corrected her aim slightly, and he signaled her to take the shot. The report of her weapon rang out, followed by a yelp from Virgil, one of the middle brothers.

"I'm freaking shot!" Virgil cried.

"Very funny, Lambert!" Jimbo shouted. "I'm gonna break yer damned kneecaps, and then let your girlfriend seduce me instead."

Beau's jaw hardened. Jimbo was going to regret that comment.

Tessa chambered another round, sliding the bolt closed quietly. Beau held up a hand, signaling her to wait. She nodded and settled into the motionless waiting state of a sniper.

The boys took a half dozen steps, right into the sweet spot of the log that was going to swing down out of

the tree tops and slam them all into the swamp right…
about…now.

The crash was spectacular as all four Kimball boys
were swept off their feet and into the swamp. They came
up sputtering and cursing, and handguns glinted dully
in the scant moonlight.

"Weapons," he breathed into his throat microphone.

"Roger," she replied in a bare whisper.

Okay, fun and games over. Beau picked up his shotgun and sighted in on the first Kimball splashing ashore.
He murmured low to Tessa, "Fire at will."

She pegged Virgil again, but this time the guy fell to
his knees, clutching at his throat. Ouch. Tessa was not
playing nice anymore. For his part, he aimed at Jimbo's
crotch and nailed the eldest Kimball in the junk with
a beanbag round. It would hit with the force of a prize
fighter burying a fist with all his might into the guy's
crotch. Jimbo doubled over gasping like a chicken with
its neck half wrung. Beau reloaded quickly, and Tessa
did the same beside him.

They peppered the Kimballs for about the next sixty
chaotic seconds as it slowly dawned on the Kimballs
that they were under actual attack. The brothers clustered together back to back, peering into the darkness
without the benefit of night vision devices.

His and Tessa's superior technology, training and
teamwork spelled big trouble for the Kimball boys.
Tough. They were thugs and bullies. High time someone gave them a little taste of their own medicine.

Beau jumped to his feet and ran to the second firing
position as a gunshot rang out over his head. He was reluctant to fire live rounds because, unlike the Kimball
boys, neither he nor Tessa would miss.

"I'm running low on rubber ammo," she transmitted under a round of noisy gunfire from the Kimballs.

"Go long for the pass," Beau murmured.

He lay down, covering fire of fast, continuous shots from the second sniper rig and glimpsed the lime-green blob of Tessa running low to the right as she left the primary hide and headed for her secondary firing position.

As she reached an opening in the trees, he lobbed a spare mag of rubber rounds her way. "Ammo incoming," he announced.

She looked up just in time to grab the magazine and keep running without breaking her stride. *Booyah. Perfect pass.*

"You missed your calling, Lambo," Tessa panted. "Should've played football. You'd have made a great quarterback."

She must have reached her next sniper nest, for pops from her rifle started up, along with yelps from the Kimball brothers. They'd decided earlier not to make tonight easy for the Kimballs. This encounter was about sending a message to the brothers to leave him and Tessa the heck alone.

He'd also used this ambush as a training opportunity for Tessa, working out infil and exfiltration points, optimum firing positions, field of fire problems and a host of other tactical considerations. Which was to say, the Kimballs weren't going to know what had hit them when this ambush was over.

He'd made absolutely sure he and Tessa would win because the idea of her getting shot panicked him more than he wanted to admit. He only prayed that once the Kimballs got serious and started shooting live rounds she would realize this wasn't the career field for her.

He and Tessa pinned down the brothers in painful, but nonlethal, crossfire for about two more minutes. Beau had just started for the third hide when something slammed into the side of his right knee. A screeching scream of metal on metal split the night air and the Kimballs hooted with glee.

Damn. He was shot.

Chapter 12

Beau's knee collapsed out from under him and he pitched over whether he wanted to or not. Using quickness and agility honed over years of training, he managed to turn the fall into a roll from back to belly, landing in a firing position.

He ignored the searing pain in his right knee and fired off a pair of beanbags in quick succession. A series of rubber bullet shots, one right after another, came from Tessa's position. Man, she was reloading fast. Must be pissed off that a lucky ricochet had hit her partner.

As he flexed the joint experimentally, he felt his pant leg for wetness that would indicate heavy bleeding. It bent without increasing the pain, and his trouser fabric wasn't soaked. There was blood, but nothing life threatening.

He smiled a little. Never thought he'd be so glad to have a knee brace on his leg. The titanium had protected him from taking a slug through the knee that would have truly messed up the joint forever. Hey. He always said he'd rather be lucky than good.

Another gunshot zinged past uncomfortably close to his head. All right. Enough of this garbage. He keyed his throat mike and breathed. "Go live. One shot. No kill."

Which was easier said than done. It took a fine shooter at the top of his or her game to actually hit a specific target on the human body. Even simply aiming at the center of mass on a human was no guarantee of a hit for most people. But Tessa was within twenty yards of the nearest Kimball, and she was a fine shooter at the top of her game.

"Roger," Tessa replied low in his earpiece.

It took about fifteen seconds for her to load a Teflon-tipped, low-grain-load sniper round and take aim.

The shot rang out stunningly loud in the night after the soft rubber rounds. Simultaneous with the shot was a scream. Interesting. She'd gone after Jimbo. Good choice. He'd always been the ringleader of the bunch. If Jimbo could be persuaded to bug out, the other boys would follow him.

"Son of a bitch! Bastard shot me bad! I'm bleedin' all over heah'. Git me to the boat. Jeebus, I need me a doctor. Gimme yo' shirt, Travis. C'mon, now, I'm dyin'."

Beau listened in grim satisfaction as Jimbo ranted and cursed all the way back to the dock. The other Kimballs eventually horsed Jimbo into their boat. A motor roared, and silence settled around the peninsula.

"Clear your quadrant," he ordered Tessa.

He hobbled through a sweep of his quadrant of the backyard and made sure no Kimballs had stayed behind to give him and Tessa a nasty surprise of their own. Searing pain shot through the joint when he reached the back porch and tried to bend his knee to take the first step. Nope. His knee was done.

"I'm clear," Tessa reported.

"I have a small problem. Make your way to me."

She joined him, clearing her way as she went. Good girl. "What's up?" she said low.

"My knee's hit."

She moved quickly to his right side and wedged her shoulder under his armpit. With her help, he made his way into the house. She took him into her room and helped him sit down on her bed. Quickly, she pulled out their first-aid kit—a medic's crash kit with excellent supplies, thankfully.

"Can you get your pants off, or should I cut them?" she asked.

"Honey, any woman who looks like you will never have any trouble getting me out of my pants."

"I see the bullet didn't ding your sense of humor."

He gritted his teeth as she fumbled at his crotch. "How about I unzip my own trousers?" Otherwise, she might end up joining him on this bed for a little unscheduled sex, shooting agony in his knee or not.

She sat back on her heels to watch. He peeled his camo pants down over his hips, and her hands were abruptly there to help skim them down his legs.

"Ahh. Well, no wonder your knee hurts," she announced. She ripped free the thick Velcro bands securing the brace and lifted it away from his leg. As soon as she did, the knifelike pain in his joint subsided.

She held the brace up and relief rushed through him. The bullet had damaged the titanium, causing a sliver of the metal to tear and bend inward so it jabbed the side of his knee. A thin gash in the side of his leg was trickling blood down his calf.

"Lemme clean that up and get some butterfly bandages on it. I don't think it's deep enough for stitches." Tessa turned away to dig in the med kit.

He used the moment to allow the panic he'd been holding at bay to flow through him, give him a short, hard shiver, and then to drain away. He'd thought for a minute there that it was all over for him as an operator.

He watched in relief as she cleaned up and bandaged what was, in effect, a boo-boo on his knee.

"All better," she announced.

He bent the joint a few times, and it was blessedly mobile and relatively pain free with that sharp piece of the brace out of it. "Right as rain, Nurse Wilkes," he declared.

"Does that mean I can yell at you for scaring me now?"

He shrugged. "Guys are going to get shot and injured all the time in the field. Get used to it."

"Yeah, but they're not you," she muttered under her breath.

"I told you not to—"

She cut him off and said defensively, "I know, I know. Don't fall for you. I remember. But that doesn't mean I can't be concerned for you."

Dammit. She *had* fallen for him. And then he became aware of something strange. A knot of warmth in his gut. What the hell was that all about? He was *not* glad she was worried about him! But that little lump of warmth wouldn't go away no matter how much he swore at it or threatened it.

Tessa's heart dropped to her feet as an angry expression flitted across Beau's face in response to the idea that she might have fallen for him. Why was he so dead set on her not having any feelings for him? Was he that determined never to open himself up to love?

The *L*-word startled her. Whoa. Where had that come from? She wasn't looking for love any more than he was. A real relationship with a decent guy who rocked her world in the sack? Maybe someday. After the Medusas. Beau had shown her that much was possible with a man, for which she was deeply grateful. But true love? Not a chance.

She bent her head, studying his knee intently, to hide the dismay in her eyes from his all too perceptive stare. She unzipped his combat boots and unbloused his pants, then pulled his pants the rest of the way off his legs. No sense knocking off the bandage and starting his cut bleeding again just when she'd gotten it stopped.

Beau stood up, putting her gaze exactly crotch-high on him. All she had to do was lean forward. Pull his underwear down, and take him in her mouth. Even as the thought crossed her mind, his male parts stirred, swelling rapidly behind the thin Spandex.

Hands gripped her shoulders. Lifted her slowly to her feet. Her unwilling gaze traveled up his body, taking in the washboard abs, the bulging pecs and broad shoulders. A finger touched her chin, tilting her face up, forcing her to look him in the eyes.

"We good?" Beau murmured.

Jeez. How to answer that? They would be great if he would just kiss her and forget about the whole "Don't fall for me" thing. She ended up mumbling, "Umm, yeah. Sure. Fine."

"I don't know much about women, but I do know one thing. When a woman says nothing's wrong, something's always wrong. And when she says she's fine like you just did, she's emphatically not fine. Talk to me. What's going on?"

She winced. If only he wasn't so direct all the time. She knew better than to try to lie to a special operator—they all had training that included knowing how to lie and how to spot a lie. She opted for partial truth. "I want you, Beau. Right now."

"Post-mission adrenaline got you jacked up again?"

Actually, she'd been shockingly calm out there earlier. Which she was secretly pretty darned proud of. Tonight was the first time she'd ever shot a real bullet at a real human being. At the time, she'd been so focused on protecting Beau that it hadn't dawned on her what she'd done.

But now that he mentioned it, adrenaline was, indeed, screaming through her. And it was demanding an outlet in no uncertain terms.

"I feel as if I could run a marathon right about now," she confessed. She risked a glance up at him. "Or have epic sex with you. Your choice."

He laughed, low and sexy. "Best sex you'll ever have is right after a scare-you-to-death mission. And they do get a lot scarier than chasing off those yahoos tonight."

Whatever. She wanted sex. She slid her hands up under Beau's T-shirt against hot, naked male flesh. "Didn't you get even the tiniest adrenaline spike out there tonight? When your knee brace got shot, maybe?"

His arms swept around her and she gasped as his hard body abruptly was plastered against hers. "I might have a little spike," he murmured in her ear. "You'd better check."

Laughing against his chest, she let her hands roam down his back to cup his tight, muscular rear end. She'd never been much of a caboose girl, but dang, he had a nice one. Her hand slid inside the waistband of his athletic shorts and around to his front. She plunged her hand downward and was rewarded with a fistful of erection so hard and so hot it could definitely deliver the kind of sex she had in mind tonight.

She pushed his shorts down while he tugged his T-shirt over his head. He stripped her with shocking efficiency. The man sure knew his way around women's clothing. And around women's bodies. In moments he had her moaning in his arms as his hand slipped between her legs. Clever, clever fingers that man had. In turn, she gripped him tightly, running her hand up and down the iron and velvet shaft.

He backed her up against the wall, looping her right leg over his hip. He slammed up and into her with a groan as she shuddered in delight and arched into him.

"Again," she demanded breathlessly.

He obliged, sandwiching her between the wall at her back and his driving thrusts from the front. She wrapped one hand around his neck, tangling her fingers in his hair. He captured her other hand with his, lacing their fingers together and plastering the back of her hand to the wall above her head. He all but lifted her off the floor with the force of his thrusts and she opened herself to him eagerly, driving down onto him with abandon.

"Come for me, baby," he growled in her ear. "Scream for me."

That was all it took. She buried her face against his neck and cried out her pleasure as an orgasm tore through her.

"I could do this all night long with you," he growled. He spun her around, dumped her on the bed and followed her down, impaling her from behind this time and pounding into her like a jackhammer.

He drove her over the edge into bliss again, and amazement coursed through her. He did it so easily to her. A few kisses and a few strokes of his magnificent body inside her, and she was lost.

"More," she panted, well aware that he had not found his own release yet and greedy for more herself.

"I don't want to hurt you," he ground out.

"I promise you are not hurting me," she gritted back. "Please."

He rose to his knees, gripped her hips and lifted her onto her hands and knees.

"Tell me if it's too much," he muttered as he positioned carefully. "I'll try to hold back—"

"Don't you dare!"

Beau made a strangled sound halfway between a laugh and a groan. And then he drove into her and all humor fled in the face of the towering pleasure abruptly building between them like a firestorm. It swept away everything in its path, leaving only the two of them, their bodies straining toward each other, and the promise of release so powerful they wouldn't be able to stand before it.

Faster and deeper he drove into her. Harder and higher she pushed back onto him. Their bodies collided over and over, each time wringing a cry of delight from her throat. Her blood burned through her veins like molten magma seeking escape. Higher and higher the heat and pressure built until her body felt as if it couldn't contain it all anymore.

Beau grabbed her hips and slammed into her one last time as he pulled her back toward him, and completely uncontainable pleasure ripped through her as her entire being exploded. He shouted and drove into her one last time as the pleasure utterly and completely consumed them both. She shivered as he shuddered against her, pouring his entire being into her and taking everything from her in return.

Beau collapsed onto his side, taking her with him and tucking her against his front, spooning with her like they had that very first night in the motel. She was gratified to feel him breathing as hard as she was. Well, then. Sign her up for adrenaline-fired sex any day.

"See what I mean about the adrenaline?" he said lazily.

"Why, yes. Yes, I do," she managed to answer.

He laughed quietly and his arms tightened affectionately around her.

The two of them were so much better at communicating with their bodies than with their words. She didn't have to hear him say he had feelings for her, too, when he made love to her like that. Goodness knew she poured her heart and soul into it, as well. Nope. She had no need for words from him. His demonstration of passion and tenderness and caring and desire spoke volumes.

They lay there together for a long time, wreathed in contentment.

Eventually, she roused herself enough to ask, "Think the Kimballs will be back for more tonight?"

"Nah. Jimbo thought he was dying. He'll want to get patched up before he comes back for more. Where'd you shoot him, anyway?"

"Right shoulder. Round passed through cleanly from what I saw."

"Yup, that'll lay him up for a few days. The other

boys won't make a move against us without him to lead the pack."

"Not the self-motivated types, huh?"

Beau nibbled her ear lightly. "Hardly."

She turned in his arms to face him. "So you're saying we have all night to rest up before they try again?"

"I am."

She smiled up at him. "So. How fit are you Spec Ops types? Is your recovery time from strenuous exercise as good as everyone says it is?"

The corner of his mouth curved up in the soft glow of the kerosene lamp. "You looking to find out?"

"Hey, I run triathlons for fun. I know I can recover on a dime."

His grin widened. "Is that a challenge, Wilkes?"

"I guess it is, Lambo. Whatchya got?"

Beau climbed toward consciousness lazily, a little disoriented at registering himself lying in a bed with a lush female body draped over him. And not just any body. Tessa's glorious body. It was a damned fine way to wake up in the morning.

She moved a little, half-waking, as well. Her hand stole across his chest and dipped lower, tracing the sharp indents of his stomach muscles, which tightened under her touch. As did other portions of his anatomy.

They'd gone at it for a good portion of the night last night. He would think his body had had enough, but apparently not. This woman was hard to get enough of. Honestly, he didn't think he would ever tire of her. There was always something new to discover about her. Another layer of personality, another dimension to their passion. And the miracle of it all was that she seemed to be as addicted to him as he was to her.

He was abjectly grateful that she didn't seem to require romantic speeches and grand declarations of his feelings. He was a thousand times better at showing how he felt, and thankfully, she seemed to understand his unspoken message.

As he became more alert, less lazily half-asleep, it dawned on him to wonder exactly what he *wasn't* saying to himself about his feelings for Tessa.

Tessa's leg was already thrown across his thigh, and she pressed herself upright, sliding the rest of the way across his hips to straddle him. She smiled down at him sleepily. "Morning, handsome."

"Mornin', beautiful."

Her dark hair was wavy and tousled around her face and shoulders, her breasts peeking out from among the silky strands. She looked like a Siren smiling down on him and was as irresistible as one. It really was a minor miracle that she not only found him attractive, but was also bold enough to take on a guy like him romantically and meet him halfway.

Strike that. No romance here. Just sex. Lots and lots of truly amazing sex. *No feelings. No strings.* He repeated the mantra to himself over and over.

But then his traitorous hand had to go and reach up, to trace the seductive curve of her breast through her tousled hair. Maybe when he retired he would take up painting and spend a few decades trying to capture the perfection of that shape. His body stirred, and a slow, sexy smile spread across Tessa's face. He grinned back at her. She had a hell of an effect on him. He couldn't remember ever being this insatiably drawn to a woman before.

She shifted her weight and slid herself down onto his eager erection, her body tight and warm around him. She rocked her hips lazily and a groan of pure pleasure slipped between his lips. She rode him slowly, her movements languid as her body undulated upon his. He watched her ride him, as lazy and sultry as the morning. His gaze narrowed as he grew harder and his body tightened almost painfully. Good grief, the pleasure she gave him. She knocked his world so off-kilter he hardly knew which way was up.

"I think I could do this forever." She sighed blissfully.

"I know I could," he replied fervently.

She opened her eyes and smiled down at him. He stared back at her, his soul stripped bare. He was defenseless in the face of her sensuality. She was everything he'd ever dreamed of in a woman and more. Hell, she could shoot Eisenhower's eye out of a dime at fifty yards and then do this, riding him into complete oblivion. She was perfect.

The pleasure built and built, and Tessa threw her head back, losing herself in the love she was making to him. He reveled in the myriad expressions flitting across her face. She was so open, holding nothing back as pleasure, wonder and even a bit of awe shone in her eyes and curved her mouth into ever more delirious smiles.

No feelings. No strings.

She looked like a goddess come to life, calling forth sexual responses from him that he didn't even know he was capable of. Her internal muscles tugged at him hungrily, and his hips rose to meet her. His entire body clenched, on the edge of detonating. Her hips rocked forward and down as she impaled herself more deeply than ever upon him, gripping his entire length tighter and tighter.

No feelings. No strings. No feelings. No strings.

He thrust up into her, seeking her core with a desperation he hadn't known he could feel. There. Heaven. He'd touched Heaven. Tessa threw her head back and keened in pleasure as her body spasmed hard around his, her internal muscles shuddering and clenching, releasing and clenching again in the throes of her orgasm.

No feelings. No strings. No. Feelings. No. Strings. Dammit.

His entire body tightened and then exploded into her with such violence he almost lost consciousness for a second. Her internal muscles pumped him until he was drained, totally emptied into her, body and soul.

He fell back, breathing hard, mind blown. He'd never, in his entire life, experienced a release like that. He felt shredded into a million disconnected bits. An odd and totally unfamiliar sense of wholeness filled him. With it came a wave of peace, of rightness, that ran soul-deep.

Tessa planted her hands on his shoulders, panting, and her hair swung down around their faces like a sable curtain. Inside its shelter, the two of them stared at each other for a long, wordless moment. The intimacy of it was staggering. Based on the joy and disbelief shining in her bright gaze, he gathered her mind was nearly as blown as his.

Neither of them spoke. They just stared into each other's eyes. Hell, into each other's souls. A million words could not have conveyed what their eyes expressed.

Eventually, she murmured, "I know I'm not supposed to fall for you. But can I at least say thank you for that?"

Stone-cold fear rippled through him. It was both unexpected and unwelcome. Worse, it wasn't fear of her falling for him. It was fear of her *not* falling for him. "Yeah. Sure," he mumbled. *No feelings. No freaking strings.*

His gut clenched, this time with unpleasant awareness of an even bigger problem. A huge one. She might not be falling for him, but he sure as hell was falling for her.

Chapter 13

Beau had taken his turn in the shower, helped Tessa cook up a giant pile of pancakes and done his part to help devour them when his phone rang. He pulled it out and frowned at the caller ID. Torsten. Guilt speared through Beau's gut. *Busted.*

Which was ridiculous, of course. Gunnar couldn't possibly know what he and Tessa had been up to most of last night and this morning.

What, then, did the boss man want? To date, Torsten had been mostly hands off with Tessa's training, trusting Beau to figure out what to do and get it done.

"Hey, sir. How's it going?"

"It's going. I have a question for you, Beau. How's our girl's training progressing?"

Lambert said with definite reluctance, "She's doing better than I expected."

Tessa smiled broadly over the dishes she was washing in the sink, and Beau rolled his eyes at her.

Gunnar asked seriously, "Would you say she's Medusa material? I need you to be dead straight with me."

"As much as I'd love to say no, I can't. She's taking to this stuff like a fish to water."

"That's fantastic news. I was pretty sure she had the right stuff."

Beau snorted. As if Gunnar Torsten was ever wrong about such things.

"Here's the thing, Beau. I need her operational as soon as possible."

He frowned, warning bells clanging in his gut. It might be okay in theory to think about making a Medusa of Tessa, but with the reality abruptly staring him in the face, Beau was shocked to realize he actually hated the idea. A lot.

More to the point, he hated the idea of her going anywhere near harm's way.

"Why do you need her operational?" he managed to mumble.

Gunnar answered grimly, "I'm going to have a mission for her sooner rather than later."

"Use someone else," Lambert replied sharply.

"She's the perfect candidate for the job," Gunnar replied tersely.

"She's not even a baby Medusa yet," Beau snapped back.

A long silence ensued. Beau wasn't about to be the one to break the stalemate, since Tessa's actual life might very well be on the line.

"I'm sorry, Beau. I need a woman on this op. It's been a year in the making, and we've got undercover guys in place, lives on the line. It's going to take a woman to close the deal, and she's the only one I've got right now. In a couple of years when I've got a whole team of Medusas to choose from, of course I wouldn't consider sending out someone so inexperienced." He added, his voice waxing ragged, "But I lost my whole Medusa team six months ago. I've got *nobody* else but Tessa Wilkes."

Beau exhaled heavily. He got where Torsten was coming from. He just didn't like it. Hell, he hated it.

"I want to bring her in, Beau. Hook her up with a Spec Ops team. Train with them. We need to prepare her as much as possible as fast as possible. A plane will arrive at the airfield in…four hours plus or minus ten minutes. I need both of you on it."

Beau stared at his disconnected phone in disgust. He'd never had a choice at all over whether or not Tessa got thrown into the deep end of the pool. The damn plane was already en route to come get her. Great. Just freaking great.

Tessa couldn't remember the last time she'd felt this amazing. The sex with Beau had been mind-boggling. For better or worse, it had been more than mere sex. They'd made love with each other.

Even Beau seemed to have been affected by it. She'd never felt such a connection with any man before. It was scary and wonderful and overwhelming all at the same time. How on earth he could resist that, she had no idea.

Beau was quiet over breakfast. Withdrawn. As if he was thinking deep—unpleasant—thoughts. She would lay odds he was thinking about her because he glanced over at her from time to time when he thought she wasn't looking his way.

Please, *please*, let him not be regretting sleeping with

her. If she'd learned nothing in her life so far, it was that life was too short to dwell on regrets.

Take her, for example. She would never regret sleeping with him. Yes, she understood that she couldn't have him and be a Medusa. She knew that someday she would have to choose between the two. But that day was not this day. Today she would enjoy being with him. Maybe she would initiate the sex tonight.

"Penny for your thoughts?" she murmured.

He just shook his head.

Drat. Beau could lock down his thoughts and feelings like nobody's business. She would give a million dollars to know what was going on inside his complicated head. But no amount of money would induce him to share, of course. The man lived for his secrets.

Not that she didn't have a few of her own. Like the fact that she'd actually enjoyed being in a firefight with the Kimballs last night...nearly as much as she enjoyed having sex. Well, maybe as much as regular sex. What she and Beau did together was in a class all its own. Nothing compared to that. Surely, he felt it, too.

Their connection was intense. What she felt, he felt, and vice versa. It was as if they were inside each other's heads when they made love. What pleasured one pleasured the other. It was kind of freaky. This morning the more pleasure she'd given him, the more she'd experienced herself.

Maybe that was the difference between sex and making love. Sex was about taking as much feel-good for herself as possible. But making love with Beau was about giving as much pleasure as she could. And in return, the pleasure she received increased dramatically. Who knew? It wasn't as if she'd had any healthy, love-based relationships around her growing up or in her own life to date to learn it from.

Stop. Rewind. Love? Since when was love on the table between her and Beau? It was one thing to fall for him— as in to like him a lot and be crazy infatuated with him. Infatuation was about lust and hot sex. Tearing clothes off and sweat and naked flesh slapping together.

But love? That was long-term stuff. Commitment and sharing life stories. No secrets. Exposing everything about herself to another human being and knowing everything about that person in return. Was she ready for that? Not so much. And besides. No way would Beau go for it. Right?

Relief calmed the panic attack clawing at the back of her throat. Nope. He would never let her inside his emotional fortress of solitude. She was just caught up in the spectacular sex. Yeah. That was it. No love here. No, sirree. No feelings at all. She was a lone wolf.

Except she'd liked working in concert with him last night in the ambush. A lot. It felt great to move as one with Beau, to know what he was thinking without having to speak. She didn't need him to tell her that they'd clicked perfectly as a team. She'd *felt* it.

And then in bed…

Was that what made last night and this morning so special? Teamwork? Connection? Sympatico? One thing she knew for sure. Whatever it was, it was freaking amazing.

"Earth to Tessa. Come in."

She looked up at Beau, startled.

"Do I want to know what you were thinking about?" he asked.

"Nope."

She really wished they could talk more openly with

each other. But they were caught in this weird limbo of teacher/student versus man/woman. And it wasn't like either one of them was the type to talk out their feelings at the drop of a hat. It was part of what made her comfortable with Beau and likely made him comfortable with her. Still, it wasn't a recipe for great communication or solving relationship problems.

His gaze flickered, looking troubled for a moment. Then a mental door closed in his eyes and he was abruptly all business.

Chapter 14

Beau sighed as he locked the back door behind him. The old house was buttoned up, the power turned off, until he came back next time. Assuming there was a next time. What would it be like to leave here and know that, barring a freak boat accident on the way to town, he would make it back here safe and sound every time? What an odd concept. A disturbingly alluring concept, all of a sudden.

He followed Tessa down to the dock. She practically ran to the boat and climbed aboard like a puppy eager for a ride in a car. Cripes. Was he ever that enthusiastic about anything?

He dumped his gear in the boat beside hers and cast off the lines. "Listen, Tessa. You have to take your next training seriously. Just because you made it past me doesn't mean you're there yet."

She looked at him quizzically. "Now you *want* me to make it onto the Medusas? What gives?"

He sighed. "I want you to be happy. If doing this thing makes you happy, then I want it for you."

"Easy for you to say now that you can't stop it," she retorted.

His first impulse was to flare up in anger. But she wasn't wrong. He schooled his voice to calm. "You're right. If I've been a pain in the ass out here, it was only because I want the best for the Medusas. It's nothing personal."

"I should hope at least some of what we've done out here was personal," she responded.

He couldn't help but smile a little. "That part most definitely was. One thing I can say unequivocally—I've never met another woman like you. Not even close."

She smiled at that, and he was shocked to realize his throat was tight. Rather than try to talk more and end up embarrassing himself, he started the engine and turned his attention to navigating out of the bayou.

He was sad to go. His time out here with her had been magical—if a person thought playing commando was fun. Which he did. And which, amazingly, Tessa did, too.

Yup. She was one of a kind.

And she'd chosen him. It was enough to humble a guy. Make him feel abjectly grateful for their time together.

Aww, hell. Who was he trying to kid? He was going to miss her like crazy, and he was scared to death that he would never find another woman even remotely like her.

They rode in silence to the marina in town, where he docked the airboat. They transferred their gear to his Jeep and drove in silence to the airfield.

* * *

It seemed like a lifetime ago that she'd arrived here, exhausted, furious and with a chip on her shoulder the size of Louisiana. And now she was leaving at least part of the way to becoming a highly classified female Special Forces operator. She took inventory. Did she feel different?

She was fitter now. Stronger. More observant of her surroundings, more self-possessed, more confident in her ability to handle any crisis that came her way. And, she allowed reluctantly, she was more relaxed about men. More at ease in her skin. More comfortable with the idea of being a reasonably attractive woman and able to enjoy the right man.

Too bad the right man had been sulking ever since they left the house and had retreated very, very deep into his emotional man cave.

The plane Torsten had sent was already there, waiting. Beau cut the Jeep engine, and the night sounds pressed forward, a familiar cacophony that would forever be the sound of long nights of loving Beau Lambert.

He picked up Tessa's bag and carried it to the business jet, passing it to a pilot inside, then turned to face Tessa. Nodded once, tersely.

Her stomach jumped with butterflies as she waited to board the Learjet. The good kind. She and Beau were moving on to the next step of the process. She paused for a moment to stare into the trees, listen to the night sounds and smell the swamp one last time before she left.

From behind her, Beau said quietly, "This is where I leave you."

She whipped around to stare at him. "What the hell are you talking about?"

"Congratulations. You did it. You made it through your own private version of Qual training. You're ready to go work with a full-blown team and get field experience."

Vividly aware of the pilot standing in the doorway of the jet behind them, she spoke under her breath, urgently. "What's going on?"

"You're going to train with your temporary team. Until a full team of women is assembled, you'll have to work with men. That could take a year or more." He shrugged. "The price you pay for being the first woman chosen for the new team."

She opened her mouth to protest, to demand that he come with her, or that she go with him, but he cut her off quickly as if he was afraid of what she might say.

Was he afraid of the pilot or afraid of words that could not be unsaid? Words like, I love you—

"I have orders of my own from Torsten. There's a job elsewhere he needs me to do." Beau's jaw worked for a minute, and then he continued, "You wanted to be a Medusa. This is part of being one. Leaving with no warning. No time for a personal life. Living at the beck and call of Uncle Sam. Suck it up, buttercup."

"Can I at least have a hug?"

"I don't know. Would you hug Gunnar Torsten?"

She squeezed her eyes shut briefly. Pain sluiced through her. He was right. She knew it. But God, this hurt.

"I'll see ya 'round, Wilkes."

That was it? I'll see you later? Not even a simple "Good luck"? Nothing?

Numb with disbelief, she stumbled up the steps and

paused in the doorway. She turned around to say…she didn't know what…but to say something.

But Beau had already turned around and was striding away into the night.

He didn't look back.

Chapter 15

Six months later...

"Welcome to Morocco, Tessa."

She turned to look up at Gunnar Torsten, barely recognizable sporting a thick beard, which had been dyed brown to match his dyed hair. Gone was the high and tight military haircut, replaced by shaggy hair that looked like it hadn't been trimmed in a while.

"Nice hair, sir," she commented.

He grinned briefly. "The rest of the team is this way. They're eager to get the full in-brief. I waited for you two so I don't have to repeat myself."

Neville Thorpe had picked her up at Marrakesh Menara Airport, a stunning terminal made of white concrete diamonds filled with glass and light. She followed him through the tall wooden gates of a white stucco house now, into an open-air courtyard and up two flights of stairs to a thick-walled room furnished with rugs and piles of pillows on low platforms.

Tessa nodded a greeting to the other men lounging around the room, who smiled back at her. *That's right. A woman has finally cracked the all-boy's glass ceiling.* A moment's pride passed through Tessa, but then she set it aside. She had a job to do. They all did, apparently.

Cole Kettering, the team's computer expert and resident hacker, strolled over to give her a hug. "Lookin' good, Wilkes."

"Quit trying, Webby. I'm *way* out of your league." Cole's field handle was Webster, but she tended to shorten it to Webby. Truth be told, he was more like a brother to her than any of the other guys on the team.

Torsten called them over, and they gathered around a rough-planked table that looked older than this ancient house. Gunnar spoke from the head of it. "I brought you into this op, Wilkes, at the suggestion of a CIA profiler who has studied our target for years. She believes you will throw him off balance and that he won't suspect a woman of being a military plant."

Tessa turned her attention to the files Torsten passed out to everyone at the table. Hers was substantially thicker than everyone else's.

"Open them," Torsten ordered.

She lifted the cover to reveal a picture of a Middle Eastern–looking man with a shaved head and silver-rimmed spectacles.

"Nasser Malouf," Torsten said. "Former employee of international arms dealer Hassan Al Dhib."

Beside her Webster sucked in a quick breath and asked sharply, "Is Al Dhib our target?"

"Affirmative," Torsten answered. "Turn to the next picture."

She did as he said and stared at another Middle Eastern–looking man, this one with a thick black beard and heavy brows.

"Tarek Sadiq. He's Malouf's contact inside Al Dhib's inner circle. He's a powerful man in his own right, and possibly more violent than his boss. He's going to be willing to get his hands dirty and will kill with the slightest provocation. If he distrusts you *at all*, you're dead. Understood, Tessa?"

She nodded. Her cheeks felt tight and butterflies flitted in her stomach.

Torsten continued, "Marco and Ray have already been introduced to Sadiq by Malouf."

Marco Giordano was a quiet Italian guy who passed for Middle Eastern with his thick, black beard and fluent Arabic. Ray Torres was the team's ordinance specialist and built like a brick mountain. They'd been the point men on this op, posing as terrorists in the market to buy black market weapons, making contact with Nasser Malouf. They'd been cultivating Malouf for months, cautiously angling closer to Al Dhib, the ultimate target. But they'd hit a wall.

Torsten was speaking again. "As you all know, Marco and Ray tried to get a meeting with Al Dhib, but it was a no-go. Al Dhib wants an End User Certificate for any weapons Marco and Ray plan to buy before he'll meet with anyone."

End User Certificates were documents generated by governments promising that any weapons purchased would be used for legitimate purposes by that government and would not be sold to anyone else. And they were priceless in the world of illegal arms sales. They passed liability to the government that issued the certificate and away from the black-market dealer who sold the weapons.

Torsten added, "Al Dhib has also demanded to meet with Marco and Ray's boss. If you'll turn to the third picture, that's Hassan Al Dhib."

Tessa stared down at a well-groomed man of perhaps fifty-five years of age. His hair was iron gray, and his Western-style suit was impeccably tailored. But it was his eyes that captured her attention. They were flat, cold, calculating and as lethal as any she'd ever seen. This was a cold-blooded killer.

Tessa frowned. "Where do I fit into all of this?"

Torsten answered, "You're going to be Marco and Ray's boss, a high-ranking member of the VRM—the Venezuelan Resistance Movement. You're the one who will meet with Al Dhib."

All of a sudden, the profiler's suggestion that a woman would throw off their target had a context and made total, terrible sense. A woman highly placed in a violent protest movement would surprise Al Dhib.

The bad news was that he was bound to be suspicious as hell of her, too. Tessa asked, "How am I supposed to convince this Al Dhib guy that I'm the real deal?"

"The additional documents in your file are an exhaustive intel report. They include everything the CIA knows about the VRM. You'll need to memorize all of it before your meeting with Al Dhib."

"And when am I supposed to meet him?" she asked.

"No idea. Could be a few days, could be a month. But whenever his people call to set up the meet, you'll have to be ready to go."

"What about the End User Certificate?" she asked. "Do we have that?"

"It should arrive tomorrow sometime."

She leaned forward. "What's my angle going to be? Am I a political fanatic, a seductive sexpot or something else altogether?"

Torsten referred to his notes, but Tessa suspected he had every word in his file memorized already. Gunnar was a frighteningly brilliant guy. "Al Dhib appears Westernized on his exterior but is a traditionalist at heart. Which means he'll be an extreme chauvinist. He'll try to assert sexual dominance over you and use his status as a powerful man to bully you."

Horror rattled through Tessa. Sexual dominance? Brief, terrifying images of burly, drunk thugs groping her and pushing her around flashed through her mind. She shoved the images aside. It wouldn't be like that. She was an adult now. A freaking Medusa. She could defend herself. No man would ever hurt her again.

Torsten continued, and Tessa tuned back in. "You'll need to be both a fanatic and willing to do anything— including have sex—to get what you want."

Oh, God.

"I don't expect you to actually sleep with him, of course," Torsten added quickly. "I leave it up to you how far you want to go in flirting with Al Dhib. But you may need to convince him you'd go that far."

"Gee. Thanks," she responded drily.

Torsten shrugged. "I actually recommend that you *not* sleep with him. He would perceive it as an abdication of power and would take merciless advantage of you in negotiating the actual deal. Also, sleeping with him would open us to accusations in a court of entrapment."

"Well, then," Tessa choked out past her sawdust-dry throat. "We wouldn't want to entrap poor Hassan."

Chuckles floated around the table.

"You'll be fully wired for sound," Webster volunteered. "We'll try to send in Marco and Ray with you. But my guess is they won't be allowed into the actual meeting between you and Al Dhib."

Torsten leaned forward. "Expect him to quiz you at length on the material in that folder. He'll kill you if you make the slightest misstep."

"Lovely," Tessa murmured. "Anything else?"

Torsten grimaced. "I'll leave the shopping trip to find suitable clothing for the meeting up to you."

"What? You don't know what all the girls are wearing this year to high-end arms deals?" Tessa quipped. "I'm disappointed in you."

Torsten threw her a quelling look while the other men at the table grinned.

She scooped up the folder. "If you don't have anything else for me, I'd better get going on my homework."

Torsten nodded. "When you feel ready, we'll all quiz you on the contents of the folder."

That sounded ominous. She expected it would feel more like an interrogation, and that the guys would do everything in their power to trip her up. Which wasn't a bad thing. Not when one misstep would, indeed, get her killed.

In a distant part of the house, the doorbell rang.

"One more thing," Torsten said casually.

The tension level leaped all around the table. She looked around, and suddenly, none of the guys would meet her gaze. What did they know that she didn't? Frowning, she looked back at Torsten. Here came the zinger the rest of the guys were already in on.

"One more person will be joining our team."

She swore mentally. She didn't even need to ask who it was.

Footsteps sounded on the stairs behind her and she turned around grimly.

"Hey, Tessa," the newcomer said.

An urge to stride over and punch Beau Lambert in the face almost, but not quite, overcame her. Instead, she leaned back in her seat and crossed her arms defensively, drawling, "Well, well, well. Look what the cat dragged in. If it isn't Beau Lambert."

Chapter 16

Beau schooled his face to show nothing. But it was freaking hard. The rest of the team—*his* team, *his* buddies, dammit!—surrounded her, subtly closing ranks to protect her.

From him?

What the hell? He was one of them!

Huh. Apparently, in his six-month absence, the dynamics in the team had shifted. Tectonically. Their body language shouted that she was theirs now, and that he'd better not mess with her, or else he'd have all of them to answer to.

And to think he'd been worried about how other operators would react to her. Apparently, they loved her like she was their own little sister.

Great. No Special Forces guy on earth was sane when another man eyed his baby sis.

He tried to talk with her after the briefing broke up,

but the other guys adroitly stepped between him and her and dragged him away to hear all about his trip to Ecuador and what it took to get the Ecuadoran generals to cough up the End User Certificate.

As if any of them gave a damn about that. They were running interference for Tessa, the assholes.

By the time he managed to extricate himself from them, Tessa was ensconced in the library with Torsten, going over the information she was supposed to memorize.

Supper with the team was more of the same. Ray and Marco made a point of sitting on either side of Tessa, using their bulk to hem her in like they were her designated bodyguards. As for Tessa herself, she was quieter than he remembered from before. Oh, she joked around with the guys and was clearly at ease with them, and the guys all obviously liked her. But she'd matured as an operator in his absence.

She was even more cut physically than she'd been six months ago, her face more deeply tanned and her eyes…well, she definitely had total awareness of her surroundings now. Her eyes were never still and took in everything and everyone around her, constantly assessing, calculating risk, identifying exit points, tactical weaknesses…

She exuded a quiet self-confidence she hadn't had in Louisiana, which was saying something because she'd been pretty damned confident, even then. She looked like a full-blown Medusa now. Pride in her accomplishment filled him.

No doubt about it. She looked fantastic. Even more attractive than ever.

He'd really tried to get over her and to end his feelings for her while he'd run around South America in pursuit of an eco-terrorist the Ecuadoran government desperately wanted to get its hands on. It had been a trade. Deliver the bad guy in return for the End User Certificate Al Dhib had demanded.

Even in the jungles of South America, Beau hadn't stopped dreaming of Tessa. She was the first person he thought about in the morning and the last person he thought about at night. And *nothing* he'd tried had worked to rid him of his addiction to her.

After supper he timed his departure from the dining room for when Tessa slipped out to go to the restroom. He turned the other direction and sprinted around the four-sided courtyard to meet her on the other side. He rounded a corner and all but plowed into her. He grabbed her shoulders to steady her and himself.

"Let go of me," she snapped.

"Sorry about that," he murmured. "How are you doing? You look great. Guys treating you okay?"

"I'm fine. The team is fine. Everyone's fine. What are you doing here?" she demanded.

Ouch. She sounded more than a little annoyed to see him again. At least she wasn't completely disinterested. He would take anger over apathy. At least there was little passion left for him to work with.

"I got the End User Certificate Al Dhib is demanding before the deal with him can go forward."

"So now that you've delivered it you'll be leaving?" she asked hopefully.

His brows twitched into a frown. "Look. I'm sorry I had to go. But we knew that was going to happen. Why are you busting my balls because I had to go back into the field and you had to finish your training?"

Her green eyes narrowed until she looked distinctly

like a cat about to tear a rat limb from limb. She bit out, "I'm not mad that you left, or that I had to go to training."

"Then what?"

She rolled her eyes. "Men. You're all such morons."

"Help me out here. Why are you mad at me?"

"Because you didn't say goodbye. You just turned your back and walked away from me like it was nothing."

"Jeez, Tessa! It wasn't nothing. That was the hardest thing I've ever had to do!"

She shrugged, unimpressed. "Whatever. I'm done with you, anyway."

Except she was breathing hard, and her pupils were dilated way too much for the ambient light conditions, and her hands were clenched in fists. He leaned in, backing her up against a wall. He put a hand up beside her head and leaned in even more. He growled, "Then why don't you look done with me?"

She slipped out from under his arm and moved back from him. "How does done look? Tell me, so I'll know how to properly convey that I'm over you."

He laughed shortly. "Liar."

She glared at him before spinning on her heel and stomping away from him. He watched her rear end twitching in irritation as she stormed away from him, enjoying the sight. God, he'd missed her. He'd even missed her quick temper and sharp tongue.

Beau jumped about a foot in the air when a voice said from behind him, "She's a looker, isn't she?"

The British accent announced that it was Neville Thorpe. Beau's fist itched to slam into the guy's teeth. He was impatient to follow after her and finish the unfinished business between them. Which was to say, he wanted to make up with her and get into her pants in the worst way. He turned to speak to his teammate, in a hurry to get rid of the guy as fast as humanly possible.

"How'd she do with you guys?" Beau managed to ask reasonably civilly.

"Better than any of us anticipated. She's a natural."

Beau sighed. "Yeah, she is."

"Must've been rough being alone with her in the middle of nowhere for months on end," Neville commented.

The guy had no idea. Of course, it was entirely possible that Neville was fishing to see if Beau would give away anything extracurricular that had gone on between him and Tessa in Louisiana. Beau merely shrugged. "She was a fast learner. Good student. Made my job easy."

He turned to leave, to follow after her, when Marco rounded the corner. God dammit! Was the whole team determined to keep the two of them apart?

"Hey, Beau! Welcome back. How'd South America treat you?"

"Same old, same old." He tried to look past Marco to see if he could spot Tessa, but he couldn't peek around the guy without obviously leaning to the side. Tessa was gone. Damn.

"Tell us more about Louisiana," Marco said, crowding Beau back toward the dining room.

"Not much to tell. I ran Tessa all over the place, dragged her through swamps and did everything in my power to get her to quit." He shrugged. "And she didn't."

"How long were you two out there?" Webster asked.

Twelve weeks, three days and a sunrise. "A few months. Three, maybe. I lost count," Beau answered aloud.

"Wow. Rough duty, running around with her like that," Ray chimed in suggestively.

Crap. They all seemed to be fishing for details. At

least that meant Tessa hadn't kissed and told on him. Which was good news, at any rate. She hadn't felt obliged to nuke his career.

Beau looked around at the group. "She was a good recruit. Worked hard. Did her best. Showed talent for the business. Same stuff all of you have seen in her."

Quickly after that declaration, the guys started wandering off to their own pursuits. Thank God, no one was going to come right out and ask him if he'd slept with her. He would have lied, of course, but not only were these guys trained to sniff lies, they also knew him very well. If anyone could spot the tells of him lying, it would be this crew.

He diverted the conversation to getting a rehash of the earlier in-briefing he'd missed. And as soon as that was done, he claimed jetlag and retreated to his bedroom.

He stretched out in his bed, deeply alarmed at what Gunnar Torsten was planning to ask Tessa to do. The entire US Government had been after Hassan Al Dhib for years, and he'd proven too paranoid, too highly connected, too damned slippery, for anyone to catch. The bastard had left a trail of dead bodies in his wake every time he was forced to elude the authorities.

Why Torsten thought this time would be different, Beau had no idea.

All the next day he tried to get another moment alone with Tessa, but the whole damned team decided to help quiz Tessa. They all memorized the Venezuelan Resistance Movement file and peppered her with questions, phrasing them in ways meant to trip her up or take her by surprise.

He had to admit, she was good. By the next evening she knew the file backward and forward and could practically quote the entire thing verbatim. More important, she had instant recall of even the most trivial details. She was ready to face Al Dhib's interrogation—or at least as ready as the team could make her.

It was a waiting game now until the call came in from Al Dhib's henchman to set up the meet.

As night fell over Marrakesh in a wash of dust-laden crimson, he sat on the third-floor balcony, overlooking the courtyard below, its fountain bubbling sleepily.

Tessa strolled through the courtyard, and he was reminded of how beautiful a woman she truly was. Her dark, wavy hair flowed loose around her shoulders tonight, and she wore a pale pink *gandouri*, a loose caftanlike garment made of some filmy, soft material that flowed around her body like water.

Seeing her like this made him wish he'd taken more time to find this woman under the warrior.

He leaned forward over the balcony and took advantage of the tall space's excellent acoustics. "You look beautiful," he said quietly.

She looked up at him sidelong, slanting him a look that was pure seduction. One corner of her mouth turned up, and she looked positively Mona Lisa–like—except totally hot—in that moment. "Thanks," she replied, her voice low and husky.

He all but pitched over the railing as his body roared to life and demanded that he carry this woman off and make slow, passionate love to her all night long. He opened his mouth to invite her up to his room when Gunnar Torsten strode into the courtyard without warning.

Torsten said, "There you are. Tessa. Ray's about to call his contact to let him know we have the End User Certificate. Wanna come listen?"

"Of course."

Torsten looked up at Beau, pinning him with a stare.

Crap. Gunnar knew Beau had been up here watching Tessa. "You coming down to listen, Lambo?"

"On my way."

He jogged down the steps, swearing every step of the way. Torsten had to be aware that there'd been something going on between him and Tessa in Louisiana. The guy didn't miss a thing, after all.

Beau rounded the corner into the living room and everyone was there.

Torsten asked him, "And the generals who signed the EUC know to expect a call from Al Dhib? They'll verify its authenticity?"

Beau nodded. "Their phone numbers are even included in the document."

"All right, then," Torsten declared. "Everything's in place. We're ready."

Marco said briskly, "Let's pull the trigger, then, and catch this bastard."

Low-level panic had been humming through Beau's gut all day, and it exploded now. He should speak up. Voice his objections. Tell them all to come up with another plan, one that didn't involve throwing a rank amateur into a deadly situation she was no way, no how, prepared to handle.

Of course, Tessa would disagree. And furthermore, she would never forgive him if he yanked the rug out from under her when she was so close to becoming operational. Better than most people, he knew just how stubborn she could be. She would die before she admitted she was in over her head. Dammit.

Later. He would pull Torsten aside. Have an honest conversation with him about his reservations. Convince him Tessa wasn't ready to go into the field. And that she certainly wasn't ready to go into the field alone and face off against one of the world's most dangerous men.

"Make the call, Ray," Torsten was saying.

Nonononono. Beau watched in dismay as Torres pulled out a cell phone and called Tarek Sadiq to let him know the End User Certificate had arrived and the meet with Ray's "boss" was a go. Tessa being that boss, of course.

Curses flowed through every corner of Beau's brain, but there was nothing he could say to stop this runaway train. Everyone else seemed to think it was a just peachy idea to throw Tessa to the wolves like this. Couldn't they see? Didn't they know she wasn't trained for this?

Sure she'd had a few months of running around in the field with the rest of the guys. But he knew what initial training with a team entailed, and it was mostly how to divide up the jobs of a mission and avoid shooting each other. The mental toughness required to go undercover and maintain a cover identity against a hardened arms dealer was a totally different ball game.

"Okay," Torres announced. "The meet's on for tomorrow night. Tarek will call me with a location an hour or so before we're supposed to be there."

As Beau continued to scream silent objections in his head, the others pored over a map of the city, guessing all of the places Al Dhib might choose for the meeting and planning contingencies for pulling Tessa out of each if the meeting should go badly.

Ideally, Ray and Marco would be allowed to stay with her during the meeting with Al Dhib. They wouldn't be armed, for surely Al Dhib's security team would disarm them. But they were both highly trained hand-to-hand combat specialists. And they could still be lethal with improvised weapons like a broken glass, a heavy ash-tray or even a ballpoint pen.

In all fairness, Tessa was also a trained martial artist. She wouldn't be completely helpless, either.

Still. Three unarmed soldiers against a small army of Al Dhib's bodyguards, all armed to the teeth? If even one thing went wrong, it would turn into a suicide mission.

He couldn't lose Tessa. He'd just found her again, dammit!

Of course, he didn't want to see Ray or Marco die, either. They'd been teammates of his for years, and he considered them brothers.

But Tessa—that was different. He would die, too, if something happened to her. He'd been responsible for training her and clearing her to go on with her training. If she died, it would be on his head. He would have killed the woman he lov—

Whoa. Hard stop. The woman he *what*?

He couldn't even bring himself to think the *L*-word.

It was bad enough they hadn't been able to keep their hands off each other. And if he had anything to say about it, they would get back to that state of affairs as soon as possible. But that was just healthy lust and mutual attraction. When had it turned into…more?

"You with us, Lambo?" Torsten asked from the head of the table.

He jerked his attention to the satellite image of Al Dhib's residence lying on the table. The white stucco structure, a freaking palace, was surrounded by manicured gardens, huge fences and dozens of roaming bodyguards.

"Ingress and egress points are limited to here and here…" Torsten droned.

None of this planning mattered. Not one bit. If the

meeting with Al Dhib went south, Tessa and the other guys would be dead before they could get out of the room.

Beau pretended to play along with the idea that they could save Tessa if the meeting imploded, but neither his heart nor his head was in the charade. He was relieved when the planning session broke up, and he retreated to his room immediately afterward.

He stretched out on the low platform bed and stared out the window. Light pollution from the city obscured all but the brightest stars, and the night sounds of Marrakesh washed over him. Cars, the occasional siren, a church bell—there must be a Coptic Christian church nearby, calling for the last prayer of the night.

The sounds faded but not his panic over Tessa's meeting nor his sense of utter helplessness to stop this travesty of sending her to her doom.

The moon, a waning crescent, came into view.

It wheeled out of view again. And still he lay there trying to figure out a way to pull Tessa out of the meeting. Hell, every guy on the team knew the Venezuelan dossier as well as she did. Why couldn't one of them take the meeting and pretend to be Ray and Marco's "boss"?

He knew the answer, of course. Tessa was half-Venezuelan herself and had spent time there as a kid. She was by far their best bet to pass for a Venezuelan revolutionary.

Tessa not only was the right nationality, but her gender would also unquestionably startle Al Dhib. Beau could only pray that it would throw him off enough that the arms dealer would terminate the meeting without ever doing a deal. Then maybe Tessa had a chance of escaping alive. Maybe.

He didn't know how long he lay there, tossing and

turning. Hours. It had to be approaching 3:00 a.m. when he heard his door latch squeak faintly and jerked to full combat alert.

The door eased open just far enough to admit a slender figure in gym shorts and a baggy T-shirt.

Tessa.

A dozen emotions roared through him. Lust. Frustration. Satisfaction. Relief.

But mostly relief.

Wordlessly, he held up the thin blanket, and she slipped under it and into his waiting arms. He wrapped her in his embrace wordlessly, too emotional to do anything else at first. She matched the urgency of the embrace, clinging to him like her life depended on it.

She didn't need to speak. Her first mission as a Medusa was tomorrow, and it was going to be dangerous as hell. She would be on her own to spar with one of the world's most dangerous men. Of course she was tense. Nervous. Scared, maybe.

For all he knew, her adrenaline was so jacked up that this was a pure sex visit.

He didn't care. If she wanted to use his body for meaningless sex, he was all over it. He would take her any way he could get her. And if he was lucky, she would receive the unspoken message he was trying desperately to send to her, that he still had feelings for her and wanted to be with her for the long-term.

"Why can't you sleep?" she muttered. "I know why I can't."

"I'm worried about you," he admitted.

"At some point a person who's been learning to swim has to get thrown into the deep end of the pool. You guys can train me forever but eventually, I have to go out on missions and learn the rest of being a Medusa in the field."

"This shouldn't be your first op," he growled.

She shrugged. "It is what it is. And it's not like any mission we do is easy."

We. She was, indeed, one of them now. He bit out, "I still don't like it."

Her palm slid up his chest and came to rest cupping his cheek. "I know. But Gun saw something in me. He thinks I've got what it takes and even you agreed I'm Medusa material."

"If I'd known how I was going to feel about you, I'd have washed you out the first day I met you."

She sat up indignantly. "Seriously? Are you really that selfish? You would have denied me achieving my lifelong dream because you were afraid?"

He huffed. "You know it's not like that. This—whatever it is between us—isn't just sex. Believe me. I've jumped in and out of the sack with enough women for just sex to know the difference."

She subsided slowly, lying back down beside him. "Agreed," she said reluctantly.

"What? You've had meaningless sex with women, too? *Hawt.* Can I watch next time?"

She poked him in the ribs, and he rolled over on an elbow to tickle her back. She muttered "Uncle" quickly, which was just as well. It was hard to engage in a tickle war in silence. And he shared each of his bedroom's side walls with one of the other guys' rooms.

Propped on one elbow, he stared down at her in the faint starlight. Man, he never got tired of looking at her. He pushed her hair off her forehead gently, reveling in the way her cheekbones cut the darkness and the curve of her jaw seduced the night. He leaned in to taste her full lips, to sink into her heated breath, to lose himself in her and to forget what she was going to attempt tomorrow.

"I didn't come here to talk," she murmured.

Fair enough. He hadn't invited her into his bed to talk, either.

She reached up, wrapped her arms around his neck and pulled him down to her as her mouth and thighs opened to welcome him.

His thoughts still spun. Not only did her life rest on her performance, but the future of the Medusas might very well depend on how tomorrow went. That was a crap-ton of pressure to carry around. The kind of pressure that led to miscalculations and mistakes. The kind that got good operators killed.

She nipped his lip with enough force to yank his full attention back to her. He smiled against her mouth. She was right. If he was in bed with the hottest woman on the planet, the least he could do was pay attention to her.

He pushed her sleep shirt over her head and skimmed his hands down her hips, taking her shorts with them. He discarded them somewhere across the room. She returned the favor quickly, stripping his shorts and T-shirt off, too. And then they were body to body, flesh to flesh.

She was sleek and warm against him, and his entire being strained toward her. He wanted to engulf her, to pull her into his heart where she would always be safe. To protect her forever.

Which she was having none of.

Using a slick wrestling move, she dumped him onto his back and straddled his hips, taking control of their kiss. Amused, he let her. Frankly, her assertiveness was a huge turn-on.

He reached up to cup her breasts, and as she leaned forward, took them into his mouth one at a time, lick-

ing and sucking her nipples into hard, excited peaks.
Tessa was breathing in little gasps now, and she arched
her back, offering her chest more fully to his mouth.

He suckled at her breasts gently, then hard, then
gently again, laving the nubs with swirling strokes of his
tongue until she moaned under her breath. He ignored
her tugs at his hair. She wanted to kiss him again, but
he wasn't done with her body yet. He lifted her by the
hips, nibbling his way down to her waist, relishing how
it tucked in sweetly to muscular abs that were, at the
moment, soft and welcoming.

Laying his hand on her belly, he relished the magic
of her body. Life maker, life giver. Mother, lover, warrior. Somehow, she managed to encompass all of them,
and he stood in awe of her for it.

Her fingers wound into his hair again, but this time,
she wasn't taking no for an answer. She slid up and
pushed him downward at the same time. *My, my, my.*
She'd gotten bold in her old age.

He slid between her thighs and lifted her hips to meet
his mouth. God, she tasted good. Salty and sweet. And
her folds were already plump and swollen, the bud of her
desire a hard pearl hiding between them. He swirled his
tongue around it and she gasped.

Hah. Thought she'd exhausted his bag of tricks, did
she? He still had a few tucked up his sleeve. He sucked
at her hard enough to make her hips rock forward involuntarily.

Her thighs trembled and she breathed in short, sharp
little gasps that drove him out of his mind. She came
apart on him, shattering violently, both hands slapped
over her own mouth to keep from crying out.

He eased his ministrations, laving her flesh softly for
a minute until her breathing settled slightly. And then

he did it all over again. After her next hard orgasm, she toppled over onto her side, panting.

"You're not worn out, are you?" he teased. "I'm just getting warmed up, babe."

"I sincerely hope so," she responded breathlessly.

He surged up over her, his thigh between hers, her body pinned deliciously beneath his. "What do you want?" he asked her low.

"You know darned good and well what I want."

"Tell me."

"I want you. All of you. Until I can't remember my own name."

He all but came apart then and there. But he gritted his teeth and hung on to sanity. Barely. If she was going to die tomorrow, he was by golly going to give her the night of her life.

Huh. The married guys talked about farewell sex being the best sex they ever had with the possible exception of homecoming sex. He got it now.

He trailed his fingers down her belly and between her legs, stroking her slick folds, teasing her ultra-sensitized core.

"More?" he murmured.

A short laugh. "Jerk!"

He laughed quietly and started all over again, bringing her right to the edge of an orgasm and then retreating. She caught on fast, though, and grabbed his shoulders with all of her considerable strength, wrapping her muscular legs around his hips.

"If you even think about trying that again, I'm going to have to hurt you, mister. I need you inside me. Right now."

Laughing under his breath, he leaned down to kiss her. "You're amazing. As the lady wishes…"

He reached over her to the nightstand and with one hand found a condom. He ripped the packet open with his teeth and rolled on protection. Neither of them were likely to have any diseases, for they were medically tested all the time. But neither of them needed a surprise pregnancy, either. Assuming Tessa was even fertile at the level of intensity she exercised at.

He rose up on his knees and positioned himself at her eager entrance. "Ready?" he murmured low.

"I was born ready, soldier."

She reached up over her head and grabbed two of the elaborately carved spindles that formed the headboard. Her eyes glowed like embers, sensual and wild, daring him to take her.

He plunged forward. Hard. He seated himself to the hilt in her tight heat and paused to absorb the heady glory of making this woman his. Her internal muscles pulled at him hungrily, silently begging for more. He fell forward onto his hands, one on either side of her head.

She stared up at him and he stared down at her. He would like to say he knew what she was thinking, but she'd changed in the past six months and held her cards a lot closer to the chest than she had in Louisiana. He silently tried to communicate how much he'd missed her and how badly he'd wanted her. It was anybody's guess if she got that message or not.

He withdrew partway. Paused for an endless, agonizing moment, and then plunged home again. She groaned under her breath, and he was shocked to realize he'd done the same. Man, the pleasure this woman dragged out of him. It was unlike any other sex he'd ever had.

"Again," she commanded.

One corner of his mouth turned up. "So pushy."

"You're gonna see pushy if you don't get busy."

Laughing silently, he plunged into her again, this time setting up a slow, mind-blowingly incredible rhythm he kept up until he couldn't think and practically couldn't see.

He could only feel her body against his, welcoming him home. Absorbing him into her. Quivering with lust, exploding around him. Showering him with stars and galaxies. Flying him to the edge of forever and back.

And still he drove into her, faster and faster, deeper and deeper, reaching for more, and yet more, of the ecstasy he found in her arms and in her soul.

Wonder filled his mind as a massive tsunami of pleasure rolled toward the shore of his mind, a place where only Tessa waited for him. Only him.

His hips slammed into hers uncontrollably. He was no more capable of holding himself back than he was of holding back the sun from rising or the moon from setting. His body was not his own. He was lost in the love they made between them, transported entirely out of himself and into her. Into the one entity they became when they joined like this.

Higher and higher they rose, faster and faster they rolled toward that far shore. He felt them reaching the pinnacle of the wave. Cresting. Starting the curl and the long, wild ride into oblivion.

Sensing the final explosion coming, he gave himself over to it. With a final, apocalyptic thrust into Tessa, her hips rising violently to meet his, they crashed into ecstasy together, obliterating each other. Their shared orgasm tore them apart, ripped the wings from their backs and flung them earthward into a long, blissful free fall through wave after wave of exquisite pleasure.

He let it all roll through him. Imprinted every magical second of it in his mind. He realized they were floating in a haze together. Light. Weightless. Simultaneously exhausted and energized. Separate and one. Alive and something else altogether that transcended flesh and bones.

"Wow," Tessa breathed against his shoulder.

He registered vaguely that he must be crushing her, but her arms and legs gripped him tightly when he bunched his muscles to move.

Wow, indeed.

Mind. Blown.

They lay as one for long minutes, joined in body and soul. Words weren't necessary as they reveled in the wonder of what they'd just shared.

Eventually, he rolled onto his back and tucked her against his side where she cuddled close, one leg thrown lazily over his hips, and her arm resting across his chest.

Thought gradually, sluggishly, began to return, and with it, worry.

No. He wouldn't think about tomorrow. Not yet. They had tonight, and he was damned well going to enjoy every second of it.

Tessa seemed of similar mind, for she made no move to get up or to leave his arms, his bed, his room. She seemed content to just be here with him. He couldn't remember the last time he'd been this relaxed, and she felt every bit as boneless draped across him.

Which was why they both jumped violently when his door opened without warning. Gunnar Torsten loomed in the doorway and growled, "What in the bloody hell do you two think you're doing?"

Chapter 17

Tessa lurched, starting to sit up before she remembered she was naked, and snatched the blanket up around her chin. *Ohgod, ohgod, ohgod, ohgod. Not good.*

Correction: terrible.

End of the world disaster.

Was it all over? Had she blown everything? Her life, her career…the mission? A litany of cursing repeated in her head—

"My office. Five minutes. Both of you. With clothes." Torsten backed out of the doorway and closed the door silently.

Tessa rolled out of bed and snatched on her T-shirt and shorts, grateful Beau didn't say anything as he yanked on cargo pants and a T-shirt. Her hand went to her hair, which was a wild as it ever got. Crap. She darted out of Beau's room on bare feet and down the hall to her own room for a hairbrush.

She stared at herself in the mirror in dismay. Her lips were pink and swollen, her cheeks flushed and her hair…it shouted that she'd been having hot sex mere minutes ago.

Swearing, she dragged a brush through her mane and corralled it into a ponytail. The whole mess poofed like a poodle tail. Of course. Because it was important to look like a clown going into the butt-chewing that spelled the end of all her hopes and dreams.

She shoved her feet into a pair of sandals and trudged downstairs to the first floor where Torsten had set up shop in the house's library. As she passed the burbling fountain, she spied a man-shaped shadow lurking on the far side of the courtyard.

Neville materialized out of the darkness. He must be pulling watch right now. "Pre-mission jitters?" he asked quietly.

If only. "Gun wants to see me."

"Don't let him intimidate you. He's got the big picture. He may talk a tough game, but he'd die for every one of us. Including you."

She nodded miserably. Too bad that devotion probably didn't extend to court martial offenses.

"As for nerves, we all get them before missions. Ray and Marco have both been roaming around tonight, too."

Great. Maybe they'd heard her and Beau going at it. She thought back, tried to remember if they'd made any noise. But the sex had been so all-consuming, she honestly couldn't remember if either of them had cried out.

Her face heated up, and she turned away from Neville with a nod of thanks. Might as well face the music. Delaying the inevitable wasn't going to make it any easier. Her heart felt like molten lead trying to burn its way through her diaphragm and drop to the ground.

She knocked quietly on the closed door to Torsten's office.

"Enter."

She stepped inside. He was seated behind his desk, writing on a pad of paper. Beau already sat in one of two wooden chairs in front of the desk. Torsten pointed with his pen at the second chair and went back to writing.

She sank onto the edge of the wooden chair and perched gingerly. Risking a glance at Beau, he was already looking at her. Apology shone in his eyes.

Torsten laid down his pen and leaned back in his seat, staring at both of them. His pale blue eyes were colorless in the pool of light thrown by the single lamp on his desk. His stare casually shredded her. She might as well have swallowed shards of glass. Tessa'd had plenty of interrogation training and instruction on how to resist torture, but nothing had prepared her for the waves of guilt inspired by Gunnar Torsten's steady, emotionless stare.

"It's my fault, Gun," Beau said abruptly, breaking the taut silence. "Throw me under the bus, but don't wreck Tessa's career."

Torsten's right eyebrow lifted and that icy gaze shifted to Beau. She sagged in relief. But she couldn't let Beau take all the heat. It had taken two to tango, after all.

She spoke up. "It's not his fault. We both share the blame." She noticed out of the corner of her eye that Beau was glaring at her. Tough. She didn't need him to protect her from the consequences of her actions. She was an adult, thank you very much. She continued grimly, "I was a fully willing participant. We both knew we were breaking the rules."

Torsten leaned forward, planting his elbows on the desk, and bit out, "You do realize I could court martial both of you for this."

Beau nodded. Tessa followed suit.

"Lambo, you've had a distinguished career without a blemish on it. Until this. I sent you out into the bayou alone with Lieutenant Wilkes because I trusted you *not* to do precisely this."

Tessa winced and Beau flinched. Betraying this man's trust—disappointing him—was almost worse than if he'd raged at both of them.

Torsten pinned her with an icy stare. "And you do realize that you've not only set a terrible precedent for yourself, but for all the women to follow you into the Medusas."

"Yes, sir." Not that she thought for a second that a display of contrition was going to have any impact on Torsten.

He flung himself back in his chair, his accusing stare shifting back and forth between her and Beau. It took every ounce of willpower she had not to squirm under the intensity of his scrutiny. Making excuses would only make things worse. They'd done the crime, now they had no choice but to face the penalties.

"Tomorrow's meeting requires your *full* attention, Wilkes. How am I supposed to believe you'll give the mission 100 percent if you're indulging in personal distractions?"

She took a deep breath and spoke as honestly as she could. "I couldn't sleep, and I went to Beau's room in search of a distraction that would help me get some sleep. In my opinion, breaking the rules was worth the risk if it meant I would go into tomorrow decently rested and alert."

Torsten's laser stare shifted to Beau. "What's your excuse, Lambo?"

Beau shrugged. "No excuse, sir. I love her."

He *what*? She barely managed to keep her jaw from sagging open.

Torsten made a sound of disgust. "How the hell can you know what you feel for her? You two got together under the most stressful of circumstances. Since the beginning of recorded history, men and women thrown together in high-stress situations have been sleeping together to relieve the tension. You have no way of knowing what you really feel because you let your need for an outlet get the best of you."

Torsten continued grimly, "It's all well and good for you to make grand declarations, but you two have never been together in normal circumstances. I don't accept your statement that you love her."

She opened her mouth, although she had no idea what to say. Not that it mattered. Torsten cut her off with a hand slashing through the air.

"I don't want to hear anything you have to say, Wilkes," he snapped. He exhaled heavily and continued more calmly, "I put the two of you together and alone under exceptional stress to see if something exactly like this would happen."

Oh, my God. It had been a *test*. And she and Beau had failed. Spectacularly. The humiliation in her gut degraded into abject disgust at herself. She should have known Torsten was up to something like that. She should have seen it coming. God. She'd run face-first into his spiderweb.

A horrifying thought struck her. Had Beau seen the trap coming? Had he been a willing participant in entrapping her? She glanced over at him, and chagrin was painted all over his face. Thank goodness. At least he hadn't, with cold calculation, seduced her with the intent to destroy her career.

Right?

She mumbled, "You knew if we got caught it would tank my future…you never did want me to go operational…"

Beau surged to his feet to stare down at her. "After what we just shared, you can say that? What the hell is wrong with you?"

She closed her eyes, her humiliation complete. The last thing she wanted or needed was to air her dirty laundry with Beau in front of Torsten. "For the record, I believe you. But I had to know."

"And *this* is why workplace romances in the military are forbidden," Torsten commented drily.

Beau sank into his chair, but simmering fury still rolled off him.

There was nothing she could do about his anger. She *had* to ask the question, to see how he reacted to it. His fury had flared real and immediate. He hadn't slept with her as a ploy to torpedo her career. Nope, she'd torpedoed her career all by herself. She squeezed her eyes shut. The mortification of it all. And the disappointment in herself—

"Wilkes," Torsten said sharply. "You've got me over a barrel."

Her eyes popped open. "How's that, sir?"

"I need you to complete the mission. But I need your head in the game."

She was shocked that he would consider moving ahead with her operating as a Medusa, even if it was only going to be this one mission.

He reached up to pinch the bridge of his nose in what looked like total exasperation. "Here's what I'm going to do. I'm writing Article Fifteens on both of you."

She gulped. Those were official reprimands, and she

and Beau could kiss any future promotions goodbye with one of those in their personnel files.

"I'm going to hold them in my drawer. One more screwup—or screw—out of either one of you, and I'm going to file the Article Fifteens officially."

She stared at him in disbelief. He was proposing *not* to destroy everything she'd worked for all these years? For the first time since Beau's bedroom door had opened, a glimmer of hope flickered in her chest.

"Just so we're clear," Torsten continued grimly, "there will be *no* personal relationship between the two of you as long as both of you are working on my team. None. Is that understood?"

"Yes, sir," she mumbled in unison with Beau.

He pointed at Beau. "Get out of here. And keep your damned pants zipped."

Beau stood, sighed, paused momentarily as if he wanted to say something to her, but then left without a word.

Oh, joy. She got to have a private chewing out from Torsten.

He pinched the bridge of his nose again, and she waited him out, bracing herself for the worst.

"Tessa. From the first day I saw you knock out a full workout, followed by a half marathon carrying forty pounds of gear, from which you emerged defiant and stubborn as hell, I knew you were going to make a fine operator."

Oh, dear. He was going the guilt route. He'd figured out that guilt was her kryptonite. She was a *pro* at it, and a big, fat wave of it roiled through her now.

"Part of being a good Medusa is having a certain… disregard…for rules," he observed.

She blinked, startled. He wasn't hinting at letting her off the hook, was he?

"Rebuilding the Medusas was inevitably going to result in situations like this. I just didn't expect it to happen so soon. I thought you might spend a few years on the teams before someone caught your eye."

She winced. This was worse than the birds-and-bees talk from her mother.

Torsten continued, "I get it. Lambo's a great guy. And I suppose I see why the ladies think he's attractive."

Attractive? Beau would give a Hollywood A-list actor a run for his money. Not that she was about to say that to Gunnar Torsten, of course.

"I've given a lot of thought to how I'm going to handle it when Medusas become romantically involved with their fellow operators."

And…the humiliation was back. The idea of her sex life being put under a microscope by those two was slightly beyond totally horrifying.

"I'm told there's no stopping the heart. It wants what it wants. Relationships are going to happen with the Medusas. Which leaves me in the awkward position of having to create rules for how to handle them."

What was he trying to say?

"I can't let you and Lambo be a couple while on the same team. As soon as I've got a full-blown Medusa team for you to run with, we won't have a problem. But until then, the emotional tangle is too messy. Too likely to impact an op and get someone killed. I can't let the two of you serve on the same team."

"I would expect no less, sir. Beau and I have already come to the exact same conclusion."

"Indeed? And did the two of you decide which one of you would step off the team?"

She winced. "That was a point of some debate between us. He says my career is just getting started and that I should get my shot. I say he's the more experienced operator who has the most to offer by staying."

He stared hard at her. "I need you to focus on your upcoming meeting at all costs. What is it going to take for you to do that?"

"You've already been more generous than I expected or deserve, sir."

"Agreed," he bit out.

"How about we table the discussion of what to do with Beau's career versus mine until after Al Dhib is in custody? I get that we can't work together. But maybe we can be assigned to separate teams or different theaters of operation. Or something," she added desperately.

Torsten said nothing. He had the decency to allow her the illusion that it would all work out for her and Beau somehow. That there was a way for them to have each other and to keep both of their careers intact.

He spoke quietly. "Once this mission is over and you go down for a training evolution, the pressure will be off you and Lambo. You may find that the relationship reaches its logical conclusion, anyway, and this whole discussion becomes moot."

She frowned. "What makes you think we're doomed to failure?"

He didn't hesitate. "Because of where you fell for each other. That's not real. You were blowing off steam. You both found an outlet for the pressure you were experiencing."

"So you think it's a summer fling that will fade away when the kids go back to school?" she asked in dismay.

"I know it is," he answered firmly.

Good grief. What if he was right? Had everything

she felt for Beau been a lie? Well, maybe not a lie, but not real?

"If you don't mind my asking, sir, what made you such a cynic about love?"

His gaze narrowed warningly, telegraphing loud and clear that she'd overstepped her bounds. She backed off hard, rising to her feet to go.

"Go get some sleep," Torsten ordered. "Alone. In your own room. You're going to need it."

Fitful was the word that came to mind when Neville asked Tessa over breakfast how she'd slept. Awful. Abjectly relieved to still have a job. Confused by Gunnar Torsten's take on her relationship with Beau. Terrified he might be right—that what she thought was love might be nothing more than stress-induced lust.

In a word, she was a mess.

And she was about to head into a meeting posing as a Venezuelan arms buyer, where even the slightest mistake spelled death.

The final meeting preparations got rolling around her, a flurry of action that included comm checks, last-minute oiling and cleaning of weapons and detailed reviews of the layout of Al Dhib's estate and several restaurants he was known to frequent.

The idea was for her, Marco and Ray to attempt to stay together for the meeting and not let her get separated from the herd, as it were. But Torsten was skeptical it would go down that way. He guessed Al Dhib wouldn't want to feel outnumbered and would want to feel in control of the meeting.

Marco and Ray would try to stick close by, however, so if things went to hell in a handbasket, they could charge in to the rescue. In theory.

All of their planning was theoretical. In truth, none of them knew what she would face when she walked into that meeting, and they all would be winging it. Including her. Especially her.

She spent the day practicing speaking in her mother's Venezuelan accented English. She fell into it easily, although it felt strange that one of the more embarrassing aspects of her childhood should turn into a useful asset like this.

She washed her hair and let it air dry into a curly mass typical of a Venezuelan native. Torsten handed her a plastic bag of clothing flown in from Venezuela for her, and she reeled at the scent of tonka beans that rose from the fatigue pants and tank top. Her grandmother'd had a tonka tree in her backyard and used to crush the beans and rub the juice on her wrists. It smelled of newly mown hay, grassy, sweet and herblike.

Even underwear had been provided for her. She pulled on the cheap cotton panties and bra and donned the clothing along with her own combat boots. A high-tech GPS locator had already been sewn into the bra underneath the latch hooks. She threw on a crappy, olive-drab fatigue jacket to complete the leftist insurgent look.

She was unarmed, which felt exceedingly strange after the past few months. But she would undoubtedly be frisked and possibly metal scanned. Two micro-camcorders were hidden on her—one in the pair of metal-rimmed eyeglasses Torsten handed her, and another in the religious medal she wore on a short chain around her neck. An image of Our Lady of Coromoto, the patron saint of Venezuela, graced the cheap trinket.

By midafternoon, preparations were complete.

And then came the waiting.

For the first time today, she slowed down enough

to think about last night's catastrophe with Beau, and about Torsten's shockingly reasonable reaction to catching them *in flagrante delicto*.

Why hadn't Beau made a point of speaking to her privately today? Even if just to ask her how she was doing? He hadn't even asked what Torsten talked about alone with her last night. Wasn't Beau even curious?

When faced with a choice between his career and her, had he already dropped her like a hot potato? Was Torsten right, after all? Had her affair with Beau been nothing more than a cheap fling?

It dawned on her that she'd strayed way, way off focusing on the mission. This was exactly what Torsten had warned her about last night. She had to keep her mind engaged and entirely locked in on the mission to come. She had no room to think about anything else. Not if she wanted to live to see another day.

Torsten had insisted that she not be alone today. She looked around the living room and the lethal men lounging around her. They were all pretending not to watch her, but they were failing miserably. "Anyone got some headphones I can plug into my phone?" she asked. "I forgot to pack mine."

When everyone responded in the negative, she shrugged. "Then I guess you all get to experience the Tessa Wilkes, 'Get From Mile 20 to the End' running-a-marathon playlist."

The guys groaned until she started her music, slamming heavy metal with a driving beat that would pump up a dead man. She dropped and starting doing push-ups, sit-ups and burpees to work off some of the excess adrenaline making her too jumpy to sit still. Not to mention a little sweat would inject the right amount of sour stink into her clothing.

Neville laughed. "Give the lady full marks for taste in music."

"What? You thought I would listen to dentist office music?" she demanded between sets of exercises. "Do I look like your grandma?"

Nev snorted. "You're as un-granny as any female I've ever seen."

Marco's cell phone rang, and she cut off the music. Into the abrupt silence, he listened intently, then repeated an address. He finished with, "Right. See you in an hour."

Torsten unfolded a big satellite map of the entire city of Marrakesh on the dining table at one end of the room, and everyone clustered around it. They would have only a few minutes to assess the meeting location and deploy their team to best protect Tessa.

They'd called it correctly. Al Dhib wanted to meet with her at his palatial estate.

Tessa leaned down to examine the satellite image closely. "These look like cameras mounted on top of the light poles."

Torsten used a magnifying glass to look where she pointed. "I do believe you're right. Good eye. We have to assume Al Dhib will have state-of-the-art security. Motion detectors, heat sensors, high-end biometrics for entry into any building. The works."

Low groans rumbled around the table.

Torsten continued, "Tessa, if it goes to hell, you'll help us out a lot if you can make your way outside the main house. We'll all be carrying trackers for the GPS in your bra. Take whatever evasive measures you need to, and we'll come to you."

She nodded briskly.

Beau made eye contact with her for the first time all

day. He murmured, "We're going to devolve into discussions of ingress and egress routes that don't involve you. Now would be a good time to put on your game face."

She nodded, relieved that he was at least acknowledging her existence. She moved across the room and sank onto a low hassock, legs crossed in front of her, the backs of her hands resting on her knees.

Closing her eyes, she counted down from ten to one. Released the tension from her body muscle by muscle. Her mind started to stray, and she ordered herself to think of nothing but the darkness behind her eyelids. As she relaxed and quieted her mind, she gradually achieved a state of readiness to function at optimal efficiency.

Perhaps a half hour passed before Beau's voice intruded quietly on her meditation. "Time to go, Tessa. Are you ready for this?"

Implicit in his question was a warning that this was her last chance to back out. And it was also a plea not to go. Not to put her life in danger.

"You know I have to do this, Beau. If not for me, for all the women who come after me."

He sighed. "Just...don't die."

She laughed a little. "I will do my level best not to."

His gaze met hers, and his blue eyes were turbulent with worry, pride and affection. But mostly worry.

She stared back, trying to convey silently her gratitude for all the training he'd given her, the confidence he'd instilled in her...and the love he'd shared with her.

Time stopped for a second as if even the universe knew they'd earned this moment. They gazed into each other's souls, and a lifetime's worth of happiness, of words of love unsaid, of could-have-beens passed between them. A home. Laughter. Friends. Family—

children and grandchildren. A legacy of unshakeable love to last for generations.

All of it was right there in his eyes for the taking. And so completely unattainable. Torsten had made her choice clear last night. She could have all the things Beau offered to her or she could be a Medusa. But not both.

Not both.

Was she choosing the right thing? Would she live to regret this moment, this choice? Or would she die instead and never get a chance to spend long years wondering what her life would have become if she'd chosen everything Beau was silently offering her.

The spell broke, and time resumed its normal path through the heavens.

Her chance had passed. The door closed between them.

He nodded miserably at her.

She murmured, "Keep your head in the game, Beau. I may need you before this night is over."

"I'll be there for you. Count on it."

Torsten spoke up from just beyond Beau. "We'll all be there for you."

She nodded as knowing settled in her gut. They would, indeed, be there for her. Six of the world's most highly skilled warriors had her back. And she had theirs.

This was it.

She said briskly, "All right. Let's do it."

Chapter 18

Ray drove, and she and Marco rode in the back of a piece-of-crap Land Rover that had to be older than she was. They pulled up at a guard shack outside the Al Dhib estate, and she donned her eyeglasses and the hidden camera in them.

Marco murmured into his audio feed, "Stone walls. Sixteen feet tall. One foot thick. Electrified wire at the top. Rotating security cameras placed at hundred-foot intervals. Two guards at the gate. AK-47s. Collar microphones. Earpieces. Body armor. Two guards visible patrolling in front of the mansion. Asphalt driveway…"

She tuned out the details he continued to relay to the team. She was Maria Sandoval, Venezuelan Resistance Movement member and lieutenant to Arturo X, leader of the VRM. Somewhere in the jungles of Venezuela, the real Maria Sandoval was blissfully unaware that Tessa had appropriated her identity for this evening's meeting.

Channeling her mother, Tessa muttered under her breath to herself in accented English, locking in the dialect one last time.

Ray parked in front of a humongous white stucco palace, and one of the armed guards opened the vehicle door for her. "Welcome to the Oasis," he said.

She stepped into the grand foyer and stopped to gawk. After all, a revolutionary from the poor streets of Venezuela would be impressed. If she wasn't so nervous, she would be blown away by the opulence around her. Gold gilt, crystal chandeliers and marble polished to a mirror sheen were *everywhere*.

She muttered to Marco in Spanish, "A whorehouse would be embarrassed to look like this."

He snorted. Then he said, "Look sharp. Here come the security boys."

"If you would come with us…" one of them intoned.

She started to follow a team of four heavily armed men in suits that looked made with integral body armor into a room just off the foyer. But a man with a shaved head gripped her elbow. "Not you. You'll come with me."

Crap. Two feet inside the front door and she was already being separated from Marco and Ray. Marco shot her a brief look of chagrin as she shrugged up at the giant bald man and mumbled, "Whatever."

She was taken down a hallway and shown into a small room lined with computer monitors and more armor-suited men seated before them.

No surprise, the bald man asked her to remove her army jacket. He passed the garment to another man, who ran a metal detector over it meticulously. Without being asked she spread her feet and held her arms out at shoulder height.

Baldy frisked her, and as he grabbed her breasts, she

made eye contact with him and grinned suggestively. He seemed a bit taken aback. Score one for her.

A metal detector was run all over her as Torsten had expected. Hence hiding her cameras in the two visible pieces of metal on her—the eyeglasses and necklace.

She was surprised when Baldy asked her to take off her combat boots and provided a set of soft felt slippers for her. "Worried about the floors?" she asked the man.

"Boots can be weapons," he replied shortly.

He was not wrong. On the feet of a martial artist like her, she could smash a man's face to pieces with a well-placed kick. Not that she was a whole lot less lethal barefoot. She could break concrete blocks with her bare feet.

The army jacket was passed back to her and she shrugged it on.

"This way." Baldy led her back to the foyer and up one of two sweeping staircases. A room literally thousands of square feet in size sprawled in front of her. Across the vast space, a wall of floor-to-ceiling windows looked out upon a blazing sunset. It was toward these Baldy led her.

The sun was blinding. Al Dhib must be over by the window. Which meant this was a tactic to put her at a disadvantage in meeting him. He could see her, but she was too dazzled to make out his face. Jerk.

She squinted her eyes nearly shut and kept her gaze pointed down at the floor to protect her vision.

"You may look up now," Baldy instructed her.

She lifted her gaze to the man standing before her. Hassan Al Dhib looked like his picture. Gray-haired. Distinguished. Wearing a perfectly tailored Italian suit that probably cost more than her annual salary.

But what the picture failed to convey was the massive presence of the man. He oozed power and violence.

He might as well have a neon sign over his head flashing "Danger."

Wariness coursed through her, and a surge of adrenaline made her edgy as hell. She waited for him to speak first.

"Welcome to my home, Ms. Sandoval."

She nodded cautiously.

Al Dhib continued, "I have to admit, I was surprised that Arturo X sent a woman to do this deal."

"Why? Because you think I can't make a business negotiation?" she asked in accented English.

"Because I expected his man to inspect the merchandise."

"You think a woman can't shoot a gun?" she retorted. "My people do not have the luxury of letting our women sit at home to cook and clean. We all must fight if we are to overthrow the dictator who has taken our country from us."

Al Dhib made a noncommittal sound. The bastard was probably selling weapons to the Venezuelan government, too. Ever since international sanctions had been slapped on the country's president, intel reports said the country's military had turned to the black market.

"Sit," he ordered, gesturing at a chair beside his. She mentally rolled her eyes as she realized her chair was several inches shorter than his and forced her to look up at him.

She watched Al Dhib pick up a plain manila envelope lying on a table beside him. He opened it and pulled out an official-looking document. She spied the crest of the Ecuadoran military and asked, "I assume you found our End User Certificate to be in order?"

He picked up a cell phone from the table. "We shall see." He dialed a phone number and shifted into effortless Spanish. It became clear immediately that he had called someone in the Ecuadoran government.

But it was also clear he had not called one of the phone numbers included on the certificate itself.

Oh, crap.

Huddled in the back of a step van parked two blocks from Al Dhib's home, Beau and Torsten watched the monitors showing Tessa's camera feeds. Beau looked over at Torsten in alarm.

Torsten muttered, "Please tell me your certificate went through proper channels and can be authenticated."

"I told the generals to file the document for real. Anyone who would normally sign off on an EUC should have seen this one." Beau winced. He hated a "should have" coming anywhere close to Tessa's life.

Beau glanced at Marco's and Ray's camera feeds. They were still stashed somewhere on the ground floor of the mansion too damned far away from Tessa to get to her before Al Dhib whipped out a gun and shot her if his phone call didn't go well.

A hand landed on his shoulder. Torsten. Steadying him and silently reminding him to keep his shit together. He took a deep breath and released it slowly. He had to believe Tessa would pass through this moment of crisis.

Tessa held her breath as the call concluded. She relaxed every muscle in her body and mentally prepared herself to dive at Al Dhib. The only place she wouldn't get killed immediately would be in too close a proximity to him for his security men to risk shooting.

Al Dhib said, "All right, then. It's always a pleasure doing business with you, my friend."

He pocketed his phone and looked up at Tessa. "The paperwork is in order."

She felt like a balloon with the air slowly leaking out of it as the moment of crisis drained away. "Then we're clear to proceed?" she asked her host.

"No need to be in such a hurry. In this country we take our time with business. Get to know our partners before we rush into deals. You will have supper with me. We'll talk. Drink a little wine. *Then* we'll talk business."

"My men will be hungry," she tried, in hopes of getting Marco and Ray brought up to join them.

Al Dhib didn't swing at the ball she'd lobbed at him. "I'll have food sent down to them," he answered shortly.

"Fine." Ahh, well. It had been worth a try.

Al Dhib snapped his fingers and a veritable army of servants rushed out of who knew where and laid out a feast that would feed at least twenty people.

She glared down at the long dining table and then up at her host. She bit out, "Such waste."

Torsten swore behind Beau. "She can't afford to piss him off. He doesn't trust her yet."

Beau had already gotten that memo. The way Al Dhib studied her with hawklike intensity spoke of a man still assessing his foe. But it wasn't like they could tell her to back off. They hadn't been able to risk an earbud being discovered, and she'd gone in without sound.

And that had been a good call. The scan she'd been through earlier would have picked one up for sure.

Al Dhib replied sharply, "How is this waste?"

Tessa looked up at her host. "This is enough food to feed a village in my country. Children are starving in the streets in my home."

"You live in Caracas?"

She snorted. "Hardly. I do not care to be arrested and shot."

"Where's your headquarters again?" Al Dhib asked.

Here it came. The quizzing to see if she was legit.

"Outside Solano."

"Ahh. So you have to pass through Capibara to get to Colombia?"

"No," she replied. "Capibara is north and east of Solano. There are no major cities between our camp and the border."

"Of course." Al Dhib gestured at his servants to fill her plate and his.

She stared down at the mounds of food and her stomach roiled, revolting at the idea of eating. She poked at the food with her gold fork, pretending to partake of the rich fare. Al Dhib ate in silence for several minutes while she took minuscule nibbles she hoped passed for eating.

Her host spoke abruptly. "Tell me, Ms. Sandoval. Does Arturo still have that lovely mistress of his? Consuela?"

She looked up at him, startled. There was nothing in the VRM dossier about Arturo having a mistress, let alone a wife or family. Crap, crap, crap. What the hell was she supposed to do now?

Beau lurched as Al Dhib asked about the VRM leader's mistress. He knew the VRM dossier nearly as well as Tessa did. And there hadn't been a word in it about the enigmatic leftist's personal life.

Al Dhib had effectively found a way to trip her up. She was going to die. Terror roared through him, along with a visceral need to save her from harm.

"She's busted," he said urgently. "We have to get in there and pull her out."

Torsten was equally terse. "She hasn't answered the question yet. It's possible she'll guess correctly."

"It's a fifty-fifty guess," Beau retorted angrily. "Are you willing to bet her life on those odds?"

Torsten stared back at him bleakly. "I don't like this any better than you do. But we can't get to her in the next ten seconds or so. This is going to play out faster than we can get to her. Faster than even Marco and Ray can get to her."

"God damnit!" Beau exploded.

Helplessly, he turned his gaze back to the monitors. The last thing in the world he wanted to see was Tessa's death. But by God, if Al Dhib shot her, Beau was watching it and burning the memory into his brain to hang on to for as long as it took to catch Al Dhib and kill him. Slowly. And painfully.

Agony ripped Beau's gut apart as the moment played out before him. Tessa's two cameras were utterly still, which meant she'd frozen at the unexpected question, too.

He reached out and laid his hand on the cold, hard monitor in front of him, desperate to connect with her. To let her know she was not alone when she died.

A single, exquisitely bright thought filled his mind. *I love you, Tessa.*

And then his heart shattered into a million crystal shards of agony.

Chapter 19

Tessa stared down at her plate, seeing nothing. This was it. Her life unquestionably hung in the balance. She chose correctly and lived, or she chose incorrectly and died.

Images and memories from her life passed through her mind—the moment Beau told her she was going to be a Medusa, finishing her first marathon, graduating high school at the top of her class, arguing with her mother's boyfriends, hiding in a closet as a little girl. And further back—summers in Venezuela with her *abuela*, her grandmother, a tiny woman no more than four foot ten with wise, sad eyes and a fiery spirit.

A memory of her *abuela* ranting against the violence that drove Tessa's mother to emigrate to America popped into her mind. Her granny had accused the president of Venezuela of being corrupt and making a power grab and the leftist opposition of being no better. Arturo Xaviero had been a young political firebrand back then. What had her grandmother called him?

Tessa had repeated the word and her grandmother had gotten angry. Told her never to say it again. *El maricon.*

She'd since learned that was an extremely offensive version of calling a person gay—

Tessa's gaze jerked up to Al Dhib's across the golden table. She said briskly, "I'm sorry. You must be mistaken. Arturo does not have a mistress. Nor does he have a wife, for that matter. He's gay."

Beau exhaled gustily along with all the others in the van as Al Dhib resumed eating.

"Son of a bitch," Torsten muttered from behind Beau. "How did she know that?"

Beau answered, "She spent time in Venzuela as a kid. She must have heard it somewhere."

He watched in profound relief as Al Dhib presented a decidedly more relaxed expression. The quizzing stopped, too.

"After supper we will take care of the mundane financial details of your purchase," Al Dhib declared.

A chorus of quiet cheers went up in the van. She'd done it. Tessa had convinced her host she was the real deal.

Torsten murmured, "I thought she was a goner when she hesitated like that. But damn, did she ever pull that iron out of the fire. Nicely done."

"You say that like you didn't think she could pull it off," Beau commented sourly.

"You never know until someone actually comes under fire. Hell, Beau, you didn't think she had it in her when I assigned you to train her." Torsten added reflectively, "And to think I worried you two would have too much animosity toward each other for her to learn what she needed to know."

Beau shot a wry glance at his boss. They both knew *that* hadn't happened.

"You made a decision yet?" Torsten asked quietly.

Beau winced. He didn't have to ask which decision the boss was referring to. Beau and Tessa both had yet to choose between each other and their careers.

How could she not choose the Medusas over him? She'd spent practically her whole adult life working toward this dream. And now she was going toe to toe against one of the most dangerous men in the world and holding her own like a pro.

He didn't begrudge her the choice. In fact, he encouraged her to follow her dream. Huh. Who knew he was not only capable of love but also of self-sacrificing love? He didn't associate either emotion with himself.

Yet another reason to be grateful to Tessa. She'd unlocked his heart and shown him a whole new side of himself. Hell, even the idea of kids, a dog and a mortgage didn't freak him out anymore. If he didn't know better, he would say she'd helped him grow up.

He couldn't imagine ever finding another woman like her. And he highly doubted any woman would ever fire his blood like she did.

He watched the meal with Al Dhib wind down, and the arms dealer ushered her into an office. It was smaller in scale than the rest of his home, and more utilitarian. Piles of papers littered his desk—many looked like manifests for cargo shipments via sea, and Beau spied gun catalogs beside a pair of laptops.

Al Dhib waved her into a chair in front of his desk. "So, Ms. Sandoval. Let us transfer the funds for your purchase and conclude this business."

"Uhh, I don't think so," Tessa drawled.

Beau lurched.

"What the hell is she doing?" Torsten blurted.

Beau looked over his shoulder grimly. "I have no freaking idea."

Tessa studied Al Dhib intently. He was acting exactly like a man who thought he had the upper hand—smug, condescending and eager to rip off the woman seated before him.

What kind of revolutionary would she be if she blindly handed over millions of dollars to this man without even asking about the equipment, let alone examining it for herself?

If Al Dhib was going to buy her cover, she had to act exactly as if she was who she said she was.

"I beg your pardon?" Al Dhib asked warningly.

She held out her hands deprecatingly. "Millions of dollars may mean nothing to you. But to my little group, this is a great deal of money. We have worked very hard to gather it from the sweat and blood of small farmers who raise and process coca by hand. We have had to scrape together every penny I'm going to hand over to you."

"I understand, of course." Al Dhib looked irritated, but he could just get over it. He didn't get to run roughshod over her. Plus, it would *really* lock down the DEA's case against him if she could get Al Dhib and a crate of weapons on camera together.

It hadn't been part of the plan to demand to see guns, but she was nothing if not an overachiever.

"I want to see the guns," she demanded bluntly.

"What? You know about firearms?" he scoffed.

Her eyes narrowed. "I know from the butt of the weapon that peeks out of your suit coat now and then that you're carrying a titanium-gold Desert Eagle, likely a modified four-forty Cor-Bon. I also know a four-forty Cor-Bon weapon shoots a fifty-caliber round, necked down to four-forty dimensions. It provides the punch of a fifty-cal without the recoil of one." She paused for a heartbeat and then added, "Shall I continue?"

Al Dhib leaned back in his chair, grinning. "Well, well, well. The little girl has teeth, after all. I was beginning to wonder."

She shrugged humbly, wary of getting too forceful with the man. He was still a chauvinist and still a killer. And he was the guy with the fancy gold-plated pistol, while she was completely unarmed.

"Are you familiar with the weapon mounted on the wall behind me?" he challenged.

She glanced over his head and let her eyes widen as if she was impressed. Which, in fact, she was. "That's a Holland and Holland Double Deluxe Rifle. All handmade. Price tag starts at around a quarter-million dollars and goes up from there. Designed for hunting big game with a double shot so the hunter doesn't have to stop to chamber a second round if a dangerous animal is charging him. Although an excellent weapon, an equally fine performing weapon can be had at a tiny fraction of the cost."

"Can you shoot as well as you can recite statistics?" Al Dhib asked, his tone acerbic.

Whoops. She backpedaled quickly. "Oh, no. I just studied guns so I can buy the best we can afford. We're too poor to make a mistake and provide our fighters with inferior weapons." She added, "This is why we came to you. Your reputation and that of the equipment you sell precedes you."

Al Dhib nodded regally and looked mollified. *Thank goodness.* He leaned forward and punched a button on an intercom speaker. "Prepare my helicopter. We're going to visit Persephone."

Alarm slammed into her. They were leaving the estate? But this was where her teammates were deployed. Her safety net was here!

"Uhh, I have no desire to go visit anyone—" she started.

"You wish to see the merchandise, yes?" Al Dhib snapped. "I'm taking you to see it."

She leaned back in her chair, disgusted with herself. Dammit. She'd gotten too cute, and now she was going to be completely without cover.

Everyone in the van was elbows and assholes, scrambling to figure out who the hell Persephone was and where this mystery woman was located. The call for a helicopter had prompted Torsten to order all of his men back to the step van to regroup.

Beau's heart lodged somewhere in the vicinity of his throat. Tessa was being whisked away from their protection as he watched, and there wasn't a damned thing he could do about it.

"I've got it!" Webster announced. "The Persephone is a yacht owned by one of Al Dhib's shell companies."

"Get me schematics of the yacht," Torsten bit out.

Webster typed like crazy for several seconds then leaned back in satisfaction. "Got 'em. Downloading now. The yacht was featured in a naval architecture magazine a while back."

"We're out," Marco murmured under his breath.

"Driving toward the front gate now. They actually kicked us out. Made it easy."

"Where's the Persephone berthed?" Torsten demanded.

Webster typed again. "She's registered at the port of Essaouira."

"Let's roll," Torsten ordered. "It'll take us a while to catch up with her overland. Every minute head start we can get will help."

Beau flinched. But if Webster's information wasn't accurate and they headed for the wrong port, they would lose precious time that could mean the difference between life and death for Tessa.

Torsten snapped, "Ray, Marco, fall in behind the van."

In a matter of minutes the Land Rover pulled in behind them. As the van accelerated away from Al Dhib's estate, Beau thought he heard the thwocking of a helicopter retreating in the distance. God *dammit*! They were losing her.

Hang on, Tessa. We're coming for you.

Tessa watched Marrakesh, and her team, fall away behind her. The vast, black expanse of the Moroccan piedmont stretched away below her. The flight took under an hour, which wasn't reassuring. It could be several hours before her teammates caught up with her.

The problem was, every minute they were out of range of her was another minute where the transmissions from her cameras weren't being picked up and recorded. Even if she got Al Dhib and a honking crate of guns together in the same room, if no one was there to record her transmissions, this whole bonus trip would have been for naught.

The helicopter slowed and swooped down toward the coast. A city came into sight, and beyond it, the black sheet of the Atlantic Ocean. They raced across the water, and the shore disappeared over the horizon. Of course. The bastard parked his yacht in international waters. The helicopter slowed even more, coming to a hover above a sleek white yacht, similar in scale to Al Dhib's oversize home.

"Good grief. How big is that boat?" she asked, her nose practically pressed against the window.

"Four-hundred-eighty feet," Al Dhib answered proudly. "She has her own missile defense system, two helicopter pads and her own integral submarine."

She glanced over at her host. "A submarine? That must make smuggling easy."

"I move small shipments of weapons aboard the Persephone, but I never cross into territorial waters. I'm no fool. I have no wish to be arrested."

The helicopter settled smoothly onto the deck of the yacht. She stepped out, glancing around in dismay. She was all alone out here. Totally on her own.

"Can't this thing go any faster?" Beau groused over Webster's shoulder.

"Are you looking at the same road I am?" Web snapped without taking his eyes off the ribbon of crappy concrete. "These potholes could tear an axle off this bucket, and then would where your girl be?"

"She's not my girl," Beau retorted quickly.

"Yeah, right. I've seen the way you two look at each other."

Beau huffed. "Whatever. Just get us there as fast as you can."

"I'm on it, bro. She's my teammate, too."

Beau moved into the back of the van where the others were quickly planning an approach to the Persephone. Satellite imagery they'd obtained from the NSA showed the yacht to be parked just outside the international boundary of Moroccan waters.

Torsten was on his phone, yelling at someone in Arabic. He was trying to obtain scuba gear for six big men on short notice and in the middle of the night. If he could pull that off, Beau would declare him an outright miracle worker. Gun hung up the phone and joined them in staring at the yacht schematic.

"How would you go about blowing it up?" Torsten asked.

Beau replied, "Are we talking just sinking it, or turning it into matchsticks?"

"Both."

He considered the vessel. "To sink it, we would have to punch major holes in each segment of the ship." The Persephone had been built with three watertight bulkheads that would close in the event of a leak in any one section of the ship.

"And to make a flying debris pile of it?" Torsten asked grimly.

"It would take thirty, maybe forty, kilos of explosives placed at a dozen locations on the hull to guarantee getting the job done. But," Beau warned, "everyone on board would die."

"I'm thinking about blowing it after we get Tessa off it. Could you make that happen?"

Beau considered. As the team's resident ordinance specialist, he had the most training in placing underwater charges. "It would take me upward of an hour under the hull to rig it all, but it's doable."

"Do we have that much C-4 with us?" Torsten asked him.

Beau grinned. "I'm not a former Boy Scout for nothing. I came prepared."

Torsten nodded. "If Webster can roust up a UDV or two, I'll allocate one to you and your toys. First order of business will be to get you out to that ship and get it wired to blow."

A UDV was an underwater dive vehicle—a bullet-shaped gizmo with an engine, propellers and handles or a seat to drag along a diver behind it at two to five times the speed a human could swim.

What was Tessa doing now? She'd pushed Al Dhib pretty close to the edge of pissed off in the guy's office. She had to be careful, or she'd be dead before he could get to her. *Careful, baby. Tread lightly around the lion, or else he'll eat you alive...*

Tessa hefted an AK-47, examining its firing pin and ejecting and inserting an empty magazine several times. It looked like Russian military issue, and this particular weapon had seen some action. The firing pin was worn but serviceable. It had been filed some, undoubtedly to prevent it from hanging up and causing a misfire. The action of the mag was smooth—someone had worked on this weapon, probably in combat conditions—to maximize its performance.

Where had Al Dhib gotten his hands on this stuff? The presence of weapons like this in the hands of a mercenary like Al Dhib, who would sell them to absolutely anybody, made her shudder inside.

She *had* to stop him.

"The weapons are as promised, yes?" Al Dhib challenged.

"Better than promised."

"Does that mean you are ready to complete the purchase *now*?" Al Dhib asked in a faintly aggrieved tone.

"I am. Truly, I apologize for my caution. I never doubted you. But this is the first time we've done business. You understand. My superiors were cautious. Perhaps henceforth, we can do business over the phone, and I won't waste your valuable time with quality control checks."

"Come inside. You can use the ship's Wi-Fi to complete payment."

"Of course."

The CIA had set up a dummy bank account with four million dollars in it—the amount she was supposed to pay to Al Dhib. The payment would ultimately be blocked, of course. *After* she was clear of Al Dhib.

As she stepped into the ship's salon—a big room that stretched the width of the ship and had angled banks of windows stretching over the ship's prow—she noted the black bubble of a surveillance camera overhead. This guy didn't miss a security trick.

Al Dhib sat down at a table in front of a laptop, but he surprised her by signaling a bartender to pour them drinks.

"You don't want your money now?" she asked, in a hurry to get this over with and get out of here before she could slip up or he could get the bright idea to quiz her again.

"Let us celebrate our new business partnership with a drink first."

Crud. He was stalling. *Why?*

What had she missed? Her instincts screamed that

something was *wrong*. But everything had gone like clockwork. Why was he delaying like this?

Nervous as hell, she sipped at the glass a man in an armored suit set down in front of her. "Wow. That's really smooth whiskey. Better than the stuff we get in our country."

"It's scotch, and I should hope so. That's a Macallan single malt."

She shrugged. "I know guns, but drinks not so much. I'll take your word for it."

He snorted. "You're drinking a thousand dollars' worth of scotch."

She looked down at the finger of alcohol in her glass. "Well, then, I shall certainly take my time and enjoy it."

"You should sip it slowly. Savor the aroma and aftertaste."

Oh, he was *so* stalling.

Her intuition shouted at her to get the hell out of here before something went terribly wrong. She felt disaster coming. But she didn't see what form it would take or what direction it would come from.

Al Dhib refilled her glass for nearly an hour. She managed to nurse along her scotch and consume only about one glass of scotch for every three that he drank.

Unfortunately, the more he imbibed, the more aggressive he got. Flashbacks of her mother's drunk boyfriends crept into her mind and she shoved them back. She had to concentrate on *this* drunk.

"You're a good-looking woman," he announced after tossing back yet another shot of the expensive scotch.

She swore mentally. He was about to come on to her. Did she dare fend him off? Would that make him angry enough to shoot her? God knew the idea of letting him rape her held even less appeal.

"Come. Sit with me by the window. Enjoy the view with me."

The view. *Riiight*. He was going to try to get inside her pants. Crap, crap, crap. What was she supposed to do now?

Chapter 20

"I've got audio!" Beau shouted over the roar of the boat motor.

The entire team raced across the choppy ocean in a motorboat Webster had managed to scrounge up for them. Better were the black neoprene scuba suits they all wore, and the bulky UDV sitting like a beached whale in the back of the boat.

They would go by surface until they got within, say, three miles of the Persephone. Just over the horizon from the yacht. Then Beau would motor in underwater with the explosives while Marco and Ray swam in behind him. The others stood by to improvise as needed.

Marco cut the throttles abruptly. "We're here. Time to walk the plank, Lambo."

He flipped off his teammate as he hefted his oxygen tanks and put the regulator in his mouth. He fell backward into the water and surfaced immediately to take the UDV and gear Torsten and Ray passed down to him.

"Sound check," Webster's voice announced in his earbud.

Beau tapped his ear and gave his teammate a thumbs-up. The good news was their earbuds worked under water. The bad news was these basic scuba suits didn't allow for him to talk back to his teammates unless he surfaced and took the regulator out of his mouth.

"Good hunting, Lambo."

Huh. Count on it. He was blowing Al Dhib to kingdom come tonight. And Tessa was damned well making it out of this op alive.

He grabbed the UDV and twisted the throttle wide open. It pulled him along a dozen feet under the surface at a significant clip. He heard the faint rumble of an engine pass by overhead. That would be his teammates easing in closer to the Persephone to pick up Tessa's video feed.

"I have video," Webster announced a minute or so later. "Our girl's playing patty-cake with Al Dhib."

"What the hell?" Torsten asked, voicing Beau's exact thought.

"Looks like ole' Hassan is getting handsy with our girl."

Son of a bitch! Beau twisted the throttle even harder, trying to eke out every inch of speed the UDV could give him. Al Dhib was definitely dying now.

"And she's up off the couch," Webster described. "She's got the pool table between her and Al Dhib." A pause, then multiple chuckles erupted in Beau's ear.

Torsten interjected to explain, no doubt for Beau's benefit, "She just told him she doesn't like men." More laughter. "That seems to have given him pause. She's explaining now how penises are repulsive to her...in detail."

Beau couldn't smile or else he would take in a mouthful of saltwater, but he was mentally grinning from ear to ear. *That's my girl.*

Al Dhib was worse than any of her mother's boyfriends, and some of them had been massive lechers. He was going on and on about how he had a magnificent penis and she would love it. He seemed to think he could convert her to liking men. What an egomaniac. She would be tempted to laugh in his face if that goldplated pistol of his didn't keep flashing from underneath his suit coat.

She did her darnedest to act like she was actually enjoying this little game of cat and mouse. But all the while, a clock ticked in the back of her mind, a chilling reminder that something bad was going on around here behind her back.

She could only hope this delay was also working to her advantage, giving Beau and the guys time to find a way out here. Assuming they could marshal the resources to get themselves out to sea on short notice.

The salon door opened, and Baldy from the mansion stepped inside. "We have a problem, sir."

She swore silently. *Here it came.*

"Perhaps, Ms. Sandoval," Baldy said to her, "you would care to explain why your picture in the Interpol database does not match your face?"

The little voice in the back of her head started chanting in a continuous stream. *Crapcrapcrapcrapcrap...*

"You saw my dossier at Interpol?" she asked in surprise. Oh, hell. The real Maria Sandoval was on file at

Interpol? How come that hadn't come up in anyone's research dossier?

"I saw someone's dossier. It wasn't you."

She was at a loss. How the hell did she talk her way out of this one? Should she claim that her comrades had hacked Interpol and planted a photo of someone else in her place? She opened her mouth to do just that, but Baldy was speaking again.

"And perhaps you could also explain why a photograph looking remarkably like you comes up in a facial recognition search, belonging to an American woman by the name of Tessa Wilkes?"

"You're *American*?" Al Dhib exclaimed, his voice vaguely slurred. "Who do you work for? The FBI? CIA? Who?" he demanded in a terrible voice.

"I have no idea what you're talking about," she tried desperately. "Someone has set me up." She devolved into frantic Spanish, insisting on her innocence and claiming that she'd been framed. She accused the Venezuelan government, the Venezuelan army, rival factions vying for control of the Parliament...anyone she could think of. Anything to keep these men occupied for a second while she came up with an idea—any idea—on how to get out of this alive.

"You will tell me who you work for before you die," Al Dhib roared. "And then I will kill you myself."

He did realize, didn't he, that telling a person he was about to torture that she was going to die anyway gave her no incentive at all to cough up information once the torture began?

"I will use you like the lying whore you are, and then I will slit your throat," Al Dhib ranted.

Real panic slammed into her then. Not rape. It was the one thing she'd lived in terror of for most of her life.

She'd managed to avoid it all this time, but the phobia was so ingrained that her mind completely froze.

She squeezed her eyes tightly shut and wished with all her might that she was somewhere, *anywhere else*, but here.

Al Dhib's man grabbed her elbows and yanked them behind her back while Al Dhib himself grabbed the neck of her tank top and ripped it down to her belly button.

Nononononononono…

"Dammit!" Gunnar exclaimed as he watched the video feed from Tessa's one remaining camera. Her eye-glasses had been knocked off in the scuffle as Al Dhib's man forced her across the salon and slammed her face down onto the pool table. Her religious medal had slid around to the back of her neck and was pointed up at Al Dhib, leaning over her and leering.

"She has panicked and frozen," Neville announced.

Gunnar swore violently. "How in the hell is her face still on the internet?"

Webster answered apologetically, "If someone had told me she needed to be scrubbed from the internet I would have taken care of it myself."

He swore some more. "Our screwup is going to get her *killed*."

Beau's voice startled him. Lambo must have surfaced to talk. "What's happening to her? Talk to me!"

Gunnar answered grimly, "Tessa's in trouble. How much longer until we can blow the ship?"

"A distraction," Beau gasped. "Get the bastard's attention off her. I'm still a hundred yards from the ship and have to set the charges."

"We could masquerade as pirates," Gunnar bit out. "Keep Al Dhib and his crew occupied while you move in and wire the ship. Get going, Beau. We'll keep them away from her until you signal that you're done. Don't make it pretty. Make it fast."

"Buy me ten minutes."

And then Beau was gone.

Neville asked in dismay, "Can he wire the ship that fast? I thought he said it would take an hour."

"It would if he was stealthy and took his time. In the middle of a fire fight with lots of noise and nobody watching the proximity radar, he can zoom in, slap on the charges and zoom out."

"What if someone sees him?" Nev asked.

"Then he's in as much trouble as Tessa."

Gunnar ordered, "Hit the gas."

The boat all but leaped out from underneath him.

Tessa's pants were down around her ankles, her shirt was in shreds and her bra hanging was loose around her neck when her survival instincts finally kicked in. She fought like a wildcat, but was hampered by the trousers tangled around her feet. The good news was Baldy and Al Dhib seemed to think they could subdue her with their fists and didn't reach for their sidearms. The bad news was there were two of them and she was too panicked to think straight. Thank God her Krav Maga instructor had pounded reflexive defenses and strikes into her, for they were all that was saving her right now.

She landed a solid blow to Baldy's jaw that dazed him, and had just nailed Al Dhib in the nose when an urgent voice came over the ship's loudspeakers.

"We have an incoming vessel, high-speed. Appears to be pirates. All hands to the armory."

Baldy swore and staggered out of the room, and Al Dhib reached for his pistol.

He swung it viciously at her and she ducked, but it still grazed the side of her head hard enough to knock her down. She played possum and pretended to be out cold, which wasn't far from the truth.

She saw Al Dhib's expensive Italian loafers run out of the room. Silence fell around her.

She grabbed for her necklace and yanked the medal back around to the front. "I'm alive," she croaked.

If those pirates were in fact Torsten and company, they were close enough to pick up the feed from her necklace. "I'm going to try to get off the ship and swim to you." Clumsily, she pulled her pants back up and fastened them around her waist. As she struggled to sit up, she reached behind herself and awkwardly hooked her bra.

She felt better now that she was partially clothed, at least. Although her jacket was gone and her shirt hung in tatters.

She reached for the edge of the pool table above her. Her fingers wrapped round the felt-covered bumper and she dragged herself upright. But even that small a movement made the whole room spin violently.

She threw up on Al Dhib's pool table, and then sank back down to the floor in slow motion and toppled over onto her side. She would get up and leave in a few minutes. Her eyes drifted closed in spite of her best efforts to keep them open. She needed a rest. Just a little one…

Beau heard lead ripping into the water around him and flinched reflexively as he slapped C-4 charges onto the hull of the Persephone. Two more and he would be done.

"Tessa's down," Torsten announced in his earbud. "She's alone in the salon, and she was able to tell us she's alive, but we're guessing she passed out. She's lying on the floor and not moving."

Beau swore. If his panic could possibly get any worse, it just did. Over his head, separated only by a thin layer of armored steel and fiberglass, Tessa was hurt. Helpless. And he could practically reach out and touch her!

The final charge was placed.

He was supposed to swim away from the Persephone now. To leave Tessa behind to exfil on her own. But she was down. No *way* was he leaving her. Nobody ever got left behind on his watch...especially not the woman he loved.

He swam for the aft portion of the ship and the swim deck that jutted out behind the vessel. As he rose to the surface, he spotted a man standing on the white fiberglass deck, firing some sort of automatic weapon.

Kicking hard, Beau shot up to the surface, broke through and grabbed the guy by the ankle. He gave a mighty yank and flung the guy into the water, using the counter-momentum to propel himself onto the deck. He landed on his belly and rolled onto his back, reaching for his pistol in one fluid movement.

The hostile he'd thrown into the water surfaced about eight feet away, spluttering.

Beau double tapped his pistol, planting two rounds in the guy's face. The hostile slipped under the water, and an oily black slick of blood gathered in his place.

Beau scrambled to his feet, kicked off his fins and raced into the ship on bare feet. Another double tap from his pistol, and a hostile running toward him went down. Beau ran up to the guy, put one round in the back of his neck and scooped up the guy's AK-47. He paused long enough to throw the shoulder strap over his head and grab a spare ammo magazine out of the dead man's belt, and then he was off and running in search of a staircase.

Webster's schematic came to life around him, and Beau frantically counted crossing passages.

The entire ship abruptly went dark, and he yanked up his NODs—night optical devices—from around his throat to cover his eyes. The passage jumped to life. *Mistake, boys.* Men like him were most at ease in darkness. Al Dhib's men had just handed the tactical advantage to him.

He heard footsteps coming and ducked into the room beside him, an empty stateroom. He wasn't here to play Rambo and take down an army single-handedly. He was here for one reason only: to find Tessa and get her the hell off this bucket.

Footsteps pounded past and faded away. He ducked back out into the hall. There. The staircase he was looking for. He raced up it. Thankfully, all hands appeared to be out on deck raining lead down on his teammates, and the ship's interior was deserted.

He slipped across a foyer and into the salon. There. Beyond the pool table, a human shape on the floor.

He sprinted over to Tessa's side and knelt beside her, gathering her into his arms. "Baby. It's me. Open your eyes, sweetheart."

Her eyelids fluttered faintly.

"I know you hear me, Tessa. You have to wake up. We need to get out of here so none of our guys get hurt."

He'd chosen his inducement well. A threat to her teammates had her eyes slitting open sluggishly.

"Beau?" she rasped.

"In the flesh, darlin'. Can you stand?"

"Don't know."

"Let's try." He helped her to her feet, and she looped

her arm around his neck while he hung on to her waist. "God, you feel good," he muttered. "I wasn't sure I'd ever get to hold you again."

"Me, neither." She sighed.

"C'mon. Let's blow this popsicle stand."

"Literally?"

He glanced down at her. "Yeah, actually. As soon as we leave the ship, it's wired to blow."

"Sweet. Can I mash the button?" she murmured.

He smiled a little. "I think you've earned the privilege." He passed her the detonator and she tucked it in her pants pocket.

"They tried to…rape me…fought back…stopped them…then pirates…that's us, right?" she mumbled as they stumbled across the salon together.

"Yes. We're the pirates. I don't care if you were assaulted or not," he declared. "All that matters is you're alive. I don't know what I'd do if I lost you."

"Ditto," she replied, smiling back at him fuzzily.

"Here's the thing, Tessa. I can carry you, or I can cover our retreat with this AK. But I can't do both. Can you walk?"

"I think so."

"If you can finish Torsten's twenty-mile sprint from hell carrying a forty-pound pack, you can damned well walk to the rail of this ship and jump overboard," he said forcefully.

"Point taken," she said a little more strongly.

He led her into the hallway and down two flights of stairs to the nearest deck that had exterior access. It should be two decks above where Al Dhib's men had set up shop and were shooting the crap out of Torsten and the others.

Tessa staggered and paused a few steps behind him,

eyes closed tightly. She looked ready to puke. He bit out, "Barf if you need to. But dig deep. We're almost there."

She nodded faintly, lurching forward once more. Thank God. He really couldn't carry her and cover them both.

He spotted what he'd been looking for. An exterior door. He waved Tessa down the hall behind him and cleared the deck as best he could through the tiny, awkward porthole.

"Got a spare piece?" she asked from behind him, sounding a bit more alert.

He passed her his pistol and its two spare magazines, and then swung right. Tessa would know to swing left behind him, and they would defend each other, back to back.

She fired twice, quickly behind him. "Man down," she mumbled.

"Clear," he reported.

A fiberglass window blocked their access to the water here, and he murmured, "Move aft. Keep your back to mine."

"Roger."

They scuttled aft like a human crab, her facing forward and him facing aft. As they followed the curve of the ship, a man came into sight, pointing an AK-47 down at the water. Bastard was shooting at a diver. At one of his teammates.

Beau hit the trigger and sent a burst of lead into the shooter, who toppled headfirst into the water. A black shape surfaced briefly beside the fallen hostile, and Beau knew a knife had been drawn across the guy's jugular. The black shape disappeared into the water once more.

A new sound intruded into the sporadic gunfire. An

engine starting. And then the distinctive whine of a helicopter rotor revving up.

"He's getting away," Tessa cried out. "We have to blow the ship while he's still on it."

"Yeah, but so are we!" Beau called back.

She turned behind him and he did the same, facing her in the shadows. "It's our job. His weapons will kill hundreds, maybe thousands, of innocent people if we don't stop him now. We'll never get another shot at him like this. I'm willing if you are," she shouted over the helicopter's noise.

He looked her in the eye. They'd only just found each other. They were both too young to die. But maybe it was for the best this way. They would never be allowed to have their careers and have each other. At least this way they would be together when they died.

He'd always known his number would come up someday. He just hadn't expected it to be now, or with this woman. "All right. Let's do it."

He leaned down to shout into her necklace, "Everybody pull back ASAP. We're going to blow the ship. Get your ears out of the water so we don't scramble your brains."

That was all he had time for. He just had to hope their teammates heard the warning and heeded it.

Beau grabbed Tessa's hand. "C'mon! We've got one shot to make it off this ship, and I'm damned well taking it. Even if it is one in a million!"

He took off running aft to where the deck opened up to the night air. He dragged Tessa along beside him. Her steps gained strength and speed beside his, and by the time they reached the end of the deck, she was matching him step for step. It might as well have been that day on the beach when she raced him and he realized he was a little bit in love with her.

"Push the button, Tessa! Now!"

They leaped off the deck, flying out into space, hands and hearts linked in one last moment of glory before the end. Together.

Chapter 21

Tessa smashed the button through her trousers and everything slowed around her to a fraction of its usual speed. She and Beau sailed wide of the ship, out into space, flying as one. Like birds. She felt weightless. Free.

And then, from behind them, a blinding flash of light and searing heat slammed into her, a physical blow that might as well have been a baseball bat swung by the homerun champ into her and Beau.

Oddly, she never lost her grasp on him, nor he on her. Their fingers remained tightly twined together as they flew up and out, propelled by the blast wave impossibly far from the ship.

And then they were falling. Falling forever.

It took long enough for her to register that from this height, hitting the water was going to hurt like a bitch, assuming it didn't kill them both.

"Tuck your chin!" Beau yelled at her.

Right. Her training kicked in. She turned her head to the side and plastered her chin on her shoulder to protect her neck from breaking upon impact with the water.

Beau's arms went around her and yanked her close. She grabbed on to his waist with all her strength. If she was going to die, at least she was going to do it in the arms of the man she loved.

And then they hit.

The impact with the water was every bit as violent as the impact from the explosion.

They landed on Beau's back and skipped like a rock, bouncing on the water's surface, sailing several more yards, and hitting again. They bounced two more times before they finally broke through, plunging, down, down into the icy cold.

Blackness. Unbearable pressure on her ears and eyelids. The shock of submerging in an ice bath—made worse after the unbearable heat of the explosion.

Panic. Oh, God. Disoriented.

Which way was up?

Her lungs screamed for air.

She kicked for all she was worth, but she didn't move. *She didn't move!* She was going to drown!

Then she panicked for real, her mind going blank and her most primitive instincts kicking in.

Something shoved at her mouth, and she screwed her lips shut against it. Must not breathe. One lungful of water, and she was done.

The thing at her mouth shoved more forcefully, and water and metal broke through her resistance, flooding into her mouth.

And then it dawned on her. That was a scuba regulator.

Belatedly, she exhaled the meager breath she had left

in her lungs, blowing out hard and clearing her mouth. She clamped down frantically on the mouthpiece and dragged in a desperate breath. Another.

A tug at the mouthpiece.

She didn't want to let it go!

And then her brain *finally* kicked into gear, and it dawned on her very belatedly what was happening.

Beau was trying to buddy breathe with her. He'd been wearing a full scuba suit when he boarded the ship, and his tanks must have survived the impact with the water. His weight belts were holding them both down, and they were going to have to take turns breathing out of his tank.

One of his legs kicked against hers, setting up a steady rhythm. He was swimming. Why wasn't he using both legs? She concentrated and felt one of his legs hanging completely useless. That couldn't be good. But it wasn't like they had the luxury of doing anything about it right now.

She kicked, too, shifting her hips to one side so she wouldn't kick his bad leg. She hung on to his waist with both arms, while he used one arm to paddle and the other to pass the mouthpiece back and forth between them.

Gradually, she became aware of light overhead. They were coming up toward the surface. Beau swam them up until their faces just broke through to air. She looked around quickly. Burning wreckage littered the water as far as she could see.

Beau spit out the mouthpiece and transmitted over his throat mike, "We're alive. I've got Tessa. We're in the water."

She was so close to Beau, her cheek plastered to his neck, that she heard Torsten answer, "Roger. Hold your position. We have your GPS signals. We'll come to you."

Beau unbuckled his weight belt and dropped it, and the two of them were able to tread water more easily. They swam over to what looked like part of a table-top, and they threw their arms across the broad wooden plank.

Silence fell around them and they bobbed up and down gently on the swells.

"You okay?" Beau rasped.

"Peachy keen. You?"

He grimaced beside her. "I did something to my knee when we hit the water. I can't feel my foot at all."

"I don't care if your whole leg fell off. You're alive. And that's all that matters," she declared stoutly, echoing his earlier statement.

"I love you, Tessa."

"I love you, too, Beau."

He snorted and she looked at him in surprise.

He explained sheepishly, "Your camera's still transmitting audio and video. Torsten told us lovebirds to engage in hanky-panky on our own time."

"Do you mean to say the whole team just heard us?" she asked in dismay.

"'Fraid so."

"Ohmigod. Kill me now," she groaned.

"Yeah. That," he agreed drily.

"We're never going to live this down, are we?" she asked him, wincing.

"Nope. Never." He reached over to squeeze her hand. "But at least we're alive to be humiliated on an ongoing basis."

"Oh, joy," she responded sarcastically.

"Don't knock it. I thought we were dead when we jumped off that ship."

She waxed serious. "Me, too."

The sound of a motor became audible, and the team's boat came into sight. Webster and Neville hung over the side, shoving away debris as the vessel made its way to them.

The men reached down, took her by the arms and hauled her aboard. As she flopped onto the floor, she gasped, "Take it easy with Beau. His leg's hurt."

Beau was eased aboard and she moved aside to make room for him. But then Marco pushed her out of the way.

She opened her mouth to protest, but Torsten caught her frantic gaze. "Marco's a medic. Let him do his job."

She nodded as Webster wrapped a Mylar blanket around her. Funny, but she wasn't cold until he wrapped her up like a silver plastic burrito. Then the shivering set in, and it was a long, miserable ride to shore.

The remainder of the night passed in a blur. They loaded up in a step van and headed up the coast to Casablanca, debriefing along the way as a team. A British naval vessel waited for them there—a sleek cigar boat that flew north to Gibraltar at nearly a hundred miles per hour.

Beau was whisked off to a hospital in an ambulance, and she was taken to a police station. Torsten was apologetic, but she needed to record an after-action report of her entire meeting with Hassan Al Dhib while it was still fresh in her mind for legal purposes.

She was surprised at how long it took. Torsten interjected occasionally to ask questions or ask for clarifications. But eventually, the debrief from hell ended.

"Can I go see Beau now?" she asked her boss.

"I'll take you. I got a text about a half hour ago that he's out of surgery to repair his knee. He should be coming around by now. And I need to speak with both of you, anyway."

She ought to wince. Ought to be embarrassed that Gun and the others had heard her and Beau declare their love for each other. But she couldn't be sorry for telling Beau how she felt.

They had both just cheated death in a big way. Turned out that had a way of stripping life down to the bare essentials: friends and family, laughter and love.

She rode beside Torsten in the back of a British staff car to a pretty little hospital situated high on the side of the Rock of Gibraltar. The waiting room was full of big male bodies, and all the guys rose as one when she and Torsten walked in.

"Report," he ordered.

Webster answered, "Beau's right knee is trashed. It buckled when it hit the water and ripped pretty much everything. The doc has no idea how he and Tessa survived hitting the water as hard as they did. Says the scuba tanks saved his life. Lambo reports twisting in midair with the intent of hitting on his back to protect Tessa, but his leg got caught underneath him."

He'd turned to protect her. He'd sacrificed his body to save her. She knew it as surely as she was standing here.

Webster continued, "Anyway, it's not looking good for his knee. The surgeons put it back together as best they could. They think he may walk on it again, but that's about it."

"That's what they said the last time," Torsten commented.

Marco interjected, "I've seen the MRI. They mean it this time. He's done. He wrecked pretty much everything that can be wrecked in a knee joint."

Oh, no.

He'd fought so hard to come back from his last knee

injury. It had meant the world to him to make it back to his team. She knew now why he loved this life so much. Why he loved these men more than blood family.

Agony on his behalf ripped through Tessa, and she choked out past a giant lump in her throat, "Can I see him?"

Marco answered gently, "He's asking for you."

She looked up at Torsten. "Can we have a minute alone first?"

His chin dipped in a nod. But he did follow her and Marco down the hallway. The two men parked outside Beau's door while she pushed it open and stepped inside.

His eyes flew open when she murmured down at him, "Hey, handsome."

"Hey, beautiful," he murmured.

"I hear you were a big hero and intentionally took the hit for me when we landed in the water earlier."

He shrugged, but she saw confirmation in his eyes.

"It cost you too much, Beau." She gestured helplessly at the heavy bandages encasing his leg, which was propped up on pillows. "You shouldn't have done it."

He answered reluctantly, "I would do anything for you, Tessa. I was happy to sacrifice myself to protect you."

She leaned down and kissed him gently.

His hand came up around the back of her head, deepening their kiss. He met her halfway, and their tongues swirled around each other, their lips moving restlessly, their breath mingling as they came together hungrily.

They were both alive. Not unscathed, but alive. It was a minor miracle, and they both reveled in the knowledge of it.

She came up for air, gasping. "I can't ever get enough of you."

"Me, neither," he murmured against her lips. "I don't care if I have to leave the teams. I won't give you up."

"About that—" she started.

The door opened behind her and she straightened abruptly. But Beau didn't let go of her hand. She caught the defiant glare he shot toward his boss.

"Hey, Lambo."

"Hey, Gun." Beau held up his free hand to stop Torsten when he opened his mouth to speak. "Me first, boss."

"Okay." Torsten crossed his arms.

"You offered me and Tessa a choice before this op. Us or the teams. Well, I've made my choice. I choose her. Consider this my resignation notice."

She stared down at Beau, open-mouthed. "Beau. You would do that for me?"

"In a heartbeat. Nothing—nothing—in this world matters to me as much as you."

Joy broke across her entire being like the sun rising outside the window in shades of pink and orange bliss.

Torsten nodded slowly and then nailed her with a stare. "What about you, Wilkes?"

She frowned. "If Beau leaves the teams, does that mean I can stay?"

"If you'd like."

"Can I have an off-duty relationship with him?"

"You two can do anything you'd like on your own time if you're not on the same team," Torsten answered. "But about that—"

She and Beau stared at him expectantly.

"I've got a few more women coming into the pipeline that I think are going to make it to the Medusas. I'm going to need someone intimately familiar with the capabilities of women operators to act as their operations supervisor. I was thinking you'd be perfect for the job, Beau. What do you say?"

"What if Tessa has to work an op I'm running?"

Torsten shrugged. "I'll take over in those instances. I don't want to lose either of you. You're both valuable assets."

Tessa smiled down at Beau. "Hey. I'm an asset now."

"Honey, you're a Medusa, through and through."

"I'm your Medusa," she replied. "And you're mine."

"Damn straight," he retorted.

"God save us all from you lovebirds," Torsten groused.

Beau and Tessa's laughter mingled together and chased Torsten out of the room.

Beau moved over carefully, and Tessa climbed into the bed beside him, taking her place at his side. And she was never leaving that spot again. Ever.

Even if missions carried her half a world away, her heart would always be right here. With him.

Epilogue

Tessa tipped her face up to accept a kiss as Beau handed her a paper plate loaded with more food than she could eat in two meals. "I love you, Beau, but you have a very warped sense of what a normal human being can actually eat in one sitting."

"Ahh, but you're not a normal human being."

Laughter and conversation flowed around them as the two newest recruits to the Medusas, Piper Ford and Rebel McQueen, plus Torsten's teammates and their various significant others enjoyed a backyard barbecue to christen Beau and Tessa's new house. They'd pooled their savings, which were considerable given that neither of them had ever slowed down for long enough to have actual lives before they'd found each other, and they'd bought a cute little bungalow a few blocks from the beach near Camp Davis.

It allowed Beau to walk down to the beach and swim,

which was good therapy for his knee. It also allowed him to watch the women Medusa trainees and learn their individual strengths and weaknesses before he sent them on actual missions.

Tessa twirled the diamond engagement ring on her left hand that Beau had surprised her with last week, on the six-month anniversary of her first mission. She'd come a hell of a long way since she'd staggered into Beau's arms trying to climb out of a Jeep.

But then, he'd come a long way, too. He was now a born-again believer in the value of women special operators, and was hard at work profiling missions where women would be of particular use.

More to the point, he'd learned how to love, and she had the extreme good fortune to be the woman who'd cracked the code for him. As for her, she couldn't imagine entrusting her heart to any man but him.

Her cell phone vibrated in the hip pocket of her jeans, and, simultaneously, all the other women on the back patio reached for their pockets. The men present groaned in unison.

"It's go time, ladies." Gunnar Torsten looked over at her and smiled warmly.

Beau leaned down to kiss her deeply and then murmured against her mouth, "Go get 'em, Lovebird."

She groaned. She hated her field handle, but it wasn't like she'd been given a choice in the matter. The rest of Gunnar's team had stuck her with it, and no amount of offered beer or monetary bribes could talk them out of it.

She pushed to her feet and snatched one last kiss. "Hold down the fort for me, Beau."

"I'll be here when you get back."

She smiled at him, her heart full to overflowing.

"Come back to me," he murmured as had become their tradition.

"Count on it."

With a last nod, she turned and headed out with her teammates into the gathering dusk.

She was a Medusa. And it was time to roll.

* * * * *

Be sure to check out the next Mission Medusa romance,
Special Forces: The Spy,
available next month.

Other books by Cindy Dees:

Navy SEAL Cop
Undercover with a SEAL
Her Secret Spy
Her Mission with a SEAL

Available now from Harlequin Romantic Suspense!

Before she could decide, Spence wrapped his arm around her
shoulder, yanking her against his side.

"Mia yelped.

So much tension shot through his body that she could feel it
seeping into her own muscles.

"What're you doing?"

"Using you as camouflage," he said, looking away from his
prey just long enough to give her a smile.

"The guy ran from me once already. I don't want him getting
away again."

"Again? What do you mean, again?" He wasn't going to chase
the man through this building, was he?

"He crashed your party last week to confront Alcosta, and now
he's at the man's office. If the guy means trouble, what do you
think the chances are that he wouldn't show up again at one of your
Alcosta fund-raisers?"

Mia frowned.

Well, that burst her sexy little fantasy.

"Are you sure it's the same guy?"

Taking her cue from Spence, instead of twisting around to
check the other man out this time, Mia dropped her purse so that

when she bent down to pick it up, she could look over without being obvious.

It was the same man, all right.

And he wore the same dark scowl.

"He looks mean," she murmured.

The man was about her height, but almost as broad as Spence. Even in a pricey suit, his muscles rippled in a way that screamed brawler. Cell phone against his ear, he paced in front of the elevator, enough anger in his steps that she was surprised he didn't kick the metal doors to hurry it up.

"I'm going to follow him, see where he goes."

"No," Mia protested. "He could be dangerous."

"So can I."

Oh, God.

Why did that turn her on?

"Maybe you should call security instead of following him," she suggested. She knew the words were futile before they even left her lips, but she'd had to try.

"No point." He wrapped her fingers around her portfolio. "Wait for me in front of the building."

"Hold on." She made a grab for him, but his sport coat slipped through her fingers. "Spence, please."

That stopped him.

He stopped and gave her an impatient look.

"This is what I do." He headed for the elevator without a backward glance, leaving Mia standing there, with worry crawling up and down her spine as she watched him check the elevator the guy had taken before hurrying to the stairwell.

Oh, damn.

Don't miss
Navy SEAL Bodyguard *by Tawny Weber,*
available June 2019 wherever
Harlequin® Romantic Suspense books
and ebooks are sold.

www.Harlequin.com

HRSEXP0519

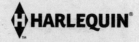

Love Harlequin romance?

DISCOVER.

Be the first to find out about promotions, news and exclusive content!

f Facebook.com/HarlequinBooks

🐦 Twitter.com/HarlequinBooks

📷 Instagram.com/HarlequinBooks

📌 Pinterest.com/HarlequinBooks

ReaderService.com

EXPLORE.

Sign up for the Harlequin e-newsletter and download a free book from any series at **TryHarlequin.com.**

CONNECT.

Join our Harlequin community to share your thoughts and connect with other romance readers!
Facebook.com/groups/HarlequinConnection

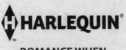